EACH INCIDENT APPEARS TO BE SEPARATE:

- a high government official falls ill with a terrible and dreaded disease,
- an American citizen vanishes without a trace from a lonely railroad station,
- a parachutist drops through the silent night into the shelter of a dense forest.

Only the plotters know that these isolated happenings are all part of a master plan...a daring attempt to overthrow a cut-throat dictator who does not hesitate to maim or murder anyone who makes a try for freedom.

"Suspenseful . . . exciting . . . one dramatic climax after another"
—BOSTON HERALD

"Almost unbearable suspense"
—NASHVILLE BANNER

"First rate"
—ST. LOUIS POST DISPATCH

"Don't miss it"
—LOS ANGELES MIRROR NEWS

the plotters

by ALAN CAILLOU

toExcel
San Jose New York Lincoln Shanghai

The Plotters

All Rights Reserved. Copyright © 1960, 2000 by Alan Caillou

No part of this book may be reproduced or transmitted in any form or by any means, graphic, electronic, or mechanical, including photocopying, recording, taping, or by any information storage or retrieval system, without the permission in writing from the publisher.

Published by toExcel Press,
an imprint of iUniverse.com, Inc.

For information address:
iUniverse.com, Inc.
620 North 48th Street
Suite 201
Lincoln, NE 68504-3467
www.iuniverse.com

ISBN: 0-595-09142-3

chapter 1

It's hard to decide just where all this trouble really started.

I suppose, in truth, it was on that first escapade when I found myself involved in one of those comic revolutions that are always going on down there, giving a hand to a wounded rebel out of nothing more political than a distaste for seeing a man bleed to death on your own front doorstep; or when I came back and wrote those virulent articles that painted me —quite incorrectly, I insist—as a man who might be interested in such things as justice and the human rights of the individual. I say incorrectly, because the truth of the matter is that you can only afford to fight for these abstractions if you have the strength, and the courage, to defend yourself against the massive and inexorable retaliation that is bound to come ... and the fear of which sent me into hiding like any common criminal, with not a friend foolhardy enough to raise a finger to help me.

Or perhaps it began when I found myself stranded, out of a job, and broke as usual, in a crummy water-front hotel here in La Guaira, which is the nearest the ocean comes to Caracas. They'd sent me to Caracas, my paper that is, to do a series of tourist articles. You know, the usual guff that any hack journalist can write on a weekend tour of the bars and night clubs, with free drinks if you remember to mention the right places, and some extra money on the side if you're not too fussy where it comes from. It's not much of a job, but I'm not much of a journalist either. And they pay all your expenses, once you're there; though I had to fix my own passage with the skipper of the most dilapidated freighter you ever saw.

Anyway, I reached Caracas in a blinding heat wave that made the sweat run down my chest under my shirt, and after a little while I filed home some stuff I'd written on the boat, because, hell, I used to live in Caracas and I know every tavern, every night club and every tourist trap here. But I went overboard about Digger's Place, because Digger is an old friend of mine, and—wouldn't you know it?—my editor had been out there a year back and Digger's Place was precisely the spot where he'd run into a little trouble and lost his pocketbook. I must admit, with due respect to my friend, that it is a bit of a dump. So I found myself out of a job again, and the cable office wouldn't even accept my wire asking about the half-fare back home the paper had agreed to pay.

But an enterprising man can always manage to earn enough to keep body and soul together fairly honestly, though I certainly wasn't making any fortunes. I couldn't get a permit to look for a proper job—with one of the big oil companies, I thought—but I showed the tourists around and bought souvenirs for them, and fixed them up with dates, that sort of thing. I did some Spanish-English translations and lived off my old friends when times were hard, and before I knew it a year had gone by and I was still living from hand to mouth and wondering where the next week's expenses were coming from. But it's like that all over South America. Lassitude, *laissez faire*, tomorrow-will-take-care-of-itself, call it what you like.

All the same, it was tough, and, when I found this fellow following me, there hadn't been any food in the house for the last two days.

Food? Hell, there hadn't even been any gin.

I was talking business with a tourist who wanted to see the sights, and we were sitting at a table in one of those rather drab little bars down on the Calle Caluso, where a tall thin girl from one of the islands was slowly peeling off her clothes to the halfhearted accompaniment of the worst band on the continent. Her long limbs glistened with oil, or sweat, and they were richly brown and well-muscled, but she was quite a beginner at the game. My tourist was watching her avidly, and probably thinking about his wife. If he had one.

I got up and went over to the band, and told the drummer to send the girl over to our table when she was through, and then I stood at the door for a moment, smoking a cigarette and sucking in the cool night air. A neatly dressed man in a silk suit was strolling along the alley that led to the bar, attracted by the garish red neon sign that was flashing over the door. It's a funny thing: a red neon sign on a main street doesn't mean a thing; but put it halfway down a dark alley and everybody wants to see what goes on there.

He was a very dignified sort of man. *Distingué*, I suppose, is the word. His hair was thick and well-groomed, a little bit gray, and he had a small gray mustache. It occurred to me, then, that I'd seen him once or twice before lately, always sitting close by where I happened to be, and there was a sudden unaccountable feeling that something was wrong.... Perhaps it was because he looked a bit out of place in this grubby quarter—not with the out-of-placeness of the tourist who is excitedly slumming (and dressed in his oldest clothes, just in case) but somehow too nonchalantly sure of himself. It's funny how you get a feeling about these things. I owed quite a lot of money all over the town, and some of the collection agencies are not very fussy about the way they gather in their clients' delinquent accounts. This was the first thing that came to my mind; I suppose it was the air of efficient ruthlessness that he seemed to have. Or perhaps it was just my guilty conscience.

He stopped close by me and looked at the nudes that were pasted up in a glass case on the red brick wall, and I turned away and began to move inside. He looked at me then and smiled quickly.

He said, pleasantly enough:

"I'll be at your apartment at midnight. It's important to you."

He was sauntering off again before I could recover from my surprise. I just had time to see that the alleyway was deserted, and then I went hastily back to my tourist to get away from what I was sure was a nasty thought. . . .

You see, Caracas is full of all kinds of rackets, some mild and only semilegal, and some quite violent and lucrative, and there aren't so many people like myself, unemployed and with what you might call an international background, who can be called upon for the odd jobs that turn up from time to time and which are too risky for the known characters to handle.

A long time ago I had realized that sooner or later I would be faced with the problem of joining one of the rackets. People like me were too much in demand there. I knew that I would be approached by one of the mobs that handle the narcotics, or the gun-running, or the brothels, or the smuggling. . . . And I knew that I would have to make up my mind about it pretty carefully. I couldn't afford to keep on living off what I could scrounge from the tourists, and yet I'm not—how shall I put it? Tough enough? Dispassionate enough? At any rate, these ventures were big-scale and pretty deadly, run by some high-caliber mugs of the old kind who'd found that Venezuela was a profitable place to operate from. It's not that I have too many moral qualms, of course, nothing like that at all. It's simply that I was scared to get mixed up with one of the crowds whom I knew to be powerful, well-organized and quite vicious. So far, I hadn't been afraid of every passing uniform, and I rather wanted to keep it that way, hoping from day to day that something would turn up.

So, by and large, the instruction from the distinguished-looking man in the silk suit had me excited and deeply disturbed. And "instruction" is the right word. There was something in his manner, affable though it was, that said quite clearly: *And you'd better be there, too.*

Well, there was no use worrying about it. I went back to the table. My tourist was giggling with the long-limbed girl who'd been dancing, leaning forward with his hand on her shoulder and breathing fumes of raw whiskey over the poor thing. The waiter was already bringing them some pink champagne, and a tall glass of cold tea and soda for me, and when I sipped it I saw that he had slipped a slug of rum in it, which was his way of sympathizing with me.

I was pleased about the champagne. There was a fat commission on it, and I must say that this fellow really wanted to spread himself around. His name was Vallance, and he was an insurance broker from Iowa, I think, a nice enough guy really, but a bit of a visiting fireman if you know what I mean. He was getting pretty drunk by now, and looking at my watch I began to wonder if I could get rid of him in time for my meeting at twelve o'clock. At that time of night things are only just beginning to look up in Caracas. It wouldn't have been wise merely to dump him, because in the state he was in someone would surely filch his pocketbook, and, after all, I had a certain responsibility to him.

At a quarter to twelve, I said to the girl, in rapid Spanish: "I've got a job to do. You want to take him over to your place now? I'll meet up with you afterward."

She nodded her head, but Vallance got up suddenly and said: "What a dump. Let's get out of here."

I was worried that perhaps he had understood what I was saying, but he added: "Gotta get some air. What about that place round behind . . . round behind the hotel?"

I said: "You're the boss. Wherever you want to go . . ."

He put a pile of notes on the table, and I just had time to check how much was there. I don't think the waiter would have welshed on me, but it's as well to make sure. At least, when you need the next month's rent it is. If we walked, we'd have to pass my apartment, and I thought perhaps I could park him for a while at Digger's Place, which was quite close by. I said: "You want to walk? It's not too far. . . ."

"Sure. Do me good. Get rid of some of this . . ."

He patted his paunch affectionately and stood looking at the girl for a moment. He said to her at last: "Maybe . . . maybe we'll be back later on, eh?"

So we went out into the cool fresh air, with the breeze coming up off the water, and we turned toward the hotel, but, as we were passing my place, he stopped and looked quickly over his shoulder at the deserted street, stood there swaying slightly while a fisherman passed us on a bicycle, and then said quickly: "All right, my friend, up you go. I'm in on this meeting of yours."

You could have knocked me over with a banana. I stood staring at him for a moment, with my mouth hanging open foolishly, conscious that he wasn't the least bit drunk any more but was standing firm on his widely spaced tubby legs, gently urging me toward the stairway. He said, smiling cheerfully: "Well, let's not hang around where everyone can see us."

It wasn't any use objecting, so I didn't. We went up to my apartment and the door opened, and the distinguished fellow in the silk suit was standing there, perfectly at home and at ease in my room, and we went in and shut the door quickly, and for a moment we stood there like guests at a party who don't know anybody and haven't yet spotted the bar. Except that my heart was in my mouth.

Then my tourist, Vallance, said cheerfully: "You've half met Mr. DeBries, haven't you? And my name is Vallance, as you know."

DeBries, the man who'd told me that what he had to say was important to me, held out his hand and I took it as though the circumstances of our meeting had been perfectly ordinary and normal.

Speaking to him, Vallance said briefly: "The people next door?"

DeBries nodded. "Nobody home," he said. "The walls are thin, but we can talk quietly." He turned away, then, and sat down on the sofa.

He was a tall man, with a face that I suppose you would call good. Intelligent eyes, an air of authority, a rather high-bridged nose that made him look faintly supercilious . . . there was the trace of an accent in his voice, not easily identifiable; it was more of an intonation, really.

Vallance, who had seemed incapably drunk a moment ago, was a short, fat man, going bald, with rather flabby features and an imposing paunch. He ran a hand through what was left of his hair and went to the mirror over the bookshelf, straightening himself out a little. He said apologetically: "I've had rather more to drink than I intended. . . ."

His voice was quite steady, and, when he turned from the mirror and looked at me, he was smiling with a kind of secret amusement.

I thought it was time to establish my tenancy there. I said, as frigidly as I could manage: "May I offer you gentlemen a drink?"

DeBries waved a negligent hand and said: "Mr. Benasque,

we will get down to business. First of all, let me apologize for the melodramatics, the secrecy and, of course, the intrusion. But when you've heard what I have to say, you will agree that a certain amount of care is necessary. We have a proposition to make to you, which may well interest you . . . for a variety of reasons. If it does *not* interest you, then I must have your word that what I say will be treated with as much confidence as you think it deserves. Is that agreed?"

I said: "That's a pretty liberal suggestion."

Vallance broke in. "Precisely. If you think it does not deserve any confidence at all, then no great harm will have been done. If, on the other hand, you are interested . . ."

He left it hanging. I poured myself a drink and waited.

DeBries went on with the air of a man who chooses his words carefully and does not waste them. "First of all, Mr. Benasque, we know all about you and you know nothing about us. All you need to know at this stage is that we represent a group of interested people. We are positively not employed by any government or government agency, although we do have . . . a measure of government support. Is that clear? What we are doing is not illegal—at any rate, it is not illegal *here*. You can put us down as . . . as supporters of a cause, and leave it at that. We believe that what we are doing is right . . . and we think that this is the general view. On the other hand, elsewhere it is illegal, and everywhere, it is dangerous. Do I make myself clear?"

I was waiting for the pitch. I said: "Not particularly. But I'm listening."

"All right. Now."

He was sitting there, DeBries, with a faintly professorial air, rather like a kindly lecturer in a university, with the tips of his fingers gently stroking his long chin. He went on: "Some years ago, you wrote some articles, three of them, about a man called Lazlo, José Lazlo. Do you remember what you said about him?"

"I remember."

"If you do not, then I have copies of those articles here."

He took a long envelope out of his breast pocket. I said again: "I remember all about Lazlo. Poor devil."

"Poor devil? Why do you say that?"

"He found it didn't pay to fight oppression. So he joined it. I always feel sorry for a guy who has to throw his principles overboard like that. Not many of us left."

"Oh? Have you thrown yours overboard too, Mr. Benasque?"

"They began to swamp the boat."

"And now?"

"Now I'm more interested in the prosaic things. Like eating."

Vallance broke in again. I noticed that he was always ready to speak when there was a bit of a pause. He said abruptly: "If there were another war, the hypothetical question, would you go back to the army?"

I shrugged my shoulders.

"I suppose so. Probably the safest place to be."

"And would you go back to the outfit you were with the last time?"

I could feel an uneasiness creeping over me. The reference to my wartime efforts was far too casual to be pleasant. As far as I'm concerned, the war was over a long time ago, and I have not the slightest intention of getting mixed up again with the mob I ran around with then. I said carefully: "I think they'll need a new crop of talent, in my field, don't you? We had good cover in those days, but now . . . Now, they know all about us. I'd probably do public relations for the army instead. A lot safer."

DeBries said: "Forgive me, Mr. Benasque, but I do not believe that whatever sense of patriotism you used to have . . . in the old days . . . is quite extinguished."

"Nowadays, I call it chauvinism. I'm an internationalist."

"You can afford to be cosmopolitan and still abhor what goes on across the other side of the fence. Of the various fences," he said.

"And you can disapprove without rattling a saber over it. The neighbor has a right to his own ideas. You may not like them particularly—"

"Sometime a saber is the only thing he can be cut down with."

"If he must be cut down—"

Vallance said mildly: "Aren't we losing sight of the real issue?"

DeBries nodded.

"The real issue," he said, "is this. Under the right conditions, would you be prepared to undertake an assignment in South America? One that would require a certain amount of . . . daring?"

"I'm not a courageous man."

He said, a little sardonically I thought: "We recognize the fact that courage is an expensive commodity in these peaceful times."

It was time I had another drink. I picked up the brandy bottle, which was nearly empty, and waved it at them questioningly. DeBries shook his head, frowning very slightly. I said shortly: "I can hold my liquor. If your proposition interests me drunk, it will interest me sober. But I'm not sure that it does. I'd like to know first just who you are. After that, just what you have in mind."

Vallance was sitting on the arm of the chair, dangling a pudgy leg twelve inches from the floor. He got up and walked over to the window, and pulled back the heavy red curtain that the landlady thought was so chic. He stood watching the street for a moment. The little window at the top, what the French call—and God knows why—a *vasistas,* was open, and I could smell the ripeness on the air, a pungent scent of dead and rotting shellfish that came up from the wharf. When he'd had time to think what he was going to say, he turned and said:

"Mr. Benasque, you must understand that at this stage we can give you very little information. Call this, if you like, an exploratory meeting. We are employed, quite properly, by a private agency which has—shall I say?—friends in high places. We are not employed by the government. But we do have access . . ."

I interrupted him in mid-sentence. I was getting tired of his pomposity. I said politely: "What government are you not employed by?"

He broke off suddenly and stared at me without speaking. Then he smiled and looked across at DeBries, who was carefully looking the other way. Ignoring the suggestion behind my question, he went on: "We have friends who are close enough to government to be able to assist us substantially. Because of this, we know all there is to know about you. Your war record included. We know that we can rely upon your strict ideas of security. . . . Do you remember Colonel Matley?"

"Of course; he was my boss."

"Colonel Matley put us in touch with you. If you want to check, you know where you can find him."

"I see."

"Is that good enough for point one?"

"Good enough. Point two?"

I began to wonder if Vallance was the real boss of the show. DeBries was waiting for him to speak. Then Vallance nodded, almost imperceptibly, and DeBries said slowly: "Your friendship with Lazlo was fairly strong, I believe?"

"I liked him. I thought he was a nice guy. He was playing a very dangerous game . . . doing what he believed was the right thing."

"And your association with him was purely fortuitous."

"I suppose so. I was in San Antonio to cover the road race they were holding down there, and this fellow . . . There was some shooting, a minor revolt, you know the pattern . . . and this fellow was lying on the front steps of the railway station, bleeding to death. I went to help him, and the cops shoved me back with their rifles, and . . . well, you know how it is when the police start strong-arming you. I told them to go to hell, and dragged this guy round the corner out of the range of the bullets . . . got him to temporary safety, at least . . . and a couple of them ran after me and then . . ."

It had been a terrifying experience. They'd tried to seize power, to topple the Dictator off his perch, and they'd been quashed rapidly and ruthlessly in the attempt. But when the two policemen grabbed me, one of them stuck his rifle butt in my groin and I fell down on the cobbled pavement and stared up at him as he shoved the barrel close to my face and threw the bolt. . . . There was just one moment of absolute panic, and then the policeman unexpectedly doubled up and crumpled as someone else fired at very close range, and then a small tight group of men were dragging me and the wounded man into a building, and Lazlo was there, a tall, slender man in his early thirties, standing close by the shattered window with a rifle in his hands and a cigarette drooping from the corner of his mouth. He had turned to me and said, in good English: "Thank you, my friend. If they had taken him . . ."

I had been more worried about my own position. Fortunately, I'd been on my way to the train at the time the revolt broke out, and had already picked up my passport from the hotel, and what with one thing and another they'd never found out who it was that had come to the impulsive aid of the rebels. An American, they'd said, with the lousiest description of me. . . . The revolt was over almost as soon as it had started, so, after Lazlo had hidden me for a couple of days, I came out from under and crossed over the border like any other tourist, with no trouble at all. But we'd quickly, and perhaps inexplicably, become good friends in those few frightened hours. He was a man of intense passion that was tempered by a cold reasoning and a strong impersonal love of justice. He hated the regime with a degree of fanaticism that could only lead to his death, one way or another, but his hatred was controlled by a kind of calculating assessment of the power they were up against in their attempts to exact a degree of democracy from the ruthless clique at the top.

It doesn't show, you know, not on the surface. It's the same in a lot of those republics. The travel posters show you pretty girls in flared skirts with castanets held over their heads, or long shots of magnificent scenery with a cable car somewhere in the background, and in the stores they smile and sell you souvenirs. But if you make a few friends, you quickly become conscious of sudden gaps in the pleasant pattern of well-being.

You see a terrified man being dragged off hurriedly into a closed car. Or someone clams up and moves away quickly if you say an unkind word about the secret police. Or you wake in the night to hear the rumble of tanks moving out into the country where the rebels are. . . . And none of this finds its way onto the travel posters.

Lazlo was a young man, but he was embittered by what had happened to his lovely country, angered by the beatings and the executions and the dreadful things that happened in the cellar under the army barracks.

DeBries said, looking at me carefully: "How do you feel about him now?"

"Well . . . I don't really know. He seems to have gone over to the other side. A junior minister or something. I believe he still comes out with a criticism of the regime from time to time."

"Do you feel strongly enough about him to . . . to make sure that no indiscretion of yours could lead to his arrest?"

"Of course."

DeBries took a deep breath as though he were going under water for a while. Then he said: "I am relying on your common sense—the affection which I believe you had for him. An indiscretion would mean his death, without the slightest doubt at all. Just one word from you, after you hear what I have to say . . . I cannot stress this point too much."

"I heard you the first time."

"Well, then. Lazlo did not go over to the other side. His party became so strong that it was a far more serious menace to the strong man and his tight little junta, so they made him a proposition. You may have heard something of it. They offered him an amnesty and a certain measure of the reforms he wanted if he would come out of hiding and join them. Anyone but Lazlo would have refused, suspecting—and quite rightly so—a trap. But Lazlo does not hold his own life in too great esteem when it comes to the welfare of his people. He took a chance, and joined them, knowing that it might be a fatal mistake he would have to pay for with his life. But he joined them so that he could work against them, knowing he'd be watched every inch of the way. And he has been watched. They know every single thing he does—except one. They don't know that he's still in close contact with the rebels, with his number-one man out in the mountains. He maps their strategy, he plans their policy. . . . But there's one important thing he's quite unable to do. He can't leave the country."

It was a clear and logical picture of their own little war of nerves, of the strong man tenaciously holding on to his power by cunning as well as force, and waiting for just one wrong move to bring his fist down hard . . . a sudden disappearance. . . . No, with Lazlo it would have to be an "accident."

I said: "So far I'm with you. Go on."

DeBries was watching me closely. He said: "Quite simply, we want to get Lazlo out of the country and put him back in again. I need not tell you how difficult this is. He's under constant surveillance. And I need not tell you that if word of this gets out . . . then Lazlo's hopes of survival are negligible."

"You can say that again."

"We have passed the Rubicon, Mr. Benasque. Now, you know. You know what has been kept a very closely guarded secret indeed through all the planning that has already been done."

"You must feel pretty sure of me."

"We do."

"Very flattering."

Vallance said pompously: "Our very tenuous connection with any government agency is not only remote; it is also elastic enough for us to feel that we are not rigorously bound, in cases of necessity, by the normal restrictions of human relationship."

Well, that was one way of putting it. I said sourly: "You mean, I suppose, that if I talk I'm a dead duck too."

Quite affable, Vallance was smiling and nodding his head.

DeBries was smoothly conciliatory. He said quietly: "I am quite sure that we have no worries on that account. We would not have come to you unless we were absolutely certain."

I said: "That's a point. Why *did* you come to me? Why *me*, in particular? There are hundreds of people better suited for this sort of thing. And I haven't accepted, anyway."

"No, you haven't," DeBries said. "We hope you will. Because, quite frankly, Mr. Benasque, you are the only man who *can* help us. The only man."

I was wondering what special talents I had, all unknown to me. DeBries must have been a thought reader.

"You have certain qualifications," he said, "which make it absolutely imperative that you help us. The one man who can. When the operation was first planned, we assumed that we could convince you one way or the other."

There was just enough emphasis on that "one way or the other." I felt they wanted me to bite, so I bit.

"And the . . . the other way?"

Smiling gently, DeBries took another envelope from his pocket. He said: "An ex-army man . . . ex-Intelligence . . . a friend of Lazlo's . . . if this were not enough, then, as I said before, we are prepared to pay the premium which has been set on courage. There's quite a lot of money in it for you. Quite a lot."

"And therefore, quite a lot of danger."

DeBries was frowning slightly. He said slowly: "Yes and no. The plan is a good one. I can foresee no possible hitch. And, if it goes smoothly, then the danger is quite negligible. At any rate, no more than enough to stimulate you and to excite you. If anything goes wrong, then that's an entirely different matter. Your chances of getting out of it alive will be . . . well, perhaps fifty-fifty."

He tossed the envelope onto the table. I fancied there was just enough nonchalance in the movement to indicate that he thought people who could be *hired* were not quite as good as those who were disinterestedly enthusiastic.

I said: "Seems to me quite a number of . . . of outsiders are getting themselves interested in Latin-American politics these days."

"An awakening of the social conscience."

"Seems the first thing we hear about it is a story in *Life* magazine on some guy's murder. Or the State Department's trying to locate some poor bastard who was fed to the sharks."

"A want of caution, nothing else."

"But why *me,* of all people? I could easily put you on to someone more capable."

"It has to be you. The reason why—you'll learn that in due course."

"How much is in that envelope?"

"Five hundred American dollars. It's a down payment. Whether you accept or not. There's a great deal more to come if you want it."

"Yes . . . If I want it."

"You'd have to go to San Antonio again, of course. But you've been there several times since that episode with Lazlo."

"As I said, they never found out who it was."

"All it needs is a clear brain, a cool mind. . . . The danger is quite small."

"If all goes well."

"If all goes well."

"You must feel pretty sure I'll accept. Even to tell me about it."

"We know your past, as I said. And we also know your present position."

I said bitterly: "When a man's sunk low enough, he'll do anything for money, is that it?"

Vallance the Peacemaker came in again. I couldn't help noticing how they complemented each other, those two characters; as soon as one of them started to put my back up, the other one chimed in with his pennyworth. He said blandly: "It's not that at all. It's simply that we have access to sufficient funds to make this quite a minor problem. And if money will sway you in the right direction . . . if you can put a few thousand dollars to good use . . . there's no reason at all why you should feel embarrassed about it."

"I'm not embarrassed."

"No, I didn't really think you were."

He was smiling delightedly as though he'd made a good joke.

There was only one thing to be settled, in my own mind. Knowing it was a bit abrupt, knowing that he'd realize what I was thinking of, I tried to make it as casual as possible. I said: "You seem to know what I was doing during the war. Information like that isn't easy to come by. Mind telling me what *you* were doing then?"

He answered without hesitation. "I was in a similar organization."

"On the same side?"

He raised his eyebrows, and it made his face look like one of those balloons they give the kids to advertize someone's breakfast cereal. I think he was genuinely surprised.

"Of course," he said. "What did you think?"

Then he recovered his aplomb and said, smiling: "Paid by the same war department."

I liked the way he said it. It was an indication that he, too, thought enough about money to accept it, that he was a mercenary along with the rest of us. I said: "All right, then. When do you want my answer? I'd like to think about it."

"If you could let us know by tomorrow sometime . . . I'm afraid you can't be told any of the mechanics until later on. You do understand that, don't you?"

Using a term we had in the old days, I asked: "What is the element of risk?"

He smiled broadly, then.

"The chance of success," he said, "is estimated at ninety-five."

"That's pretty good."

"Times are not as hard as they used to be."

I remembered how we used to do it. We'd decide to drop some poor enthusiastic devil into Germany, or Italy, or France, with instructions to contact our agents there or set up his own little outfit. We'd gather round the long table on the top floor of the office and thrash out every conceivable problem that he might have to face—whether he spoke the language well enough to fool the Gestapo . . . whether his cover was watertight . . . whether we could really trust the contacts we'd laid on for him . . . whether he was the right man for the job. . . . Then, at the end of it all, the colonel would tot up all our votes and announce: "A sixty per cent chance of success. Send him."

At one time, no operation was permitted unless the estimated chance was over eighty. Then the figure dropped to sixty, then to fifty. There was a time, in Italy, when things were going badly, when I was at a meeting where the figure turned up as eighteen. I remember that Colonel Matley's face had gone as white as a sheet. He rubbed a hand over his eyes and thought a long time and then said, very shortly: "Send him." There'd been an awful pause, a dreadful silence, round the table. Then someone had begun to protest and the colonel had cut him short. "If the estimated chance was one in ten," he had said, "I'd still have to send him. It's vital." Then he had gathered up his papers with that determined air he always put on when he knew that he could not afford to argue, and we all filed miserably out of the office, knowing that we had just voted to send a man to an almost certain death in the hope that he could find out just one little thing that the planning staff had to know.

So when Vallance said, smiling broadly, "The chance is ninety-five," I began to feel better. I felt, too, the excitement and the stimulation that DeBries had spoken of. And the money . . . You know how it is when your creditors are pressing you and you don't know even where the next month's rent is coming from?

I said: "I can tell you now. I'll do what you want."

DeBries was suddenly kinder than he had seemed before. He said cheerfully: "Good. Excellent. Splendid. And it's really quite simple. But . . . the question of discretion, eh? Of security?"

"I can keep my mouth shut."

"I know you can. Otherwise, we'd never have approached you in the first place. I can assure you, a great deal of planning has already been done. Incidentally, Vallance and I will be coming with you."

"So . . ."

DeBries stood up and held out his hand. When I took it, his grasp was firm and friendly. I thought he was rather a nice guy, if a little bit stuffy.

He nodded to Vallance, who went to the window, looked out and nodded his head. At the door, DeBries turned and said: "I'll contact you again in a day or two. Of course, you'll be under surveillance for the next few days, but you won't mind that, will you? As a matter of fact, you've been watched for the past two weeks."

He sounded quite apologetic about it. He went out quickly and shut the door behind him.

Vallance stayed by the window for a little while, watching the street, saying nothing, and I stood there waiting for something to happen. Nothing did.

At last, after several awkward minutes had gone by, he said: "Well, I guess I can go now."

As we shook hands, he said cheerfully: "You'll like DeBries when you get to know him. A sound man. And I'm glad to have you with us. Colonel Matley spoke very highly of you."

"I was the only man in the mess who could drink harder than he could."

"Well, we'll meet again in a couple of days. . . ."

"DeBries . . . What is he, English?"

Vallance said, smiling: "You ought to know better than to ask questions like that."

As soon as he had gone, I put out the lights and threw up the window sash. Vallance was just emerging from the doorway of the apartment block. He was reeling slightly and singing quietly to himself, staggering along cheerfully just as he had done when he had carefully guided me home.

I remembered the envelope and closed the curtains again before I switched on the lights and opened it. It contained five hundred dollars in American bills. I thought it was nice of DeBries to remember that I could get a better rate of exchange than he could. Five hundred dollars is a nice round sum in bolivars if you know your way around. You have to do a little smart trading in a back room down by the docks, because there's a special rate of exchange for each of the major exports which is set by the government—a different rate for each item. So, if you buy cocoa at one rate and sell petroleum at another, brother, you've made twenty-five per cent in ten minutes. But don't let them catch you at it.

I put most of it back in its envelope and slid it behind the bookcase, and tucked a ten-dollar bill into each of my jacket pockets. I didn't see why I shouldn't go out for the rest of the night and amuse myself. It was a long time since I'd been able to afford the things I like so much—sitting around in the night clubs chatting with the girls and drinking real liquor instead of the phony stuff the waiter brought you when you tipped him the wink that you wanted the money instead.

I went over to a place called "El Turc' Aterrador," which you can translate roughly as The Terrible Turk. It was run by my old friend Digger, who was a sort of leftover from an Orient Line ship that called in at La Guaira some twenty years back, so everyone called it Digger's Place, which was a lot easier to say in the small hours of the morning. There was a girl there, called Madeleine, who was a particular friend of mine. Not a pro, you understand, but a nice girl who worked days in a model agency somewhere, and, when times were bad, put in a bit of overtime around the bars. She was a quiet, reserved sort of girl, with lovely gray hair that was supposed to be natural, and quite possible might have been. I'd never seen any hair dye in her place, anyway.

She was a good friend. She was always ready to buy you a drink when you were broke, and for the last few weeks I'd been rather indebted to her. The last time she'd been up to my place, she'd brought a basket of groceries with her; that was fine, but she'd also had the grace to joke about it instead of being rather embarrassed as she ought to have been. I was very fond of her.

She was tall and rather slimmer than most models, with a way of walking that was absolutely fascinating. She'd learned, of course, in the modeling school, but she got her exquisite features from nature. She was French, and God knows how or why she ever came to Caracas.

We had a late supper together, and I gave her some money, not very much, but just enough to make her feel she was sharing my good fortune, and we had a few drinks with Digger.... I told them I'd picked up a fat commission from one of the clubs up in the Plaza Bolívar . . . and later, when I was lying wide awake in bed, smoking a cigarette and enjoying the hedonistic warmth of Madeleine's fragile body beside me, I wondered if I was asking for trouble, tying up with DeBries and Vallance. Even if I was, I figured, it was worth it, just to be able to pay my own way again. It gets you down, being broke for too long.

But some of those politicos were pretty fanatical on the subject of interference from outside. Recent history proved *that* point conclusively enough. . . . But then again, as DeBries had said, it was a lack of caution that betrayed those morons. And from one point of view I was better equipped than most. My background was . . . Well, how shall I put it?

My father was Maltese, my grandfather was Spanish, my mother was French, and I was brought up in England. It's a mixture, isn't it? We lived in France most of our lives, and when the war came they sent me to Algeria. Then the French started fighting each other and I got thrown into prison, over the Darlan business, but some OSS boys thought they could make use of me, and finally I got back to Paris and pulled off a couple of jobs and the next thing I knew I was a hero. It was all quite casual and accidental, and I never did discover what it was that made them so pleased with me. Of course, I can speak half a dozen languages and have just enough fear of getting hurt to make me wriggle out of tight corners when better men might prefer to die nobly. . . . Colonel Matley, my old boss, once told me that a dead agent was a bad agent; it was a comforting philosophy, because it meant that you could always justify running away when things got too tough. But by and large, I'd kicked around enough to make me feel I might be able to make a go of this South American thing. Whatever it might turn out to be.

And the casual disregard these characters seemed to have for money was nice to ruminate on. It seemed to be flowing easily enough, and if some of it could be made to meander my way. . . . I wondered where it came from. Oil? Coffee? It could be anything. Most of the merchant barons had a finger in politics, and all it needed was a drop in the world price of cocoa and then, almost overnight, some tin-pot army colonel had seized power and was holding the president at pistol point, in the barracks. Unless the president had seen it coming and was on his yacht racing north; with the hold full of currency, as usual.

Well, it was none of my business. I was just a hired hand. Madeleine stirred beside me and I turned my attention to more important things.

chapter 2

I didn't see DeBries or Vallance again for nearly a week. In fact, I'd almost begun to believe that they must have changed their minds about the whole thing.

Meanwhile I bought a few copies of the newspapers from down there in an effort to find out what Lazlo was doing. All I found was an article he'd written condemning some Pan-American pact or other that the politicos were working on. He seemed to be Minister of Press Affairs, which was a new one to me. I suppose it was a sort of Propaganda Ministry, and it occurred to me that if our own government was the one Vallance was *not* employed by, then this would be a good place for us to have a friend.

This was a thing I'd been thinking about quite a lot. DeBries had said something about the sense of patriotism I used to have. Patriotism? There's nothing patriotic about helping one group of Latins fight another group of Latins. Unless . . . When I had refused to gather in that piece of bait, he'd changed his tactics and said no more about it. I remember that the first words I learned in English, almost, were a jingle that went:

> Big fleas have little fleas upon their backs to bite 'em,
> And little fleas have lesser fleas, and so ad infinitum.

It occurred to me that if I started looking for all the fleas on this particular piece of mutton, I might come up with some pretty exotic answers. Behind the ambitious officers' group of the moment, there was always a major industrialist, or a trade union; and behind that there was always a group of exiles who sat in expensive hotels in Miami or Havana. Or in Caracas. And behind them there was always a diplomat hovering, the sort of man whose picture never gets into the paper but who has an unlimited expense account that the head of some state or other always approves with no questions asked. And when the brutal battle was over and the corpses that had been dragged through the street had all been burned or buried out of sight, then in distant places there was talk of spheres of influence, accompanied by a great deal of satisfaction and self-congratulation. Well, it was none of my business.

I spent quite a lot of the five hundred dollars, which, to tell the truth, isn't a great deal of money in Caracas, where the cost of living is probably higher than anywhere else in the world. I paid off a few debts, reimbursed the friends who'd come to my rescue, and Madeleine and I had a fine time together. We took to dining in rather better places than I'd become accustomed to, and we went for drives up on the beautiful mountains that lie across the river, with the whole of the magnificent Chacao valley spread out as far as you could see. We had a favorite spot halfway up the mountain where there was a huge mango tree set just above a wide belt of *moriche* palms where there was usually a group of *cholos*, or half-castes, who always seemed to be busy making their beer out of the sweet, ripe fruit. I used to lie on my back with an arm over Madeleine's shoulder, and stare up into the tree at the faintly yellow fruit that hung heavily among the dense dark leaves, looking for one with a reddish tinge that was about to fall, for we had a silly little thing about them—a lovers' game, if you like. We never made love under that tree until one of the mangoes fell, and sometimes I would have to climb up into the firm, resistant branches, and thud the weight of my shoulder against them to shake some fruit loose, listening to Madeleine's delighted laughter below.

We were very happy during that first week, and for a long time thereafter.

I asked Digger about Vallance. He knows everybody in Caracas, but he shook his head and said: "Vallance? That the digger you've been showing around town?"

"The little fat bastard."

"No. Never saw him before. Why?"

"Ever hear of a fellow named DeBries?"

Digger went on straining the rice wine he was making, that he used to pour into bottles labeled Liebfraumilch or Anjou for sale at imported prices. For a long time he didn't say anything, and then he said sharply to the girl who was sitting at the bar: "Well, haven't you anything to do? Go and get your costume fixed."

The girl, a refugee from some place in Europe who hardly spoke any civilized language, slid off her stool and went sullenly to her dressing room. Digger said at last: "You mixed up with that mob, Mike?"

"You know about them?"

"Not much. DeBries is a pretty high-powered digger, boy. Oil. Coffee. Manioc. Rice. Anything with a lot of money in it."

"Legal?"

"Well, some. But once in a while . . . Let me tell you something. You know Caracas as well as I do; everybody minds everybody else's business for them. You want to know all about some joker, all you do is pass over a few bolivars and you've got his life's history, what he eats for breakfast, who his girl friend's two-timing him with . . . the works. But a couple of years back . . . were you here then?"

"Two years ago? No, I was in Brazil."

"Ah, yes. Well, I had occasion to help a friend out who had some deal on with DeBries; I dunno what it was. But I sent Miguel, that lame digger who used to work here, remember? I sent Miguel to make a few discreet inquiries, and at the end of a week he'd found out precisely nothing. I bawled the bugger out, of course, and he tried again, and . . . Someone killed him, Mike. I got word that he'd been killed off for asking too many questions. About DeBries. You can make your own deductions."

"Left, right or center?"

"Ha! Wherever the money is, boy. But if you're tangling up with that monkey, just watch your step."

"Well . . ."

"And don't tell me about it. I don't want to know."

23

Digger's wife, Rosa, came waddling in and took her place at the cash register. It was a sure sign that it was eight o'clock and the bar was officially opening. Rosa was the biggest woman you ever saw. From the top of her head she began to swell out so that round about the neck she was already a couple of feet across, and from then on down it just got wider and wider until all you could do was gape at her. She used to brag that she took a size fifty-four bra, whatever that means, because certainly she'd have to make up those things for herself. Out of surplus tentage, probably. She was a jolly creature, who was always laughing, except when she was suddenly and unexpectedly and viciously savage. She kept a close fist on everything that happened in the bar, and knew all there was to know about *everything*. Digger was terrified of her, big as he was, but long ago they'd come to a sort of understanding; Digger was allowed to play around with all the girls he wanted, but apart from that he had to ask his wife's permission for just about every single thing he did. I think she realized that there wasn't much she had to offer him, in the field of passion that is, and felt that if she let him find all the warm beds he needed then he wouldn't bust out in any other direction. Surprisingly enough, they were very happy together.

Digger wheeled her stool close to the cash register and said: "Mike's been asking about DeBries."

She swung the might of her shoulders round at me and put a pudgy hand on my knee. She said cheerfully: "Watch out you don't get hurt, Mike. Get into trouble there, and ain't nobody gonna help you. Nobody."

"Not even you, Rosa?"

She was suddenly serious. "Some things you ain't joking about, Mike. That man's one of them. What you do to Madeleine today, eh?"

"How's that again?"

Rosa started chuckling to herself. It showed first in a gentle vibration of the shoulders that was soon picked up by the chins, and then the massive breasts began rolling from side to side and you knew that Rosa was laughing. She said: "Never see that girl look so good. What you do to her, Mike?"

I knew she didn't want to talk about DeBries.

It was funny how friendly Digger and I had become, and it started in the queerest possible way.

Digger, like most of us poor expatriates, had a finger in many pies, and one of them was stolen gasoline. Now in Venezuela, which lives off petroleum, this isn't a healthy racket at all. It's not the police you have to worry about so much, it's the Company boys, the accredited investigators.

They're not fussy about their methods, and stealing their gasoline was rather like dining off sacred-cow steak in Calcutta. They used to color it, a faint purple, usually, or sometimes yellow, so that if they found your boat full of colored gasoline they knew exactly where it had come from. Only the boys used to strain it through a loaf of bread, and it came out clean as a whistle.

Anyway, Digger had this big store of stolen gasoline in a barn out on the other slope of the Silla de Caracas, which is the twin mountain that overlooks the city a couple of miles to the north. There are some very deserted spots up there, quite hard to get to, and I was prowling around up there one day looking for some of those pale gray orchids that fetch such a fancy price in town, when I was suddenly aware that the place was lousy with cops, all moving in on this barn that was set in a hollow among the breadfruit trees. I lay doggo and watched through my binoculars, and I saw Digger drive up in a jeep with a load of tires on the back. The track that led to this place passed quite close to where I was hiding, and the police were all on the other side of the hill, so I ran down as fast as I could and when Digger stopped I told him what was going on over there.

I hardly knew him at that time. But he was . . . well, one of *us*. He high-tailed it out of there as fast as the jeep would go, and when I went into his bar that night he told me all about it. He asked if I'd like to come in with him on this gasoline racket, and when I refused I think he was rather touched that I wasn't going to blackmail him into an arrangement. I learned later that he'd also moved his stuff out of there in a hurry, but when he found out that I wasn't talking, he moved it all back again and settled down once more into the comfortable little rut of his sideline. I think it was Rosa who'd told him he could trust me to keep my mouth shut, in spite of the big rewards the Company men were always offering for information like this. We became very close friends after that.

He was a big, burly Australian who always seemed to need a shave. He had tattoo designs all down his forearms, and a chest on him like a beer barrel. He used to fancy himself as a hell of a man with the women, but the truth of the matter is that it was Rosa who made sure the girls were friendly to him; she liked her Digger to be happy all the time, and this was the easiest way to do it.

One night Madeleine had a late appointment with some photographer or other, and I went home about midnight.

Vallance was there. I had the sense not to ask him how

he got in, and I must admit he was apologetic about it.

"Didn't want to hang around outside," he said. "I knew you wouldn't mind...."

We had a drink together, and he said: "Nice girl, that Madeleine."

I didn't feel like discussing her with him, so I said nothing. Changing the subject abruptly, he said: "We've had a man on your tail. Interesting to know if you've spotted him?"

"As a matter of fact, I haven't. I was particularly interested. In the army you took the efficiency of the colonel for granted; it was never in question. But now it's different. I'm a free agent. I'd like to believe that the people I'm working for know what they're doing."

Vallance said politely: "And you don't believe we do?"

"I'm damn sure there were times when your man must have lost me."

He swilled his drink round the glass and examined it as though he were wondering why I didn't get better gin now that I could afford it.

"Not once," he said. "Every minute of the day. We know what you've done, whom you've seen . . . every minute of the day."

"Oh, yes? Where was I last night?"

He stared at me as though he found my questioning his word somewhat distasteful. Then he said coldly: "You mean El Calvario?"

El Calvario is the big public garden up on the hill. It gets very lonely in some patches, after dark, and I'd gone up there with the specific intention of finding out if I was being followed or not. I'd double around, cut back and forth under the banana trees, slipped in behind the greenhouses. . . . I was quite sure I'd shaken whoever was on my tail.

Vallance went on: "I heard you'd given him quite a time. But it was a dangerous thing to do, Mr. Benasque. It seemed to our man that you were deliberately trying to get away from him, and had he been in real danger of losing you . . . He's not the kind of man who normally has the prerogative of discretion, but now that you know as much as you do . . . It's not safe for us not to know your every movement. He came very close to killing you last night."

I felt my mouth was open and closed it sharply. I said: "Well, I'll be damned."

Pressing home his tiny advantage, he said: "The taxi driver you pick up on the street. The guard at the museum. The street urchin who shines your shoes. The policeman who directs the traffic. The teller in the bank. You want me to go on, Mr. Benasque? There are thousands of them who are with us. Hundreds of thousands. Do you really think it's a child's game?"

I said lamely: "No . . . it's not that at all. . . ."

"And there was a time last night when the approach of a stranger . . . of someone we didn't know . . . I tell you, you came perilously close to being shot."

"Just for trying to get lost?"

"The issues at stake," Vallance said pompously, "are valid enough to support the philosophy that one life is sometimes worth more than another."

He had the damnedest way of talking—as though he were putting forward a premise with which he could brook no argument. It was also arrogant and condescending, as though, good heavens, you poor idiot, don't you realize this? I kept my temper in check. After all, he'd dispersed any doubts I had about the efficiency of his organization.

He made a final point while he was winning. He said smoothly: "And there's no need to get offended when I mention your Madeleine, either. You've been seeing quite a lot of her lately, and we had to check on her too. So calm down and fill up your glass."

I had not noticed it was empty. I went to the kitchen and broke up some ice with the handle of the carving knife. When I came back, his mood had quite changed. Smiling blandly, he said:

"You're right, of course, to demand proof of our competence. In your position I would do the same. But let me tell you this. The opposition, I'm afraid, is a good deal stronger than we are. At the higher echelons, of course, we know all about them. But the man in the street who sympathizes with *them* . . . this is the imponderable. And for every hundred of us there are thousands of them. So security becomes . . . Do I make myself clear?"

"Perfectly. So you feel I can trust my Madeleine?"

He didn't know whether I was trying to mock him or asking a legitimate question. I was conscious that he was weighing every word I spoke and every gesture I made. He said: "Like most women of her class, she's completely apolitical. I don't think you'd be so foolish as to discuss this with her. Quite apart from the question of security, you'd only be putting her life in immediate danger. A thing like this . . . it only needs one word."

He was staring at Madeleine's picture on the wall. It was a new photograph she'd given me only a couple of days back. She really photographed very beautifully. He said didactically:

"It's quite different from wartime, you know. In this case,

we have a dictator whose position is so insecure that the slightest vestige of opposition must be crushed as soon as it begins to move. There's no waiting for battle orders . . . anything that begins to stir must be stepped on, at once, ruthlessly, before it has a chance to develop into a threat to the junta, and if this means killing off a few hundred innocent bystanders . . . well, life's cheap enough in these parts. . . ."

I said: "If you want to talk, we'd better go someplace else. Madeleine will be coming here soon."

He waved a pudgy hand airily, dismissing the possibility. He said: "She's doing a job for a very good photographer, one of the best in Caracas. And his customer will be there to see that he gets exactly what he wants, even if it takes all night." Seeing my surprise, he added: "One of the men from the refineries. We thought it might be better to talk here and wanted to make sure we weren't disturbed. Your Madeleine will be kept busy until I call someone and have a message relayed. Satisfied?"

I nodded. There was nothing much I could say, really. Vallance looked at his drink again and said apologetically: "I don't really like drinking gin at this time of night. I suppose you haven't got any brandy?"

"Sorry. Er . . . it so happens . . ."

"Well, it's not important. . . ."

He was walking slowly up and down the room, his eyes very restless and concerned. He turned at last and watched me over the top of his glass. He said slowly: "You're in this with us now . . . ever since you learned the nature of the objective. And your background puts you in a rather privileged position, so if you see any flaws, please let me know. We are not omniscient, so . . . I can tell you right now that there *are* no flaws, but you have a right to be certain. Let's begin with the one thing that worries you. You wonder why it has to be you, don't you? Why nobody else will do?"

"That's a good point."

He was watching me very carefully indeed, and I sensed that under his affability Mr. Vallance was nobody's fool. He had a shrewd and careful mind. He looked exactly like a prosperous businessman from the Middle West, but a man who's become prosperous because he never lets anything escape his notice. Like one of those top-flight businessmen they take into the Pentagon sometimes.

He said slowly: "Has it never occurred to you that you and Lazlo are very much alike?"

I could feel the skin crawling at the back of my neck. It never had occurred to me, and, now that it did, I didn't like what it implied. I could imagine all sorts of things, ranging from the stupidly dangerous to the downright suicidal. I suppose it must have shown on my face. Vallance smiled and said cheerfully: "Oh, I know what you're thinking. Believe me, there's nothing to worry about. But it does all hinge on this resemblance."

"But good heavens, Lazlo's ten years younger than I am."

He said grimly: "Not any more, he isn't. Don't forget he had a short spell in one of their prisons. The wonder is he doesn't look old enough to be your father. You haven't seen him for a long time now, so you wouldn't know. But I have. Look, I'll show you."

He delved under his shirt and pulled out a slim leather case. Opening the zipper, he took out a photograph and laid it on the table. It was Lazlo all right, but quite a different Lazlo from the one I'd known. He was a great deal older than the young firebrand who'd been standing by that shattered window, and he was considerably thinner too. His hair was balding, and the skin was a lot tighter over the cheekbones. There was a certain superficial resemblance to me, I suppose, but . . . Then Vallance laid another photograph beside the first and I stared at it.

It was a photograph of me, but . . . I picked it up and went and sat on the sofa examining it under the light of the yellow-shaded standard lamp. I could still feel that creeping sensation at the top of my scalp. I saw that it was not my picture at all, but another one of Lazlo. They'd added a hair piece and done something with his teeth, and my own mother, rest her soul, would have sworn it was me. Trying to keep my voice steady, I asked: "What have you done to it?"

"To the photograph? Nothing. It's unretouched."

"So?"

"He's been given a hair piece, and by the grace of God he had his front teeth knocked out by the truncheons of the secret police, when he was just a student."

When I said nothing, he added: "We simply gave him a new denture. Bigger teeth, like yours. Now you see why it has to be you. Nobody else will do."

I threw the picture angrily back on the table.

"But you don't really imagine," I said, "that I can take Lazlo's place? It's fantastic. It's so impossible as to be downright stupid."

"You don't have to," Vallance said patiently. "I told you, there's nothing to worry about. Nothing at all. It's not a question of your taking Lazlo's place. It's a question of *his* taking *yours*. That's quite a different kettle of fish, isn't it? Wouldn't you say so?"

Well, I suppose it was, and I agreed with him, though not very happily.

He said, with a tinge of asperity: "Well, if you've quite got over your fright . . . Briefly, this is what happens, without benefit of detail. One: you go into the country on your passport in the normal way. Two: Lazlo leaves the country on your passport. Three: Lazlo returns by the same means. Four: you come out in the normal way. While Lazlo is *out* and you are *in*, you remain in a prearranged hiding place, under guard. Is that simple enough for you? And safe enough?"

Ignoring the jibe, I asked: "And while I am *in*, and Lazlo is *out*, what happens if someone goes looking for him?"

"Nobody will. That's been taken care of."

"But if they should . . . They'd find me."

"No." He sighed patiently. "I told you, he is taking your place but you are not taking his. There'll be . . . a vacuum."

"How long will Lazlo be out?"

"Three days."

"And I'm in hiding all that time."

"In a perfectly safe place, under reliable guard."

"Why don't I just rent you my passport? You can have it for a hundred bucks a day."

"We want you to be seen going in and seen coming out. Please don't try and find frivolous objections."

"How do I account for my presence there in the first place?"

"You're on a business trip. There's no difficulty there. The place is wide open to tourists . . . visiting businessmen. . . . Even their own people can move about just as they wish, as long as they keep away from any area where there's actual fighting going on. The important thing is that Lazlo should spend three days out of the country without their knowing it."

"For a meeting, I take it?"

"Precisely."

"Where?"

"In Havana."

"Hardly the best place right now, is it?"

"No, I suppose it isn't."

He spoke with just the right amount of polite interest to make me understand that Havana was *not* the meeting place and that it was none of my business anyway. Which it wasn't, of course. I looked hard for any possible flaws. There was just one small thing. I asked him: "On that second trip in, when the guy with my passport is Lazlo . . . you still need a visa to go down there. Suppose they refuse it?"

"They won't. The business you're traveling on is too important to them. They need scrap iron, and that's what you're selling."

"Me? You said yourself that their spies are all over. They'll soon find out, if they're interested, that I'm no scrap-iron merchant. That's big business in these parts. Usually handled by people with expensive yachts."

"Your actual position will be less imposing. You will not be alone. You will be . . . a servant, but you won't mind that, will you?"

There was one more detail, and it was an important one. "Under guard," Vallance had said.

"The people I hide out with . . . This seems to be the danger point. How do you know you can trust them?"

He smiled and said: "I see you haven't entirely forgotten your old cunning. As you say, this could well be the danger point. But it's someone we can trust . . . someone *you* can trust implicitly."

"Oh?"

Vallance was beaming at me again. He said: "His name is Trenko. Remember him?"

Did I remember Trenko! Trenko was the man I'd dragged to safety at the railway station that day. Vallance said happily: "I thought you'd be pleased."

The whole picture was beginning to fall into perspective, a kaleidoscope clicking into clarity with every new twist of the conversation.

After Lazlo's men had pulled us both out of danger, I'd sat with Trenko in the bomb-scarred room, the only man without a weapon, terrified that the police would force their way in and find me aiding a bunch of hotheads against them . . . not even knowing what it was all about. They wouldn't have bothered to stop and ask questions.

I'd spent an hour dodging the bullets and trying to stop the flow of blood from Trenko's shattered leg. A police grenade had torn a great lump out of his thigh and he was lucky not to have lost it altogether.

Then Lazlo had said shortly: "All right, time to withdraw. Down through the cellar."

He'd stared for a moment at a wounded man who was lying in the corner, his face white with a kind of parchment glossiness to it that could only mean he was dying. He'd had a whispered conversation with this man, and then gently put a grenade in each hand, with the pins pulled out ready. I saw this fellow's eyes flicker briefly as he clutched them to his bloody chest with his fingers clenched tight around the levers and then he nodded his head a little and actually smiled as though nothing could be better for him than blowing himself up as soon as the police broke in and bent over him. It was far better than what they'd do to him, anyway, and to save a dying man . . . for what?

I'd carried Trenko over my shoulder along the dark stone alleyway that led under the house, with the reek of beer in the air and the wet feel of it sloshing about our ankles where the great casks that lined the walls had been punctured. I'd carried him out into the darkness, running blindly after the others until we reached a barricade and clambered through, and then on again to where a truck was waiting with its motor turning, waiting to spirit us away into the hills, and for the next two days I'd nursed Trenko back to some sort of health at least, and we'd become close friends, the three of us, Lazlo, Trenko and I.

When I'd left, I'd said jocularly enough: "One day I'll be back. When you're in power. You can give me the keys to the city."

He was one of those fervent rebels, Trenko, who fight against any sort of authority. Not with cold skill and a passionate devotion, as Lazlo did, but with a kind of reckless hatred of government just because it was government. If the junta was right, then Trenko was left; if it was left, then Trenko was right. It's a healthy enough attitude in a democracy, but under a dictatorship it can be pretty difficult spending your whole life automatically fighting the people in power. Because you get no respite even when your own people claw their way to the top; as soon as they're in the saddle, you're instinctively trying to upset them. If he'd become Dictator himself, he'd have felt obliged, out of moral principles and habit, to topple himself from his perch.

Conscious of the changes that must have taken place in the years since all this happened, I said: "What's he doing now? Trenko?"

"He's an honest citizen. A farmer. Quite content to knuckle under to the regime. But he runs the liaison between Lazlo and the rebels."

"And they don't suspect him?"

"No. He's a smooth operator."

"And who else is in on the scheme?"

"You and I, DeBries, Lazlo and Trenko. Apart from . . . apart from the people I take my orders from, there's no one else."

"And where do they hang out? The people you take your orders from."

"You don't really expect me to answer that, do you?"

"No, not really."

"Good."

"How does Lazlo give them the slip for three days? I thought they were watching him constantly."

Vallance smiled as though he were particularly pleased about this. He said: "He'll have smallpox. He'll be at his country home, which is only a hundred miles or so from the border. The application of a suitable skin irritant will give him the necessary hemorrhagic eruptions on the forearms, and the local doctor will diagnose smallpox. Take it from me, no one will go near his house as soon as the word gets out."

"Smallpox takes a month to cure, if it's not fatal. How come he's on his feet again three or four days later?"

"It was a false alarm. Turns out to be an allergy that caused acute eczema."

His thoroughness astonished me. I couldn't help asking: "Allergy to what?"

Vallance nodded affably. "Yes," he said, "there's the weakness, I suppose. But the allergy that causes eczema is egg whites, did you know that? And on a country estate . . . he's got a couple of hundred hens there. Satisfied?"

"The doctor must be in on this. He'd be treating him with sulfanilamide."

Vallance smiled. "But once the diagnosis is made, he'll be kept away from the house without knowing why. He'll be made to believe that someone is trying to prevent his treating Lazlo. All part of the picture of tyranny."

For the life of me, I couldn't find a flaw. It was so damnably thorough. I began to admire the executive ability of these people. And to feel, moreover, that I was in pretty safe hands. Vallance said again: "Satisfied?"

"Yes. It's a pretty damn good operation."

"All right then, let's get down to facts."

He took a map from his leather case and spread it on the table. It looked like an operational battle map, with annotations in green ink all over it. Leaning over it, looking very short and stout, he punched at it with a thick forefinger.

"Here," he said, "here. This is Lazlo's place. A sort of minor manor house, surrounded by cashew trees, some sugar cane, quite a lot of guava and papaya—the usual run of stuff in these places. The railway line which leads to the border is eighteen miles away . . . over here. On D-day minus three, Lazlo gets his attack of smallpox and is quarantined in his house. On that day, you and I leave Ponte Encino by train, cross the border. . . ."

"Did you say *'you and* I'?"

"I did. DeBries told you we'd both be along on the trip."

"Yes, of course. I'd half forgotten."

"Mustn't forget these things, Mr. Benasque, they can be

important. Now. You and I leave Ponte Encino . . . here . . . by train, on D-day minus three. We cross the border on D-day minus two, and we stop at the village of Volvoda . . . here. I shall be a cripple, in a wheel chair. I'm a businessman selling their government a load of scrap iron, and they are expecting me in San Antonio on D-day minus one. My meeting with them will be over in a few hours, and you and I will return, passing through Volvoda again, on D-day. Now, the train stops there just before eleven o'clock at night, and this is when and where we go into operation.

"Lazlo, with Trenko at his side, will be waiting, concealed, near the railway station. It's a tiny place, just a watering stop, with one elderly man to sell tickets, pump the water, sweep the place out from time to time . . . everything. The watering process takes well over half an hour, and you and I spend that time on the platform, such as it is, with you wheeling me up and down in my wheel chair while we wait. But at this point, you have to go to the toilet.

"By now, Lazlo will be in the toilet, wearing his hair piece and his new teeth, and dressed in precisely the same clothes as you. It'll be a sort of uniform. You stay in the toilet, Lazlo comes out and takes over the wheel chair, Trenko picks you up as soon as the train has left, and takes you to the hide-out; and Lazlo continues as my male nurse across the border, with me to see that nothing goes wrong. Three days later, we repeat the same thing in reverse, and the operation is over. Well?"

I poured myself another drink and slumped on the sofa to think about it. It had all the elements of thoughtful simplicity, right down to the use of a wheel chair. Knowing what the answer would be, I asked: "The purpose of the wheel chair?"

"It justifies my having someone with me, by my side, all the time. He'll be constantly with me."

"Lazlo's English is good, but not that good. Suppose some border guard or other asks him a few simple questions?"

"I'm carrying a letter from their Department of Munitions. I'm an important man, a VIP. And if they want to ask my servant any questions, they can damn well do it through me."

There was just the right edge to his voice to prove his point. He was the high-powered traveler who thought that all foreigners could understand you if you shouted at them loud enough. All the same . . . if anything went wrong here they'd find my passport on Lazlo. I said, not expecting much of an answer: "Why the hell don't you just make a passport specially for him? With the connections you seem to have . . ."

Vallance said primly: "The operation will go forward precisely as planned. As I said, we want them to see you going in and to see you coming out. Just to make doubly sure."

I stared at the ceiling again for a long time, then closed my eyes and thought about it some more.

It was simple, neat, tidy, efficient. I wondered if it were perhaps too simple. The trouble with a straightforward operation is that you're inclined to forget, in the backwash of its simplicity, that all around you are dangers you'd be more aware of if they faced you at every turn. One man goes in, another man goes out. . . . Why not? Those sleepy little border towns between one republic and another . . . high in the mountains where the air is thin and lethargy is the order of the day . . .

I liked the smallpox, too. It was the one dread disease that would send the secret police scampering for cover. They'd keep their distance too, with images of the Plague hammering at their memories, a scared little group of frightened men sending in their reports as usual but mutually agreeing with a kind of tacit understanding of one another's fear that no one would actually go near the house until the man was better . . . or dead.

But could it be so easy, to get a carefully watched and important man out of the country—a minister, for God's sake—and then to put him back in again? "A lot of money in it," they had said, and I know it was the thought of the money that made me throw away the sense of caution I was born with, and, with it, my last hopes of a normal, decent death in bed.

I should have remembered the *Life* magazine stories and the indignant inquiries from the State Department. I should have remembered that wounded man lying there in San Antonio with a smile on his face while he clutched two Mills bombs to his chest; or the stories that Lazlo had told me about what they had done to his girl . . . and, for that matter, to him too. But I didn't. All I could think of was the money and what I could do with it. Maybe I'd go back home to Scranton, Pennsylvania, maybe even take Madeleine with me. Or to Paris instead, if she wanted, anywhere away from this rat-infested cesspit where you had to steal or scrounge or pimp to make a living.

It was the money, all right, and nothing else. I didn't see why, if I played it carefully . . . that's the way money makes you lose your sense of perspective. The danger and the terror seemed small and far away, at the furthest extremities of a pair of converging lines, like specks at the end of a Dali landscape. But if the truth were known, they were looming over me at that very minute, close by and large and horrifying. It was the money.

I said: "All right, when do we get operational?"

"Very soon now. As a matter of academic interest, how does it strike you?"

"Thorough. Simple. Don't see why it shouldn't work."

"It's got to work, Mr. Benasque. A lot depends on it."

There was an unexpected vehemence there suddenly. Looking at him curiously, I said: "Your interest in this thing . . . It's rather more political than anything else, isn't it?"

"Quite the contrary," he said quickly. "I'm a paid employee, just as you are."

"Uh-huh."

"But my sympathies . . ."

"Of course."

"And we didn't discuss the question of payment, did we?"

"We did not."

"We will, in the course of time. Meanwhile . . ."

He pulled a package out of his breast pocket. It was bulky enough to set my pulse moving faster for a moment. He put it on the table and stood up, slipping his thin leather case with the map in it back under his shirt. He said: "There's enough there to keep you going for a while. We'll be getting in touch with you again. Can I use your phone?"

"Of course. It's in the bedroom."

"Yes, I know."

I stood there trying not to pick up the envelope until he had made his call. Through the open door I heard him dial and say briefly: "Any time now."

When he came back, he held out his hand and said: "They'll be finished with your Madeleine now. We've given her a busy night, haven't we?"

I took his fleshy hand and said: "Academic interest again. What's the skin irritant that produces smallpox sores?"

His face brightened into a delightful smile. He said: "You know, believe it or not, I was half hoping you'd ask that."

"Well, what is it?"

"The oil that lies between the two skins of the cashew nut. There are cashew trees all round Lazlo's place."

"You don't miss a trick, do you?"

"We can't afford to, Mr. Benasque. We just can't afford the luxury of mistakes. And if I might make a parting suggestion?"

"Security?"

"Precisely. Make no mistake about it. This is far more deadly than it ever was in the old days. You haven't got an army standing behind you now. No Geneva Convention . . . Do I make myself clear?"

"You do."

"One word is all that's required . . . one intemperate word. They fight with claws, not gloves."

"You've made the point."

"And they're all around us. So . . . Just stand by till you hear from me."

"Am I still under surveillance?"

"Yes. But now, it will be for your own protection. We have too much interest vested in you. You're a precious commodity. We'll see you again soon."

When he had gone I opened the envelope. This time it contained two thousand American dollars.

Madeleine came home shortly afterward and told me that the client of her photographer had been hanging around there, a nice-looking young American tourist who had something to do with a fashion magazine in the States. He'd been very fussy about what he wanted, and wouldn't let the photographer alone to get on with his work; otherwise, she said, she'd have been back a couple of hours ago.

I had intended to go out on the town a bit, but Madeleine looked so lovely that I decided to stay home instead. She let her long gray hair down over her shoulders when we got into bed, and I don't think I ever loved her as much as I did that night. She never wore anything in bed, and with that strange-colored hair and her long white body, incredibly smooth and lustrous, she looked like a porcelain figurine, but warm and supple and very much alive.

I was really beginning to fall very much in love with her.

In the morning, I went out to a public call box and put through a call to Colonel Matley in the States. I knew I'd never get him in Cape Canaveral, so I left a message at his home in Jacksonville, Florida, giving him the number at my apartment. It took a long time for my call to get through, but I was surprised how fast his answer came back.

I just had time to get back into the kitchen to put the coffee on when the phone rang. I took it quickly so that it would not wake Madeleine. It was the colonel all right. He said breezily: "Hullo, Mike, hear you're looking for me. What's on your mind?"

I said: "I rather hoped you were expecting to hear from me."

"Oh, that. Well, I was, last week. When I didn't hear, I thought you must've turned them down."

"You know about them, then?"

"Sure I do."

"Are they . . . legal?"

There was just a brief hesitation. Then he drawled: "Do you mean legal, or legitimate?"

Well, that was a fine distinction. I said: "Either."

"Well, they're pretty legitimate."

"Any connection with anyone we know?"

"Not the slightest, Mike. Not the slightest."

"Unofficially."

"Unofficially and officially. This is purely a personal matter. Just doing a favor to a friend of a friend of a friend."

"How's that?"

"They wanted somebody for a job, that's all, with qualifications that you have."

"Then the old outfit isn't tied up in it?"

"Hell, no. I don't even know what it's all about."

There was just enough hasty insistence that the department's hands were white as snow to make me believe that maybe they were just a little bit muddy, in patches. I couldn't help laughing. The colonel said quickly: "All I do know is . . . just take it easy, Mike. Remember all the things I taught you, that's all."

"O.K., Colonel. I'll do that. Family O.K.?"

"Sure, fine. How's Caracas?"

"Expensive. Too many tourists."

"I'll come and look you up one of these days. Will you buy me a beer?"

"You bet."

"So long, Mike."

"So long, Colonel."

The same old Matley. When he rang off, I reflected a bit on the way things were shaping up. It was almost like being back with the old outfit again. Only now, they paid you better.

Madeleine came sleepily into the kitchen with a yellow bath towel wrapped around her white body. She went straight to the coffee percolator and lifted the lid and then went back into the bedroom without saying a word. I followed her in and stood at the bathroom door while she took her shower, just admiring her perfection. I went back to the kitchen when I smelled the coffee coming through, and I put a couple of bread rolls into the oven and took the butter off the ice, and then Madeleine was standing silently beside me again, looking incredibly lovely in a dark green dress with a sort of off-the-shoulder, Grecian look to it.

One thing I liked about Madeleine: she always dressed decently. Some of the women in a place like Caracas, where it gets pretty hot most of the time, tend to slouch around the place in a housecoat, or a kimono, or some other shapeless nonsense they think is comfortable. But not Madeleine. In all the time I knew her, I hardly ever saw her except properly dressed or properly undressed.

chapter 3

Ten days later, things started moving, with a vengeance.

I was up at Digger's barn on the Silla, helping him shift some drums of gasoline ready for delivery to one of his customers. They were stored in the lower part of this old barn, under the heavy planks of what was the main floor. It was a sort of cellar, quite low-ceilinged and with an earthen floor, but it was long and spacious, and although it had been constructed as a crawl-space, it acutally made a very good spot to hide things, because unless you knew it was there you'd never think of looking under the floor for a lower story.

We had to roll the drums up a sort of wooden ramp onto the main floor, and then up another smaller one to an elevation that led outside, so that a truck could load quickly in the darkness and get the hell of there fast. It was hard work.

It was just about twilight when we finished, and we sat on the stone wall of a big shallow well that lay quite close to the barn, wiping the sweat off our necks and chatting about this and that and drinking whiskey out of Digger's flask.

I'd had a few qualms about going up there when Digger asked me to give him a hand, because I knew that I was being watched by Vallance's men, but then it occurred to me that Vallance was not likely to interest himself in such petty nonsense as stolen gasoline; after all, everybody has a little side line of some sort; you must have, to pay the rent. And I didn't like to try and wiggle out of it because Digger was always worried that the *cholos* who helped him out from time to time might give him away, one of them, to the cops or to the Company men. So I shurgged my shoulders and went along anyway.

We rolled up twelve of the big drums, and replaced the one that Digger always kept up in the loft for his own use, and what a job that was! It was up a long ladder, and we had to haul it up on a rope and tackle, but he liked to keep one up there because it was a good hiding place and it saved opening up the heavy floor boards every time he wanted to fill the tank of his own car.

Anyway, we were sitting on this thick stone wall, drinking and chewing the rag about nothing in particular, when suddently someone fired on us from the cover of the woods close by. My reflexes seemed a bit slow, because I just sat there shocked into a sort of immobility with surprise rather than fear, conscious that a bullet had struck the broken-down wooden cover over the well, quite close to my head, just as the noise of it sounded. I turned and stared at the direction it had come from, and Digger said: "Christ, the coppers . . ." and then another shot sounded and a piece of flint flew up close beside my feet. Whoever it was seemed to be a lousy shot, but there was precious little consolation in *that* fact.

Then I felt Digger's arm over my shoulder as he slipped off the wall, and we both tumbled together into the well itself. As I said, it was quite shallow, no more than ten or twelve feet down to the water level, and then only a couple of feet or so of water and sand. We splashed to the bottom and crouched there looking up at the round ring of the sky above us for a moment, and then drew close under the protective cover of the overhang, pressing ourselves against the wet stone and staring upward.

Digger said: "Can't be the coppers, you know. Can it?"

I knew damn well it wasn't and I shook my head. Digger looked at me for a while thoughtfully and said: "If you're in trouble, Mike . . . You know you can call on me, don't you?"

"Sure, Digger, sure."

He said nothing for a while and then mumbled:

"This won't do my spring water any good, will it?" I knew then that he just wasn't going to ask any more questions.

We stayed there for an hour or so, waiting. But nobody came, and at last we climbed out, soaking wet and filthy with sandy mud, and we stood around until we were a bit drier and then took off for home. Digger wanted me to spend the rest of the evening in the bar, warding off pneumonia, but I had other things to do. I was furious, and my anger was increased by the knowledge that I didn't know where to find Vallance and would have to wait for him to call me. Which I knew he would do.

Sure enough, the phone was ringing when I reached the apartment. It was Vallance at the other end. He said cautiously: "You know who this is?"

I said: "Too damn well I know. What the hell was the idea of that nonsense this evening?"

There was a little pause, and then he said: "Did you think that was us?"

"Who else, for God's sake?"

"Well, it wasn't. I've just heard about it. My man was up there, but couldn't see who it was."

I could feel the fear creeping into me again. I said unhappily: "Well . . . if it wasn't your man then who the hell was it?"

"I wish I knew. You haven't been talking out of turn?"

"Of course not."

"No, I thought not. Let me make a few inquiries. I'll contact you again in a day or two."

"But wait a minute—"

It was no use. He'd rung off.

I never did find out who'd fired those shots. I saw Vallance again the next day, and he was puzzled and therefore worried. He liked to know exactly what was happening all around him, and a little gap like this in the weave of his knowledge was a thing that made him unhappy indeed. I asked him if it would affect the operation at all and he shook his head.

I said: "Seems an awful long time between the conception of the idea and its execution."

"I know. Too long. But it can't be helped, I'm afraid. Your nerves bad?"

"No. Just like to get started, that's all."

"We all would, Mr. Benasque. But it won't be long now."

It wasn't.

It was one of those bright and cheerful nights when everything seems to turn out well. Digger had bought a deer from one of the *cholos* who'd been out hunting, and Rosa, his wife, who was a pretty good hand with a skillet, had made some *bigarade*, which is a sort of braised steak marinated in the oil of the small sour wild oranges that grow out in the valleys near Caracas.

We all sat together, that night: Madeleine and I, Rosa and Digger and his new mistress, who was a pretty little dancer he'd seduced away from one of the more fancy clubs up in town, about seventeen years old or so and quite attractive, though a bit empty-headed. I'd just bought Madeleine a new dress, which turned out to be a felicitous choice; it's easy to go wrong on a thing like that, only this one pleased her immensely and she looked lovely in it; and she was consequently in very good form. Digger was pleased as punch with his new girl friend, and even the rather tatty floor show was going unusually well.

A new spotlight had been installed that played on one of those spherical revolving mirrors, and somehow it gave the place an air of slightly dilapidated romance that was generally missing. Even the orchestra was playing in tune, which was most unusual. Digger's girl, whose name was Lala something-or-other, got up to do her act, slipping out of her dress carelessly as she approached the little raised platform that served as a stage. Perhaps I was a bit drunk, because Digger was pouring the good wines instead of the usual crabby stuff and I'd had rather a lot. But I seem to remember more than anything else, just then, the spectacle of Lala with her hands pressed tight to her young breasts, cupping them, so to speak, with her long brown fingers as though to make sure we all saw how firm and proud they were; her head was tilted back a little and her mouth was half-open, and only her hips seemed to be moving. I noticed that the music was very quiet, and the drummer was tapping out the rhythm delicately with the tips of his fingers, while his shoulders were hunched up as though he were floating on the compelling cadence of his counterpoint; there was a rapport between the girl and the drummer that was astonishing. No one at the table was talking. We were all watching the act, and then Digger looked at me with such a smug expression of possessive pride that I could not help glancing across at Rosa; she winked at me and started shaking with that funny chuckle she had.

All in all, what with one thing and another, there was a warm sensation of—how shall I put it? Of pleasing decadence . . .

It was pleasing because the really fine things we had there had all taken on a light touch of debasement, and this has come to be a rare thing. Nowadays, we're getting a damn sight too virtuous to appreciate anything. But here . . . here there were good wines—not to sip and delicately savor, but to get hopelessly drunk on. There was music—not to be coldly appraised, but to succumb to in a kind of narcotic stupor. And there were beautiful women, not to chat lightly with and doff your hat to, but to satiate yourself with in heart-pounding, loin-straining, spasmic convulsion, quite beyond the reach of any rational restraints.

Satiation. That's the word. To fill yourself with the things you want until the very excess of luxury is itself no longer endurable and you lose control of your senses. The Romans knew about it, and so did the Greeks. To them, Bacchus and Priapus were gods to be indulged and propitiated, but now . . . Now, they simper about moderation and discipline, and raise their holy hands in pious fright if anyone should want to be happy.

What use is a craving unless you indulge it?

I'm afraid the moderates would not have approved of Digger's crowd. But that night, we were slowly letting the tide of sensuality creep up around us, letting our bodies float in it, welcoming an indefinable feeling of nostalgia for something we once had or had always wanted. I suppose, if the truth were known, it was merely the beginning of drunkenness, but I felt that our role in life was passive, not active—that things were happening to us that we could not prevent, even if we had wanted to, and that we were absorbing them greedily rather than rejecting them.

It was because of this feeling that I had an instinct that something was wrong. I could neither understand it nor justify it, but it centered itself on something that seemed to be happening behind me. I turned round, but there was nothing unusual there. Then I became aware of a tall, thin man with very hollow cheeks, who was holding a chicken leg in his hand and gnawing on it as though he hadn't eaten for a month. He looked up at me once, over the drumstick, not stopping his chewing, and then looked quickly away again, and there was suddenly a feeling of acute unease. I turned back to the table and said to Digger:

"Don't look now, but that consumptive fellow over by the door . . . do you know him?"

Digger could not take his eyes off Lala. He said: "How's that?"

Rosa was looking at the consumptive man somberly. She said: "He is not from here, Mike. You know him, maybe?"

I shook my head. The uneasiness had passed just as quickly as it had come. I realized it was probably Vallance's man, and felt a little foolish. But Rosa was looking at me shrewdly. She said: "That trouble at the barn the other day, Mike. You think they maybe make trouble for you? Or maybe for my Digger?"

It was astonishing how that woman always seemed to know what you were thinking of. I said shortly: "How the hell should I know? Someone took a shot at us. Could have been at Digger, could have been at me. I don't know. Don't think I even care, not right now."

Madeleine turned her face to me and I saw a sudden anxiety in her eyes. It was the first she'd heard of it. She said nothing, but looked away again, and then put her hand on mine, and I could feel the tremor that was running through her.

Rosa called the waiter over, and whispered something to him. His name was 'Arry. He was English, but he passed for a Spaniard because of his dark complexion and black eyes, and we always dropped the aitch because, first of all, he was a cockney and that's how he spoke, and secondly because it sounded like "Arri," which is a common enough name in those parts. He was a vicious little runt, but a good man in a scrap. I saw that 'Arry was keeping an eye on this fellow from then on.

I was good and drunk when I got home that night. I emptied my pockets on the top of the dresser, and I found a piece of paper that had not been there before, with a telephone number on it and a note: *Call this number as soon as you get home.*

It sobered me up, realizing that I was on call, so to speak, even in the middle of a beautiful night. . . . I rang the number, and as soon as I said "Hullo?" the voice at the other end said shortly: "O.K. Ring off."

Wondering, I put the receiver down, and a few minutes later it rang again, and, when I answered it, Vallance was there. He sounded quite cheerful. He said: "Well, that was quite an evening you had, wasn't it?"

I said: "That guy's got consumption. He ought to see a doctor."

There was a little hesitation at the other end, long enough to set me wondering again. Then Vallance said: "What was that?"

"Skip it. What's on your mind?"

"Go to the Agencia Castelano tomorrow and ask if they have a temporary job for you. Tell them you've had a smattering of medical experience. All right?"

"Can do."

"Go there at two o'clock, and take it from there. All right?"

"Check."

He rang off without saying any more. Castelano's was one of those employment agencies, not a very big one, that found odd jobs for misfits. There was a girl there I knew slightly, and I wondered if Vallance knew that I knew her.

When I went into the bedroom, Madeleine was already in bed. She stared at me as I lay down beside her, wondering if I was going to tell her what went on, but determined not to invade my privacy by asking. It was one of her more endearing qualities; she never talked unnecessarily. She was an intelligent woman, but she felt that her prime purpose in life lay in her body instead of her mind, which wasn't at all true, really.

I forgot my worries in her embrace, and my last thought as I fell asleep was of her pale, wide-awake eyes looking into mine just before I dozed off.

Aware that I would not be seeing Madeleine for some time to come, I spent the whole of the morning in bed, just lying there with her, not talking very much, smoking cigarettes and drinking coffee, and enjoying the touch of her body.

It was a stinking hot day, with the wind in the wrong direction for the sea breeze, and I was restless as I always am in the heat. But I knew that I was falling in love with Madeleine, and I felt that I had to fill my mind with a complete picture of her to keep with me on the trip south with Vallance.

It had come as a bit of a shock to me, and I don't really know when it happened. All I know is that I looked at her one day as she sat by the window balcony that overlooked the edge of the harbor, and suddenly felt that she was closer to me than she had ever been before. She still had her own place up in the town, but she had moved some of her things in with me, and had given them my number at the modeling agency, so she spent most of the time with me. Now, she was composed and relaxed and quite motionless, with her hands held loosely in her lap, and she looked like a Domergue portrait. I was suddenly struck by an awareness that she was rapidly becoming a very important part of my life. It came with a sudden impact, unexpectedly, and I turned away from her and thought about it, knowing that nobody else would ever fill for me the place that she was occupying. It worried me at first, because I have always been frightened of getting hurt, and I knew that if I allowed my emotions, which had always been a bit gregarious, to depend upon one outlet only, then I would be helpless in the hands of one woman who could accept or reject me as she pleased. It was as though the protective demilune you instinctively build around your susceptibilities had suddenly disappeared and left you completely naked and vulnerable. Love, in its abstract form, is a pretty terrible thing, and the last thing I wanted was to be exposed to it like this.

Until that moment, my passion for her was no better than an intense admiration of her physical beauty, coupled with the knowledge that she was also a very nice girl with a lot of sympathetic qualities; it was, to put it simply, a matter of what the bluenoses call lust, with a bit of genuine liking thrown in for good measure. And seeing her sitting there as lovely and motionless as a great artist's *capolavoro*, I had been filled with an urgent need to disprove to myself that this was anything more than a purely physical emotion. I had lifted her from her chair, carried her into the bedroom and made brutal love to her, not bothering with the niceties at all, but merely gratifying an animal appetite. When it was all over, there was the faintest possible smile on her lips and a very demure look in her eyes, and I'll be hanged if I don't think she knew precisely what was going on in my mind.

So I had told her. I told her exactly the reason for my sudden onslaught, and her smile had blossomed very slowly with a kind of secret amusement, and still she did not question me. I had told her then that I loved her, and all she said was: "Are you sure, Mike? Are you sure?" And when I had said yes, I was quite certain about it, she had put her hand on my cheek with a peculiarly childlike gesture and nodded her head as though this was very proper and desirable.

So now, knowing that I would leave her for a while, I stayed with her until after midday, impressing my mind with the white etching of her loveliness. In fact, I rather overdid it, and it was nearly two-thirty before I arrived at Castelano's and asked the girl there if anything had turned up that would pay a few bucks for a while. She hadn't seen me for nearly six months, and I had a nasty feeling that I'd broken a date with her. She was a foolish girl, plump and gushing, but not too bad-looking in a Latin sort of way.

She said: "Why, Mike! A long time since you came to see me."

"I know, honey. One thing and another..."

It's awful when you can't remember someone's name. I said: "Thought I'd look for a job ... something to tide me over the next couple of weeks or so. Anything on your books that might do?"

She shook her head, conscious that her long black hair swirled very nicely.

"I don't think so, Mike. Some English lessons? Some translations?"

"Hell, I don't give a damn. Just something to pay the rent with..."

She shook her head again and made cow's eyes at me, sitting there with her finger running down a list in a tattered ledger. She transferred her attention to the page and read out: "Secretary ... secretary ... engineer ... truck driver... How about that, Mike? You want to drive a truck?"

"What else is there?"

The finger started moving again. Her nail polish did not match her lipstick. She said: "Plumber's assistant ... secretary ... male nurse ... coffee grader ... another coffee grader..."

I said: "What's that male-nurse thing?"

"Maybe this is good for you. For two weeks only. Wait, I get the slip. It's only just come in."

She took a slip of paper off the file and read:

"English-speaking male nurse ... two weeks ... accompany elderly invalid to San Antonio. Ah, yes, now I remember. He said his nurse was sick and he wants another one quick. His name Vallance, Mr. Vallance."

"Pay?"

"One hundred American dollars a week. This is good, Mike. On the black market . . ."

"Sure. Think I'll do?"

"Why not? You want this job, I fix for you."

"Do that, honey, will you? I'll send you some stockings with my first check."

She tossed her silly little head again, pulled out the employment book, and ten minutes later I was walking back to the apartment with a note to the travel service that was to give me the plane ticket. I was to pick up Vallance in Encino just as soon as I could make it there. I rather hoped there wouldn't be a plane that day, but—wouldn't you know it?—there was one scheduled at eleven-fifteen that night. They checked my passport for me, gave me my ticket and I went back to the apartment.

Madeleine was a little sad to hear that I was going away, but I told her it was a good offer I couldn't afford to refuse, with more for a couple of weeks' work than I'd normally earn in a month, and, anyway, I'd be back in no time at all. I gave her the other key to the apartment, and tried to give her some bank notes too, but she refused them. I wanted to make sure that she would not . . . well, that she wouldn't feel she had to go out and earn money while I was gone, but with her usual perception she realized at once what was in my mind and said, very gently, that she still had plenty left from the money I'd given her a little while back. And she added, with just a trace of disquiet, that it wasn't necessary to worry about where she'd be or what she'd be doing. Looking at me very steadily she said: "When you come back and while you are away, Mike, I will be here, always."

I think that, in that one brief moment, she was half ashamed of the way she used to earn her money. I knew then that she was in love with me too, and I wondered, surprised, that she had never said so. It didn't occur to me till much later that she must have felt that this was the one thing she could never say.

The barriers that our inhibitions put up around us! I wasn't going to her with lily-white hands, exactly, either.

She wouldn't see me off at the airport. She said she wanted me to say good-by to her in the apartment so my last sight of her, even for so short an absence, would be the one that I like the most. And when I went out with my Gladstone bag full of spare laundry, she was lying on the bed with her hands behind her silver-gray head and her hair all piled up, looking at me with those solemn, pale-blue eyes, her splendid breasts firm and white, and her long limbs as graceful and supple as a swan. As I hesitated at the door, taking one long last look at her, she said: "I will be here when you return, *mon amour*."

It's a funny thing. In English, "my love" sounds like any other catch phrase, and even in French it can be pretty trite too. But when a Frenchwoman really means it for what it says, then you know.... It implies so much *more*....

The plane trip to Encino was quite uneventful, although I had an attack of nervousness halfway there, feeling that *they* knew exactly what was being planned and were waiting for me.

But it was fine to enjoy the unaccustomed luxury of a good airline. The stewardesses were tall and svelte and cool-looking, with a lot of the dignity I didn't see much of these days, and the food was excellent.

It's a wonderful thing, flying over South America. Down there below you there are sudden towns with modern buildings and wide streets, and you make a turn and you're over jungle again, where little brown men still blow poisoned darts at each other. A river meanders through incredibly lush trees, with no sign of life or habitation for hundreds of miles, and then, once again, there is a broad plantation of coffee or cocoa or sugar cane or tea, with the red earth neatly tilled and tile-roofed buildings dotted everywhere.... You wonder how they can survive so far from everything, and then you realize that, just because you've spent most of your life in some port or other, this is not necessarily vital to a man's existence; that people live in the distant places too.

We made two stops en route, though for the life of me I don't remember where they were. One airport looks exactly like another in the middle of the night. All I remember is that I was comfortably fast asleep when they woke me up and told me they had to fumigate the plane, which is a sure sign you're crossing a border; it's funny how everybody thinks the bugs all come from the other side of the frontier.

It was hotter than ever when I stepped down onto the tarmac field at Encino, and there was a car from the hotel to meet me, with a liveried chauffeur, no less, who spoke quite good English; I'd been told long since not to talk any Spanish down there, which was a wise decision. And it showed the way Vallance thought. He had said: "If anyone asks you, of course, you speak excellent Spanish. But don't volunteer the information. Come to that, don't volunteer *any* information."

"Eyes and ears open, mouth shut."

"Precisely. The sum total of knowledge in the human concourse ... if one man were to give and never receive, and the other were to receive and never give . . . Has it occurred to you what an advantage that one man would have?"

I had said politely: "I never thought of it quite like that, but . . ."

So I said nothing much to the English-speaking chauffeur. He treated me with a great deal of deference at the airport, as was fitting, but as soon as we were in the car his manner changed. It was obvious that he knew I had come as the replacement for Vallance's sick nurse and was a servant just as he was. The camaraderie of servants is still in the prerevolution era, and I'm thinking of the great eighteenth-century revolutions, too.

He took me in the tradesmen's entrance at the hotel and up the freight elevator to the tenth floor, and ushered me into Vallance's suite.

It was good to see Vallance there. Somehow, he gave a mighty comforting feeling that everything was going exactly as planned. He was sitting on a couch with his feet up on a stool, and his wheel chair stood close by. He stared at me unsmiling for a while and said nastily: "Well, if you're the best they can do . . ."

I blinked at him and he said: "Do you think you can get me into my chair without breaking my back?"

I said: "Yes, sir. I've worked in a hospital. . . ."

"I should hope so. I'm paying you good money."

I was astonished at the change in his character. Where he had been affable and a little pompous before, he was now mean-tempered and thoroughly unpleasant. He flew into a rage when I started to move him, and claimed I was twisting his spinal column. The chauffeur moved forward anxiously to help, but Vallance waved his stick at him as though he were defending himself against a murderous attack, and when it was all over and he was properly strapped in his chair, he said to the chauffeur: "Take him to the tailor's and get him some uniforms. He can't push me around dressed like a goddamn tourist."

We went out together, and the chauffeur did not relax until we were on the ground floor where the servants' quarters were, and then he took me into his room and gave me a drink of whiskey and a coffee bean to chew so that it wouldn't be on my breath, and he sighed and said: "The rich ones, eh? I sympathize with you, my friend. I hope he pays you well."

"A hundred bucks a week."

"So. This is not bad. Not good, but not bad. We will make a little something together from the tailor, no?"

"You bet."

My uniforms were ready the next morning, one to wear and one spare; I felt like a ship's steward, with a jacket buttoned up to the neck. It was certainly very distinctive and would be remembered by everyone who saw it, and when I showed myself to Vallance we were alone in his room, but he held a finger to his lips in a signal to say nothing compromising. It was quite unnecessary; I had no intention of relaxing until this thing was over.

As for Vallance, he really threw himself into the act with abandon. He seemed to take a great delight in making the underlings bow and scrape to him, and if the slightest thing went wrong he flew into a terrible rage, raising his voice to a high-pitched whine and literally shouting down all opposition. The hotel staff were glad to see him go.

We hired a special car to drive out to the station, and there was a lot of fuss because the train was late. . . . As if it were likely to be on time!

Actually, it wasn't a bad sort of train. A little old-fashioned, but it was comfortable enough and there was a dining car on it that still had the original European Pullman markings; they must have bought it as surplus in Budapest or Vienna or Istanbul, and it looked like one of the coaches from the old Orient Express. It was strangely out of place on this South American train that labored so slowly up the steep grades of the Cordillera, with the high peak of the Cerro Verde towering above it like a challenging and unattainable goal for the hopelessly underpowered locomotive.

We ran into some awkwardness at the frontier. It was no more than that, but it gave me an insight into Vallance's cunning.

There was something wrong with our papers. It was about the wheel chair, if you please. They couldn't decide whether or not it constituted a wheeled vehicle under the terms of the act, and the customs officer, whose only valid reason for being there at all was that the peasants used to bring in wild coffee from over the border and mix it with the domestic product was quite sure that with an important man like Vallance he ought to show just how efficient he could be. Vallance put up with a certain amount of it, for form's sake, and then began to shout at him, and finally produced the imposing document from the Generalissimo and waved it in the poor fellow's face until he shied away in actual fright of the signature on it. Scrap iron, Vallance was dealing in, and with nobody selling the government half of what they wanted because they reneged on their accounts as a matter of public policy, the junta was not going to allow petty restrictions to hinder a man who was fool enough to offer them a year's supply on terms they knew they could wiggle out of....

But when we were safely over the border, and alone in our carriage once more, he took time out to smile a little. He had been so consistently ill-tempered, even when we were alone, that my nerves were getting frayed. I felt he was overdoing it, even though I knew that in these days of rifle-microphones and long-range cameras there was no such thing as a surfeit of precaution. The only efficiency in a place like this was in the hands of the junta. It was easy enough to believe that everything was backward just because the customs officer hadn't shaved for a week, but it wasn't so. Up at the top, they'd surrounded themselves with some pretty high-powered operators.

He said: "It's going very nicely, Benasque."

"Brother," I said. "You've certainly learned how to make enemies."

"It will pay off, you'll see. Keep your voice down."

"Yes, sir."

He giggled, then, and rang the bell for the porter. When he came, he ordered some sandwiches and a bottle of wine, and as soon as the coast was clear again, and we were munching steadily on the crisp French bread and white chicken meat, he began to elaborate on the plan ahead of us. Introducing the subject, he said: "I expect you'll be glad to see your friend Trenko again. How well did you know him?"

"I thought you knew that."

"He's a good man."

"I suppose he knows I'm coming? That it's me, I mean?"

"Surely. It was his idea in the first place. He told us that Lazlo was getting more and more to look like you. We've fixed him up with a hair piece and the new dentures.... He'll be wearing a uniform, of course, just like yours. You'd be surprised how much a uniform changes a man."

I said: "Lazlo's English is pretty good, but it wouldn't fool a real expert."

"There won't be any real experts. As long as he can understand what I say to him ... If any of the border officials start asking him awkward question, I'll be right there beside him."

"The wheel chair again."

"Precisely. It's the one logical reason to have him close at my side at all times."

Knowing I shouldn't be asking such a question, I said: "What's it all about, actually?"

Vallance shrugged his shoulders.

"You know all you need to know. My employers want him

out of the country for some briefing. Conferences, meetings
. . . And then they want him back in again."

"He's risking his neck."

"That's not a thing that Lazlo would worry about."

"I thought DeBries was coming with us?"

"He's there already."

"Oh?"

"A perfectly legitimate tourist. If you happen to see him, which you might, you won't recognize him, of course."

"Of course not."

"I mean, don't go shouting, 'Hi, DeBries!' He wouldn't like that. Wouldn't like it at all."

"Who's the boss, Mr. Vallance? You, or DeBries?"

He thought a long time before he answered, as though he were trying to read my thoughts. Then he said, proving that's exactly what he was doing: "Don't worry, nothing will go wrong. But if you must know, I'm the boss. DeBries is my number two. And to tell the truth, I'd be lost without him."

I was conscious of a suppressed excitement in him that had not been there before. We were in the middle of them, now, if anything went wrong . . . I said: "And if anything should go wrong?"

"Nothing will."

"But if it *should*. There must be a Plan B."

Vallance chuckled again, hiding that excitement under a phony front of cheerfulness.

"Of course there is. A very untidy one. Let's hope we won't have to use it. All we have to worry about now is getting to the operational epicenter and making the switch. My work in the capital is a formality, no more than that. They'll sign the orders for my scrap metal, talk me into an earlier delivery and a smaller interest on the account, and then . . . back we go."

"Why do we have to stop at this place—what's its name? On the way in."

"At Volvoda? For a last-minute check. We spend the night there, tonight. We'll get confirmation there that our men are ready. Then, on the way back, they'll be waiting."

"A small station, you said."

"Tiny. It's an ideal place for the job we have to do."

"And how do we justify our stopping there?"

Vallance smiled again; he was always pleased when I raised a point like this. He said: "We've had enough of the train for one day, and I need a proper bed at night. It's logical enough."

"Shall I see Lazlo?"

"No . . . no, I doubt it. There's a toilet at the station; a pretty grubby one, I imagine. When I give you the word you'll go there and shut the door. You'll wait three minutes, and then come out. Trenko will be waiting for you. Don't speak to him, just follow him. It'll be dark, and the station lights are pretty dim. You'll simply walk along the track behind Trenko, turn off when he turns off, and as soon as you're in the clear he'll let you know. Within a couple of hours you'll be at his hide-out."

"Sounds simple enough. What then?"

"It's a cottage, a wild sisal cutter's cottage. Trenko will stay right beside you for the full three days. And then, when he gets the word, he takes you back to the railway station, you walk into the toilet again, walk out and take your place behind my wheel chair, which by that time will be on the platform."

"Suppose someone comes to the sisal cutter's cottage while I'm there?"

"Nobody will. But if someone should, then you simply hide out among the trees till they've gone. You'll have plenty of warning."

"So Trenko still has his dogs."

"Three of them, apparently. German shepherds. And the cottage is surrounded by heavy timber. It would need an army to find you there."

He wiped his mouth with a napkin and pushed the tray away. While I folded the table out of the way of his crippled legs, he watched me and then said suddenly: "You've never asked about money."

"I know. I've already had twenty-five hundred bucks."

"Pull this off and there's a great deal more. Once we get back to Caracas, there'll be a deposit of ten thousand dollars at your bank. Make you feel happy?"

"Very. I can use it."

He said quizzically: "You're a queer fellow, Benasque. During the war you did some excellent work. You're a good journalist, you're fairly honest, and yet . . . bumming around Caracas like that . . . How come you haven't been able to make something better for yourself?"

I suppose that question might apply to almost anybody. I said: "I don't know. There's something missing, I suppose. Energy, ambition, the competitive spirit . . . call it what you like. I get restless. You struggle like hell for a while and then . . . well, you begin to say *who cares?* And then you start to take it easy again, and the next thing you know is you're broke and nobody wants to hire you. . . . Come to think of it, I make more money showing the tourists around the night clubs than I ever did writing erudite essays on the manioc business or the devaluation of the bolivar. You sit around drinking cold tea and soda water, and watching the girls in the spotlight, and the next thing you know is it's daylight and you've earned a week's rent. It's not a bad life, provided there's enough to have a real drink once in a while. The night-club owners are pretty generous, if you know the right ones. And the tourist doesn't mind being fleeced. Makes him feel he's having a hell of a good time. You try to save them money, and they think you're not showing them the best places, so they go out and hire themselves a proper guide, with a uniform and all."

"Seems a pity. Wouldn't you like to join up with us on a more permanent basis? We could make good use of you."

I shook my head.

"No, this sort of thing's all right once in a while, but I'm strictly an amateur. An occasional fling at excitement is all I want. More than enough, to tell the truth."

"Nervous?"

"Not yet. I will be, later on."

"Not to worry."

We watched the beautiful mountain scenery go by, with the serpentine sweep of the muddy Río Tolto far below us, shimmering against the rich greens and browns of the forest, with here and there a wide, open plain where there had been an effort at cultivation and where kapok trees or guava were growing. There were bananas spraying their broad leaves close by the bank of the river, and once there was a little white house built of adobe with a red tile roof that looked like a miniature Spanish mission. We passed a gang of half-naked laborers sweating in the sun along the railway track; they were chained together by the legs, and their guards had rifles, and there was a big Doberman pinscher on a leash lying under a rickety shelter of woven palm leaves on sticks. As we went slowly by them I was able to see that one of the guards was carrying a heavy leather whip, and I looked across at Vallance, but he avoided my eye. We climbed up through the mountains with the background noise of the wheels over the points as insistently rhythmic as a hot jazz drummer. When I tidied up the compartment, I noticed that Vallance's baggage had been marked in the accustomed way by the staff at the various hotels he had stayed at en route. I said conversationally:

"I see you didn't make yourself quite so unpopular at the Santa Margarita, in Ciudad Guacian."

Vallance looked up sharply. His eyes were suddenly very alert, and I was conscious that for a moment he suspected that, while he had been watching me, I too had been watching him. I hastened to clear myself.

The story was in the labels that were stuck all over his bags. You may not know about this, but it's one of the things you soon pick up when you're hanging around a place like

Caracas for very long. There's an international code which is used among the bellboys, to advise the hotels in advance just how much trouble they need take with the guests. When I was traveling myself, and was too hard up to tip decently, I used to steam the labels off my bag and paste them back on again at a different angle.

Have you ever seen a hotel label dead square on a suitcase? Well, if you have, it means you're a lousy tipper and they needn't bother to look after you too well. If they paste on two labels, one just lapping over the edge of the other, it means that you're a real terror to the staff but it's worth putting up with. But the labels on Vallance's suitcase were very neatly stuck at a precise angle across the top corner, and, brother, that's the worst thing they can say about you; and there was a second label just underneath which was on its side, and that means, quite simply, "Lots of money; play it right and you can get some of it."

I tell you, those bellboys can write a ten-page report on you, for the benefit of all other bellboys, just by sticking a couple of labels on your suitcase. I told Vallance about it. He stared at me open-mouthed for a moment and then said: "Well!"

I finished the tidying up and he said: "Well!" again, and then asked me: "So what happened at the Santa Margarita?"

Reading the message of the labels, I said: "It says here . . . It says that you're not a bad sort, really, and free with the tips. You must have fallen out of character for a moment. But it means excellent service at the next hotel. Lots of deference."

For the third time, he said: "Well!"

I derived a great deal of pleasure from that exchange. I'd grown to think that he was so much better than I was at almost everything. It was satisfying to know that there was at least one small thing he was not so well-informed about.

A little while later, staring into the valley below us, flanked on each side by thick forest, he said: "There's Volvoda."

There was just enough whine in his voice to indicate that we'd better get into character again, and by the time we pulled into the tiny, grubby, disorganized halt, he was as bad-tempered and unpleasant as ever. He nearly started a civil war when they tried to help me get his wheel chair off the train, and I began to realize just how much method there was in his madness. Word was getting ahead of us along the railway line—"Look out for that old bastard in the wheel chair." There's a camaraderie on the railways, too, among the porters and the waiters, and the various *cabos*, that doesn't exist in any other sphere. As you'll find out if you ever make railway friends in one country and have to travel to another. I once went halfway across Europe without a franc or a shilling or a lira in my pocket, just because I had a friend in the business. With no meal tabs either.

Volvoda. It was a hamlet set high in the green hills, with barely a couple of dozen houses, with an adobe railway station, a broken-down post office, and a high whitewashed wall that surrounded the police barracks.

You never can tell; there's a village like this with only one man on duty at the railway, with just a sleepy clerk at the postal station, with hardly a paved street in the place, and then you suddenly see that there are two or three hundred police housed in a long stone building on the outskirts of the very same village. And the realization that this is their headquarters for a big administrative area leaves you only with the thought that you ought to be a hundred miles away from it.

Barracks . . . It's merely a place for the troops to live, but down there, in a good many of the Latin-American dictatorships, it means something else again. It means the whitewashed rooms down in the cellar underneath, where the screams you hear might come from some student who disappeared five years ago or from the girl next door who didn't come home last night. It's taken on an aura all its own; down there, you just don't talk about the barracks. You don't even think about them, and there, truthfully, lies the reason by which they can get away with it.

The mountains towered up on three sides of us, and on the fourth side there was just the open darkness of the sky with the moon on the water far, far below us. I was astonished to find the sea so close, since it seemed that we must have left it behind us long ago. Then I recalled the map Vallance had shown me, and I realized that, although it looked so near in the moonlight, it was nearly forty miles away, clear and cool and inviting through a break in the harshness of the mountains. The trees around us were mostly deciduous, with dark and somber shadows binding them together.

I was glad of the hidden darkness. If this was to be my clandestine home for three days, while dangerous things went on all round me, it was just as well that the trees were so secretive and closely knit. I have always liked the night; there's a friendly comfort in darkness that is always dispelled by the harsh light of a street lamp or the bright unfolding of the sun. Give me a dark night and I can face anything.

Vallance had summoned the porter, and thrown his weight about again, and told him, in terrible Spanish, that he was sick and tired of the disgustingly uncomfortable train and was going to leave it. The porter explained that Volvoda wasn't much of a place, and Vallance interrupted him sharply and asked if there was a hotel there, and when the porter shurgged his shoulders and said, well, of course, Señor, there was a hotel of sorts, but he didn't honestly think . . . Vallance broke in and told him nastily that he wasn't being asked to think, and that it couldn't be worse than the train anyway, and why the devil didn't the company buy itself some new rolling stock?

The porter called the conductor, and the conductor called the *cabo* and between us we got him quieted down, and then the stationmaster, who lived in a little room over the ticket office, woke up his young son and sent him running off to the hotel to fetch the only car in the village and to prepare accommodations for us.

The train pulled out at last, and my final memory of it was the plump face of the dining-car steward, leaning out of the window and winking at me and shaking his head as if to say: "Well, thank God for that." The universal brotherhood of servants . . .

Forty minutes later, we were in the hotel, and half an hour after that, Vallance was fast asleep.

I lay down on the bed in the adjoining room and stared at the ceiling.

Well, for better or worse, we were there. We were in their country where they still had chain gangs and slave masters with whips in their hands. We had passed over the frontier and we wouldn't be passing back again until the dangerous job had been done. I smoked a cigarette and thought about Madeleine. I was pleased that I had taken so much care to etch her picture on my memory, and the image of her soft ivory body was as clear as if she were beside me. Well, almost.

I put out my cigarette, turned over on my face and tried to sleep. Tomorrow, we'd be in San Antonio, talking business with the suave representatives of the junta, whose prime enemy we were going to smuggle out from under their very noses. We'd make polite conversation with them—or Vallance would, while their servants entertained his servant—and we'd take the train back to Volvoda.

An hour, the watering process took. The elderly stationmaster went forward to the pumps, and when the tanks were full he went with the engineer and the driver's mate to have a cup of coffee in his office. . . . And, all this time, Lazlo would be lurking in the shadows close by, with Trenko at his side. A cold, dispassionate Lazlo, filled with hatred for the people who ruled him, and an equally fanatical Trenko, ready to throw his life away at the drop of a hat. They'd be waiting for an unemployed journalist who hadn't had a decent job in years, a man who'd forgotten all about the loyalties and the causes which were so important to them . . . a man who was lying in a four-poster bed wishing that his girl was by his side to still with her warm, silent, generous presence the agony of apprehension and downright terror that was creeping over him.

D-day, Vallance had called it. It was very close, now.

chapter 4

I tried hard to identify the last-minute check that Vallance had spoken of.

It could have been the peasant who passed by the hotel with a donkeyload of bananas and who stopped to light a thin black cheroot, just as Vallance was staring at him out of the window; it could have been the thin column of smoke that started to rise from the hill just above the hotel at midday precisely, where someone was burning some rubbish; or it could have been the plump serving girl with sturdy legs and a bust too big for her age who brought him the filtered water for his medicine.

I waited till the early evening before I asked him about it.

As I expected, there was that smug look of accomplishment on his face when he told me. He said: "At our end, all is well. But at seven o'clock we shall know if everything has gone according to plan."

I said: "I don't believe you're carrying a radio receiver."

"Naturally not," he said primly, as though I had suggested something indecent. "I gave you a little lecture the other day on simplicity. At seven o'clock, you'll hear . . . you'll hear shots on the hill there."

"Shooting?" I was startled. It seemed that guns had no place in this little scheme of ours.

"It will sound like shooting. Have you ever been near a charcoal kiln?"

"No, I don't think I have."

"They build a pile of twigs, cover it with palm leaves and earth, put a twist of grass in the top for ventilation and fire it. The resulting process of pyrolysis has an interesting feature: the wood explodes from time to time in short, sharp bursts. It should exactly like rifle fire. Exactly like it. If you get into the middle of a cluster of charcoal kilns, the impulse to throw yourself flat on your face is almost overpowering."

I said politely: "Well, that's very interesting."

Vallance ignored the remark. He said: "During the course of the morning, Trenko will start firing charcoal up on the hill there. A good kiln will last for two or three days, and keep on exploding for the first twenty-four hours or so. Trenko will have two kilns going, and, as long as the charcoal keeps exploding, everything is in order. We shall hear it, never fear. But if we stop hearing it . . . if Trenko has to burst the kilns open . . . then we're in trouble."

"And in that case?"

"In that case, we simply continue with our journey, you and I together. Satisfied?"

"Perfectly."

I had to be. He'd thought of everything. I said: "Then I take it Lazlo is already quite near here?"

"His country estate borders on the railway line. In fact, this village is part of it. Or was, under the old feudal system."

"Then the villagers must know Lazlo. By sight, I mean."

"I don't think so. He has only recently acquired the estate. It used to belong to someone on the other side of the fence. Who is no longer with us."

"The rewards of expediency."

"I'm afraid so. The big estates have been very nicely parceled out, as you may know, to the new aristocracy. This is quite a poor one, as befits a man they can't quite be sure of. But in any case, even if they have seen him before, no one is going to recognize him, in your uniform, in the middle of the night, with false teeth and a hair piece. This is another reason for which we stopped here; they'll be accustomed to the sight of you, and expecting you to leave, when our man takes over. No one will recognize him. Any other worries?"

"You seem very nonchalant about it all. I suppose that means that everything, so far, is under control? So far, so good?"

"So far, so very good."

"Then there's nothing to do but wait?"

"Exactly. I will sit out in the sun now that it's lost its heat. Kindly push me over there to the terrace, and tell the girl to bring me a brandy and soda. You'd better make sure the ice is clean."

"Yes, sir."

"And get me my newspaper out of my brief case."

"Yes, sir."

I'd been pushing him under the long shady avenue that ran from the hotel itself down to the entrance off the gravel road. It wasn't a bad little place, and I wondered vaguely how it came to be there. There was a big lake nearby, and I supposed that there'd be shooting there; at least, there were stuffed ducks all over the vestibule, looking unbelievably dusty and ragged. The sun was slanting through the tall jacaranda trees of the avenue, and playing quite prettily on the hard, red, beaten earth under our feet. I pushed him over to the terrace and called the plump girl, and she set up a small table for him, and I went with her into the kitchen and looked at the ice, and said nothing to her, letting her assume that I spoke no Spanish, and, by the time I got back to Vallance, a policeman was standing there beside him.

It gave me a little shock, but he was just standing there, staring, a surly peasant dressed in gray, with a pistol at his belt and a rifle slung over his shoulder. The serving girl came up behind me and smiled at the policeman as she put the tray down on Vallance's table, but he did not smile back at her. He just looked at her once with a slight acknowledgment of her gesture, as though it was the right thing for her to do. I was surprised that she seemed to think his attitude was correct, too; that she expected no more response from an important man like the village policeman—that it was enough that she be permitted to smile at him. . . . I suddenly felt sorry for her.

There's something in the Latin character that presupposes charm and volatility and the love of pleasure; and in the presence of the surly policeman, this pretty little peasant girl, with wide-spread, sturdy legs, and brown arms, and a full ripe breast ready for the caress of a lover, had suddenly subjugated all her natural emotions with an ease that could only have come through long practice. It was rather terrifying.

Vallance paid no attention to him at all. He sat there sipping his drink and turning the pages of the *New York Times* as though the policeman, standing no more than five feet away from him and inspecting him closely, just didn't exist. It was a little comical; the surly policeman, determined to do his job, was staring at Vallance and frowning as though deep and somber thoughts were going on in his mind, but I knew that all he was doing was simply obeying orders, with a capital "O." The stationmaster had told the police that two people had left the train, and the police had come along to make sure that they had registered properly at the hotel, that their passports had been handed in and were in order, that they weren't radicals or saboteurs or spies, that they weren't carrying anything that was Forbidden, also in capitals. . . .

It was easy to dismiss these clumsy, uniformed peasants. But I knew, too, that they could be very, very dangerous. Not because they could think, but precisely because they couldn't.

Vallance went on reading his paper without paying the slightest attention to him, and in a little while he came over to where I was standing and stared at me too. Then he said: "Spanish?"

He'd seen my American passport, of course. I shook my head slowly, and offered him a cigarette. He stared blankly at me as though I were offending his dignity, and then looked over his shoulder to make sure no one was looking before he took three cigarettes and put them in his pocket. He did not smile, but concentrated on looking dignified and stern, and then he went to the desk just inside the lobby door and had another look at our passports before he went round to the kitchen for a meal.

There was something quite frightening in the way he moved, as though he were almost not human. He used short, jerky little steps that made me think of the machine again and brought home to me the fact that he really was part of some immense and terrifying apparatus contrived for the sole purpose of molding people like plastic, and for destroying them if they refused to be molded.

A few minutes after seven, the sound came that we had been waiting for. Up on the hill, a charcoal kiln started exploding. Vallance did not stir; he did not even look at his watch. I noticed that nobody else paid any attention, either.

There were half dozen other guests sitting on the terrace, watching the cool shadows of the evening as they sipped their *apéritifs*. There seemed to be a heavy predominance of mestizos, of half-castes, among them, and I realized that down here there was still a lot of the old Indian blood. They were mostly rancheros, I imagine, with a sprinkling of hemp planters thrown in.

Vallance folded his paper briskly, snapped his fingers rudely at me, and I pushed him indoors to his room, changed his clothes for him, brought him his dinner, and three hours later we were back on the train again, straining up the mountainside to San Antonio.

Everything was going according to plan. And, as Vallance said, why shouldn't it? Even in the capital itself, in San Antonio, we were treated with respect and deference. Vallance had his long session with the minister, while I sat in the huge white kitchen drinking first coffee and then brandy. The man who took care of me was a sort of major-domo who looked after the minister's comfort while he was at work, and he spoke the comic sort of English that you never really expect to hear. He thought he might get some good practice in with me, and hence the brandy. We became very buddy-buddy in the four hours it took Vallance to get through his business upstairs, and when we left he pressed a surreptitious bottle of Martel cognac on me, which I had nowhere to hide, and so had to slip down the side of the basket at the back of the wheel chair where we kept the blankets; I felt as though I were coming back from the supermarket pushing a buggy, but, if Vallance noticed it, he gave no sign.

We spent the night in the big hotel, the Casa Montera, in one of the suites reserved for the junta, and I have never seen such luxury. Those fellows really believed in looking after number one. Even my room, a sort of servants' quarters next to the master bedroom, was as fancy as anything in the Waldorf-Astoria. They brought me American magazines, free drinks, some thin black cigars of the kind San Antonio is famous for, and one of the assistants to the manager came up and respectfully asked if I would like a lady sent in. I astonished myself even more than I astonished him by shaking my head. It was a reflex action; I am quite sure that I was not actually thinking of Madeleine just then, but it shows the kind of feeling I was getting for her. A few weeks back, such a thing couldn't possibly have happened. And even after the little assistant had gone, I remember feeling distinctly pleased that I had refused his offer. Not only did it signify an extraordinary change in my thinking, but it also gave me a feeling of—how shall I put it?—of responsibility, that gave me a very unaccustomed glow of smug complacency.

We rose late the next morning, and at Vallance's insistence I spent most of the day in his room. I think that with D-day so close, he wanted to keep an eye on me.

So close? It was *already* D-day. I could feel the excitement of it pounding through my veins. The time was on us. We were about to pull off a feat of quite astonishing audacity, and here, in San Antonio itself, with all the comfortable frills of a pleasure-loving civilization only half hiding the terror that lay beneath the surface, it did not seem possible that our plan could be as foolproof as we had believed in the distant security of Caracas. I mentioned it to Vallance, but he shut me up very angrily. Pulling nervously on my cigarette, I had said:

"Any minute now, this thing's going to really start frightening me."

He glared at me with genuine shocked surprise on his face. Then he said nastily: "First of all, call me sir. And secondly, you will speak only when I address you."

I felt the blush rising to my face. I knew it was an indiscretion, and I cannot for the life of me think what had come over me and made me say it. But nerves are funny things. They let you down when you least expect it, and they come to your rescue when you least expect it too. I said, mumbling a little: "I'm sorry, sir."

"Are the bags packed?"

"Yes, sir."

"And the car ordered?"

"For seven o'clock, sir."

"Good. Go to your room. I'll call you when I need you."

"Yes, sir."

It was a relief to get away from him for a bit, and have a quiet drink in the privacy of my own room. I wasn't looking forward to the operation at all.

It was ten-forty-two when the train pulled into Volvoda.

I had an awful scare when it suddenly occurred to me that maybe, on the return trip, the timing for the water pump was not the same, that it would stop for only a few minutes and not give us reasonable excuse to get out onto the low wooden platform beside the line.

I should have known better, of course. It wasn't the kind of thing Vallance was likely to go wrong on. And, sure enough, when it stopped and Vallance rang the bell for the porter, the man came along and told us there'd be a halt for forty minutes while the engine took on water and they checked the couplings before making the long run down to the deep valley.

Vallance said unpleasantly: "There's no air on this damn train of yours, and the smell is insufferable. Help my man get me out into the fresh air."

We got the wheel chair out with some difficulty, feeling the cold night breeze playing about us and telling me, at least, that I was sweating horribly. The stationmaster was in his office, the night was black as pitch and the weak bulb that hung outside the office door gave only a poor, yellowish light. Vallance pointed and said: "Over there . . . further down . . . under the lamp. I want to read my paper."

I knew why he wanted to get under the lamp. He wanted to make sure that Trenko would see him. One or two other passengers had left the train and were stretching their legs too, but Vallance just sat there, reading his paper without a care in the world. It was like sitting in the wings of a theater and knowing that the curtain was still down while the drama was going on. With just myself watching it, and the real audience, on the other side of the curtain, in complete ignorance of what was really happening. And knowing that at any minute the curtain might go up suddenly and disclose the whole elaborate stage and its dramatic plot. The fear of what would happen then was almost overpowering.

The suave and friendly gentlemen in San Antonio could not have been more affable; but I knew that if they learned the smallest doubtful fact about us . . . if there were one single thing that jarred with the picture we presented . . . then they would be down on us like a ton of bricks. The friendly smiles would disappear, and the violent hatreds they masked would come to the surface again, and the whole dreadful apparatus of their security system would go to work relentlessly, efficiently and ruthlessly. We would just disappear, and six months later there'd be more stories in *Life* magazine, with teams of indignant investigators blandly reassured that we certainly *must* have returned—there was incontrovertible proof that we'd crossed the frontier . . . sworn statements . . . eyewitnesses. . . .

And all the time, in the cellar under the barracks . . . how long could a man endure it? And I was doing all this for *money?*

Now, with the moment upon us, it all seemed to be going well, but there was little comfort in that; it seemed to be going *too* well. I caught Vallance looking at me strangely, once or twice, as though he were trying to gauge my anxiety.

It was too quiet. Except for a couple of passengers, the whole station was deserted, and, although this was exactly what we expected, it somehow didn't seem right. The wooden platform rang hollowly under my feet, and for one ghastly moment I wondered if Lazlo, when he came, would perhaps be wearing rubber soles that would not make quite so much noise . . . if the stationmaster would wonder how and when and why I'd managed to change my footwear. And then I realized that Vallance would have thought of that too.

I was sorry I wouldn't even see Lazlo. It would have been nice just to have exchanged even a glance, a smile for the sake of nostalgia. But I realized it was out of the question. Anyway, to see Trenko again after all these years . . .

It was my last cigarette. Before we had left the hotel in San Antonio, Vallance had made me empty my pockets onto his table, and then had made me strip down to the bare skin while he went through my clothes with a fine-tooth comb. He took my wallet for Lazlo, and with it a couple of letters and my driving license, a bill from the tailor's and another from the hiring agency. I began to protest when he took Madeleine's picture too, but he said patiently:

"Lazlo will have your passport, and he must have your other things too. In case of accidents . . . you must realize that."

I said meekly, "Yes, of course."

"And also, in case of accidents, you mustn't have anything. Anything at all."

Holding my uniform jacket up to the light, he said: "No papers, no tailor's marks, no laundry marks, nothing. Nothing at all."

"Of course. Nothing to identify the body by."

Vallance said easily: "That's it." Then he looked up and smiled and said: "You must have gone through this rigmarole a dozen times during the war."

"That's what frightens me. It was always so goddamn *necessary*."

"Well, this time it won't be, but let's observe the proper formalities, shall we?"

The night was as dark and as silent as you could have wanted. The moon, on the wane, was behind a heavy bank of clouds, and I almost wondered if Vallance had arranged for those clouds to be there too.

Then the stationmaster came out of his cubbyhole and started walking along the track to the water pump up front, swinging his kerosene lamp in one hand and carrying a coffeepot in the other, and instinctively I looked up at the room above his office where I knew his young son would be sleeping. There were no lights there, and I had the horrible feeling that the boy was at the window, watching. The fantasy grew, and next there was the squat policeman with him, smoking one of my cigarettes, and the heavy shrubbery around the station was filled with soldiers waiting for the whistle.

A ten-year-old boy? Well, back home, ten-year-old boys don't engage in politics very much, but out here . . . brother! They'd sell their own parents if the secret police told them to. I wished I had another cigarette.

The time passed with appalling slowness. All the passengers except one had climbed back onto the train, and Vallance had told me to start pushing him up and down, from one end of the platform to the other. I wondered if Trenko and Lazlo were in position, and if they felt as nervous as I did. Then I realized that, to them, this was no more than a phase in a battle they were waging all the time; it was only we amateurs who got frightened like this.

In the hotel, Vallance had said: "I'll give the word when to move. You go straight to the toilet, lock yourself in, wait three minutes and come out again. Is that clear?"

"Why don't I wait there until the train has left?"

"Because only when the train is actually leaving can I be sure that nobody who happens to be on the platform will be studying the entrance to the toilet."

"How come?"

"When a train pulls out of a station, *everybody* watches it. Have you never noticed?"

"But the people *on* the train . . ."

"They'll be in lighted carriages, the lamp outside the toilet is dim. . . . Besides, if you are seen, it won't matter. You'll be a shadow, no more."

"Why don't I get you back on the train first, so that our man won't have to do it?"

"The operation will go ahead precisely as planned."

It had been the second time he'd said that. He was so damn sure of himself. . . .

We stopped under the lamp again, and he just sat there, secure against the damp night air in his wraps, saying nothing, while I stood behind him and waited.

At last, someone blew a whistle up front. Vallance made no move. Then he looked at his watch briefly. Someone shouted out an order somewhere, and I began to panic. Then the stationmaster could be seen further along the platform, and I heard him slam a couple of doors. I whispered urgently: "For God's sake . . ."

Vallance said: "Quiet."

There was an indescribable calmness in his voice. Another door slammed somewhere, and a whistle blew again, and then the engineer let off some steam that shrilled out with a piercing hiss. Not looking at me, Vallance said shortly: *"Now!"*

As I turned away, I heard him say softly: "And good luck."

I sauntered off in the direction of the toilet. I needed to, anyway.

It was dim and smelly inside, with a galvanized strip against the wall looking revoltingly unclean in the meager light that came from the one bare bulb, a ten-watt bulb I imagined. I wondered why the hell they didn't put a decent light there; with all that water about, electricity is almost the only thing they have plenty of. And then I found the grubby cubicle that housed the water closet. I went inside and began counting the seconds. Literally, because Vallance had taken my watch too.

When I had counted to a hundred and eighty, I opened the door and went outside. The train was just pulling out, creeping slowly, brightly and noisily along the track, puffing out great clouds of hissing steam, clanking over the points, its fire hot and bright against the low clouds.

There was the shadow of a man standing at the entrance of the toilet, and for a horrible moment I thought it was the stationmaster, and then it turned and moved away and I followed it, being careful not to look at the red-yellow, nebulous brightness that hung over the train and could spoil my night sight.

It was Trenko all right. I could tell from his heavy limp, and a sudden surge went through me as I began to feel that in being scared I'd been making a fool of myself.

It was almost too dark to see Trenko, but something of the old alertness had come back to me and I could sense him just a few yards ahead of me. We moved soundlessly on the turf, down the incline that led away from the track, and I thought of the cunning of the man. I would have gone up, I think, with the instinct of the hunted man who wants to get above his enemies. And then I thought, that's where the lights from the train will be ... and there's always the question of a skyline showing through a break in the trees. ... Down below us the darkness was stygian. It gave me a wonderful feeling of confidence. As I said before, I like the darkness.

Then the ground dropped away suddenly and I stumbled and fell, and as I picked myself up I fancied I heard a subdued guffaw up ahead somewhere. It might have been my imagination, but I could sense that Trenko, hardly able to contain himself with the excitement of the meeting, and keeping just far enough ahead not to be seen too clearly, was laughing about my unsure footsteps. Then the trees were suddenly all around me and it was darker than I imagined it could ever be. I had to stop. I couldn't see a foot in front of me.

Then silence slowly came over the place as the final sounds of the disappearing train faded away and all that was left was darkness and utter quiet.

There was another long, long wait, and I knew that Trenko was making sure that the stationmaster had gone back to his office to fill in the form—the one marked *Secret*—which said, among other things:

"The two Americans who stayed here on the night of the fourteenth left by tonight's train for the frontier."

Then at last I felt his touch on my arm. It startled me, although I was waiting for it. Trenko could move like a cat in the darkness, in spite of his bad leg. He breathed a sibilant warning into my ear, and his hand tightened on my elbow, and then he gently guided me down and away from the trees where we could see more clearly.

We moved for five minutes without speaking, and then we turned and crossed the rails and moved up into the forest on the other side, and not until we had climbed for another ten minutes did Trenko stop his quick, sure movements.

I was out of breath with the climb and with the excitement. As I dropped to the ground, breathing heavily, I felt a gigantic blow on my back that nearly threw me off balance, and then, in the darkness, Trenko was pumping my hand up and down, shaking it like a madman and saying over and over again: "A long, long time, not so? A long, long time, my friend ..."

I pulled him down beside me and thumped his back and grinned at him senselessly in the blackness and said at last: "Can we talk here? It's good to see you again."

"We can talk, why not? You think someone will come

here? You think in my country people can move about where they like, when they like? You think this is America maybe? Is that what you think?"

"How are you, Trenko? How are you?"

"Good . . . good. Always pretty good, you know Trenko. . . . Sometimes things not so good, but always I am good. . . . Is nice to see you, my friend."

I thumped him on the back again and he said: "Wait . . . you got old friend here."

He whistled quietly, and the biggest goddamn dog I have ever seen sprang out of the forest at us. It was terrifying. It looked like the Avenger come upon us, a great lean beast with startlingly white teeth and gleaming eyes that leaped up on Trenko and licked at his face. Pushing the dog away, fumbling with it, he said: "You remember Betsa? Was little pup I think, no?"

"For God's sake . . . is that Betsa?"

Betsa was one of the young dogs he had had when I'd known him. She couldn't have been more than seven or eight months old, then. I said again: "That great beast—Betsa?"

"Yes, is big dog now, very good dog, best dog I got. Her mother died, you know? You remember Cora? She died . . . old age. And Brin . . . you remember Brin? I still got Brin and one other dog, new one. Soon, you see. But now you tell me about yourself. How you like this business, eh? Is good fun, no? This time we really do big job, eh? You think?"

"I think. Pull this off . . . we've done a good job of work."

"Sure we pull it off. Why not? Is good operation. They tell you, is my idea? They tell you that?"

"Yes, they told me that. Got a cigarette on you? Can we smoke here?"

"Sure we can smoke. Nobody come here. Pretty soon we move, too, best we get to hide-out. But I only got my black cigarettes. At home I got American cigarettes."

Trenko's cheroots! I suddenly remembered them. The first one I'd tried, black, evil-smelling, blue-smoked and pungent, had nearly torn my intestines out. I said hastily: "No, thanks, it's not important."

It's strange what environment can do for you. A few days ago, at one o'clock in the morning, I'd have been sitting in a stuffy, overcrowded night club, drinking phony liquor and watching some cute little chick dancing behind a fan, with not a care or a thought in the world except how much my cut of the night's drinking would come to. And now, a few days later and a few hundred miles away, I was sitting on a cold, damp mountain in the middle of a forest, surrounded by dangers so severe that it was foolish to ignore them, talking treason to a man who carried his life in the pocket of his coarse cotton jacket. And, what's more, feeling like a rebel myself.

We moved off again through the forest, with Trenko winding his way among the tall trees and Betsa, the German shepherd, softly padding along behind us, and we climbed up and up till the forest gave way to open pasture, and then we dropped down again on the other side of the hill and crossed a stream that came winding lazily out of the darkness into a little clearing, and we forced our way into the bushes again along a path that was barely visible, and then the moon came out from behind the clouds and I muttered: "Vallance probably arranged that too. . . ."

Then we came upon it suddenly. Trenko had stopped in his tracks and said, making a gesture of it: "Our house, my friend. I got food there, American cigarettes, little bit cognac. We be pretty comfortable next few days."

I stood staring blankly ahead of me, and then the dog ran forward sniffing at the ground, and I saw that there was a hut there, no more than a lean-to of planks built around a tall thorn tree and covered over with sods of turf and branches of eucalyptus.

It took on more shape and became clearer, and I saw that it was not that an attempt had been made to conceal it, but rather that the materials with which it was made blended so neatly into its surroundings that it was almost invisible anyway.

We ducked under an overhanging branch and went inside. It was quite big, a good fifteen feet square, with a narrow bench running along two of the walls. The floor, like the furniture, was of rough-cut planks, hewn straight with an adze. There was a big cupboard opposite the door, flanked by two small windows covered with heavy curtains of burlap. There was a heavy scent of eucalyptus in the place, and I saw that the lumber the cupboard was made of was freshly cut.

Trenko was hanging up a kerosene lamp and throwing open the wooden shutters, bustling around the place like a housewife, full of repressed excitement.

I said: "What is this place?"

"You know they cut hemp here? Wild hemp? Sisal? This hut belongs to a man who used to cut here, but now . . . Now it is mine. Look, you see what we got?"

He threw open the cupboard door and showed an impressive array of groceries. There was bread there, and corned beef from Argentina, with Brazilian kippers and some cans of local beans; there was a long salami, some olives, a bowl of eggs, a carton of American cigarettes, two bottles of cognac and some imported German beer—altogether it was enough to live on for a couple of months. He took down one of the bottles of cognac and showed it to me, his face wrinkled with smiles. He said:

"Maybe we open this, eh? What do you say? It is like the old times, no?"

It was strange to see him again. It seemed that I knew him well, although in fact I had only been with him and Lazlo for a few days. In that short space of time we had become good friends, but still we were friends of very short acquaintance. I felt a strangeness, a sense of unease; it was hard to make conversation.

I said: "How's the leg?"

"Oh . . . It is fine. I would have lost it if you had not . . ."

"And how's that brother of yours?"

Trenko dropped his eyes and said the brother was fine, as though he weren't fine at all. I didn't press the point. There'd been some trouble between them, I recalled. It was all coming back to me now, the picture of those few hectic, rebellious days, with sentries striding about in patched pieces of uniform —any kind of uniform that would give them a semblance of legitimacy and take them away from the border line of banditry.

I said the wrong thing again: "And that young girl he was running around with? The one with the funny eyes . . . Whatever happened to her?"

"Maria-Anna?"

"Yes, that's right. Maria-Anna. What happened to her?"

She'd been one of the band of rebels that time in San Antonio. She was a young girl, not more than sixteen or seventeen years old, a student from the big university there. She was gawky with the awkwardness of extreme youth, and her face was elfin in a way that suggested she would one day be beautiful; her eyebrows were thin, and curled up away from her eyes, and she had a way of laughing suddenly in the middle of a serious conversation as though indicating that nothing really mattered anyway. Her eyes were large and bright and very dark, and she seemed a lot older than she really was. She'd joined the rebels because of something they'd done to her father, and Trenko had sort of taken her under his wing. Then the brother, whose name I never knew, had come along and upset things a little, and while I was with them for those few days it had seemed to me that Maria-Anna was really the brother's girl. I remember that once, when I'd paid her a silly compliment of some sort, not really flirting with her but just messing about a bit, it was the brother who had glared at me and it was Trenko who had laughed with us about it.

Trenko was pulling the cork out of the cognac bottle, flicking the little pieces of broken red wax with his thumbnail. He switched to Spanish suddenly, and said: "She died. The history of my country is written on gravestones. Sometimes they belong to people we love."

"Oh, I'm sorry. I didn't know. . . . I couldn't. . . . You were fond of her too, weren't you? Come to that, I was fond of her myself. We all were. Kind of girl you couldn't help liking."

He said slowly: "I married her, you know. Just a few weeks before she died. My brother . . . There was some bad blood between us because of her, but that is all gone now. After her death he was no longer angry with me for taking her away from him. Now, we are brothers once more."

There was a long, awkward silence. At last he said: "It was another attempt, like the one you saw. But this time, some companies of soldiers were with us, and we thought . . . we thought we were strong enough to come out into the open. We did not know that this is what they wanted us to think. So a whole regiment came over to our side, and we knew that if we could capture the radio station and hold the *palacio* for a few hours, then the people would join us. So . . . so our men came in from the hills, and we took the radio station, and we brought our leaders to the microphones to call on the people to rise. And then the regiment that was with us turned against us, just as they had planned. I tell you, we were all there, all of us except Lazlo. Lazlo was not with us because he was sick . . . as you know, his health . . . But all the others were there, and when the army turned on us there was a great deal of shooting. I had married Maria-Anna only a few weeks before this, and, when she fell, I dragged her over the roof. We got away because they had miscalculated. In waiting for our leaders to come to the microphones, they also allowed the riots to begin in the streets, and it is this that saved us. Of course, they stamped it out. . . . But a lot of us got away. Galinda was killed, and Perez, and Mattéos, and Pirenda. José was captured, and so was Maduso. It looked like the end of all of us. . . . But Lazlo . . ."

There was almost a smile on his face. He went on:

"Lazlo could not be with us because he was sick, but he started a rumor that he had been against the whole revolt and therefore had not joined it. It reached the ears of the government men, and it was soon after this that they offered him the amnesty if he would join them. So you see, even from our defeats, Lazlo can extract a little victory."

When I said nothing, thinking of Maria-Anna, he was suddenly saddened again. Staring at me as though seeking approval of what he had done, he said:

"Maria-Anna was hit twice, in the shoulder and in the neck.

I dragged her over the top of the radio station, and in the streets there was rioting, and I took her through the barricades and out to the countryside where there were no police, and I sent for a doctor. But, you understand, there was no doctor who would come. The government men, angry that so many of us had escaped, had warned the doctors. What could I do? I took the bullets out of her with my knife while she was still unconscious. I had no medicines, no disinfectants . . . nothing.

"There were just a few of us . . . it was an old farmhouse. What could I do? A doctor would have led them straight to us. She recovered consciousness and I told her that if I brought a doctor . . . that without one she would die. . . . She knew what was in my mind. She knew the whole long story of the secret police. She knew that they were not men, but animals, debased and degraded beyond belief. Sadistic. Obscene. Cruel and unclean. I do not think she was frightened of them. I think that she wanted to spare me the knowledge of what they would be doing to her down there under the barracks. So at last, she died. She was not pretty, perhaps, but she was very young and . . . and innocent. They would have made great sport with her in their cellars. It was better to let her die."

What can you say? The tears were streaming down his face, quite unheeded, as though he could not always talk so freely, particularly not in front of his own people. I could sense the relief he felt that here was a friendly stranger who would not think him weak because he cried over the death of someone he loved.

I said awkwardly: "It's hard to forget these things. . . . It's even better that you should not forget."

"Of course. Sometimes, when I am afraid . . . when the work to be done is more dangerous . . . If I think of Maria-Anna, then I am a stronger man because I am not afraid to die, and so, I am more deadly to *them*. Again, it is a little victory from a defeat, and it is with these little victories that one day we shall succeed."

I tried hard to change the subject. I said: "But they tell me you're a lot stronger now. A lot of people on your side . . ."

His manner brightened at once.

"Yes. Yes, some of the army is with us now, very many of them. Only the navy and the air force . . . And over beyond the mountains, there are great stretches of territory where we have our own provisional government. And, one day, those treacherous men in the junta will fall, and then . . . Then there will be some hope for my people at last."

It's funny. Whenever Trenko spoke like that—of his cause —he subconsciously lapsed into the Castilian Spanish of the orator. It was an effort, of which he was not even aware, to lend his words the maximum of dignity. He smiled quickly and made a sudden gesture with the cognac bottle.

"But we must not talk politics on our first night together. There are better things we can do. We have no ice, but the water from the spring is cold and it is good."

He poured out two drinks and splashed some water in them from an earthenware pitcher. We clinked our glasses with a certain amount of formality and he said: "To the Revolution."

I felt like a sans-culotte watching the guillotine go up.

We talked for a while about nothing much. Trenko produced a map and showed me where the rebel-held territory lay. And we played two games of chess. Then, tired out by the excitement of the day, we lay down on the hard wooden benches and tried to sleep.

In the morning we'd get organized. In the morning, there'd be time to look around and inspect the place. For the moment, a hard bed in a grubby shack with a damn great dog curled up on the floor with her green eyes wide awake and looking for trouble.

And meanwhile, another man, with my passport and my papers and my Madeleine's picture, was pushing my boss out of the country, leaving me naked and exposed to the fearful whims of the men I had so thoughtlessly chosen to make my enemies. Speaking into the darkness, I said: "You asleep?"

I heard him turn over quickly.

"No. Not yet."

"Shall we know when our friend is safely out of the country?"

"Yes. We shall know."

"How?"

There was a note of pride in his voice: "I got a radio. I am in contact with my people in the mountains."

"And how will they know?"

"They are in contact too."

He did not say with whom. I thought it was very discreet of him.

I reflected a little on the prolonged gleam of hatred that had been in his eyes when he had told me about Maria-Anna's death, and of the people who would have made great sport with her, as he put it, and of his hatred for them.

That was it, I thought; you either accepted them, like the plump little waitress in Volvoda, or you hated them, like Trenko. Surely no one could actually be on their side. Even the plump girl . . . perhaps under that facade of acceptance, there was a rebel there too. You never could tell. Or perhaps she was even one of them. You couldn't tell that either.

I tried to think about Madeleine so I should sleep comfortably and well, but my mind refused to dismiss the fears that were mounting up inside me. It was Trenko's talk of his girl that had done it, and when I fell asleep at last I was thinking, not of Madeleine, but of the overwhelming horrors of capture that we seemed somehow to be treating so lightly. When Trenko had pointed out the rebel positions to me, on his map, they had seemed terribly far away from us. And we were very close to the huge Volvoda police barracks.

Cellars . . . It's one of the two things they seem to insist on. The other is nakedness. Take away a man's clothes, and work him over underground . . . the two seem to go together. It's something to do with the claustrophobic grave. I woke up once during the night, frightened half out of my wits by something I was dreaming, and then I went to sleep again and tossed and turned fretfully until it was daylight.

And when I awoke again, it was bright and hot and sunny, and Trenko was standing over me grinning like an ape and waving a piece of paper in my face.

It was a message telling us that Lazlo had safely crossed the border.

I sat up and stretched my arms, rubbing a hand over my face. It was a peculiar feeling; it was not hard to persuade myself that the man who had left, in my clothes, with my papers, my passport and my job . . . It could have been me. Then who was I? A number? A myth? A cipher?

The smell of coffee brought me back to my senses and I stumbled sleepily over to the table.

chapter 5

I spent the morning mooching about the shack, alternately trying to take an interest in my surroundings and feeling I had no right to be there. And when this feeling of not belonging came upon me, I thought of the money waiting for me in Caracas, and was thus able to rationalize a bit on the subject.

I sat outside in the hot sun for a while, squatting on a smooth white boulder and playing with Betsa. She was a huge dog, a good bit too big for a shepherd, with a crouched sort of bulk to her shoulders that gave her a look of immense power. She was very alert, and astonishingly well-trained. Trenko told me he used to send her ten or twenty miles into the hills sometimes, carrying messages strapped to her collar; he also told me that he had used a police uniform when he was teaching her to attack, so that now she couldn't stand the sight of one. He had two more up at his place on the Cordillera, but Betsa was his favorite and the one that habitually accompanied him on his hidden, nighttime missions.

It was good to see Trenko again after all these years; but it was a renewal of a friendship that had been more brief than I had realized. I was not really one of his crowd. I had no cause to fight for, no hatreds to vent, no slogans to shout from the roof tops. And when I thought along these lines, and made myself into a hireling and nothing else, then I felt a lot better. It was the getting *involved* that was frightening.

Trenko's shack was a different place by daylight. With the hot sun streaming down on it within the confines of the little clearing it stood in, it seemed quite apart from the refuge I had found during the night. Now, there were signs of a more orderly living around it; someone had planted some sweet potatoes quite recently, with the broken stalks sticking awkwardly out of the ground and only just beginning to bloom in little splashes of light green. There was a long thin patch of vegetables, with carrots and tomatoes and radishes, and the onions struggling bravely but running to seed. There was a wide bed of melons, just sprouting, and a few of the more-nearly-ripe ones had been nibbled at by some animal or other during the night. A hoe and a rake were lying carelessly on the red, sandy earth, and there was a broken-down well with an adobe wall around it.

On three sides, the trees came close to the hut itself, and on the fourth, the hill stretched up high above us, spreading out wide with dry grass where there were some goats, and a path zigzagged down from the top, crossing over a small stream that trickled a few hundred yards away from us.

It was hot and stuffy inside the hut, and I spent the morning sitting moodily about just outside, under the shade of a big baobab tree, and watching Trenko at work.

He was in constant contact with "his people" as he called them—the rebels who held the territory beyond the mountains. The radio itself was an American army field model, powered by an ordinary car battery, and he kept it under the boards of the floor when he wasn't using it. But on that first morning he seemed to be on the air almost all the time.

I felt like a piece of furniture, a parcel, a bundle that had been left for him to keep an eye on. He took time out, during the morning, to tell me about the progress they were making: the building up of their provisional government; their difficulties with the spies of the secret police. But by the broad light of day the romance of it all had gone. Is that the right word? I'm not sure that it is.

But it was more than ever like a play being acted out, a play in which I had no part except as a paid hand, to stand in the wings and smoke a cigarette and watch what was going on and walk across the proscenium when I got my cue.

He felt my mood, Trenko, and tried to cheer me up with stories of the people I had met with him before; but so many of them had been killed that it all sounded rather like a casualty list, and did little to improve my temper.

He got a message during the afternoon saying that Lazlo had joined the first of his conferences. I said impatiently: "And while all this is going on, what about Lazlo's house? How do you know that he hasn't been missed?"

Trenko shook his head.

"We have a man there. But you know . . . did they tell you? He is supposed to have the smallpox, and nobody will go near him, nor his house."

"But how can you be *sure*?"

We were outside, sitting under the big tree. Trenko pulled out his pistol, a Luger, and started stripping it down for cleaning. He said: "In the village, in Volvoda, we have two or three men, two or three sympathizers. Of course, they do not know what we are doing. But ever since Lazlo had this pox, the secret police who are assigned to watch him, they have been spending their days in the tavern, in the back room, getting drunk at the expense of the landlord. They are afraid to go to the house. This is what we expected."

"And the doctor?"

Trenko threw back his head and laughed.

"The doctor," he said, "is a very frightened man. Some people came to him in the night and told him that he would not treat his patient any more. They said the government doctor would do this. He thinks that someone is trying to let Lazlo die, and yet he is afraid to go the police. This also is what we expected."

"And what the hell am I doing, mixed up in a fraud like this? You know I'm doing it for money, don't you?"

He hesitated only briefly before he answered. He was smiling gently: "When I saw that Lazlo was getting more and more to look like the man who saved my life by dragging me away from the railway station, I did not think very much about it. Until one day they told me that there would be a conference . . . perhaps it would be possible for Lazlo to be smuggled over the border. I spoke to him about the idea I had, and we found out where you were, and someone took some pictures and sent them to us, and someone else decided that you would be the man to undertake this. We knew that you could not be expected to join us without recompense; why should you? And there is enough money behind us. It is not money that we need; it is men."

I liked the way he mentioned the railway-station episode. I knew that it was meant to remind me that sometimes I did good deeds for free. He was a nice guy, Trenko. He was thoughtful and patient, and under that burning passion there was an unexpected air of devil-take-the-hindmost. I suppose by Vallance's standards he was impetuous; but in my book he was also devious and surprisingly thorough.

He limped off to get some food ready, dragging his bad leg behind him, and when he came back with two bowls of cold sliced venison, I said: "What about you, Trenko? How come they let you move about like this?"

"They do not know what I do."

"How can you be sure of that?"

"They do not have—how do you say it?—they do not have the cunning to let me stay free if they think I am working against them. This is not the way they work. As far as they know, I am only a simple farmer. If they think anything is wrong—"

He drew a finger across his throat in a piratical gesture that once more relegated the whole thing to a limbo of theatricals. Again, I had to remind myself of the money.

He asked me if I had a girl in Caracas, and I told him a little of Madeleine. Not everything, you understand, because there were some things about Madeleine that Trenko just wouldn't have appreciated. He talked for a while about Maria-Anna, and as we squatted on the red earth, washing out our bowls with fine dry sand, there was a bond between us again and I wondered how it had ever seemed to be absent.

The first sign of trouble came late that afternoon, when the sun had turned to a watery yellow and was low over the ridge of the hills to the west of us.

It was a gleam of light, no more, so suddenly gone that for a moment I thought perhaps I had imagined the whole thing, and then I knew, even in the sudden flash of panic, that I must not stare at the point from which it had come. If it was, in fact, what I took it to be.

I turned away and sat down close to the stubby trunk of the big tree that Trenko was using as a watchtower, feeling my heart suddenly beating fast. He was inside the cabin, feeding the dog, so I called out: "Trenko! I think we may have trouble."

He had the sense not to show himself at the door. His voice

was strained and low. He echoed: "You think we have trouble?"

I got up and sauntered in as nonchalantly as I could, though my heart was thumping hard. I said: "What's on the hill behind us up there? Anything? Anything with glass in it?"

His lined face was deeply troubled.

"You see something up there?"

"Just a flash of light."

"You mean . . . glasses? Binoculars?"

"Binoculars."

"You sure?"

"No. I'm not sure. But something flashed up there. At least, I think it did. I just saw it out of the corner of my eye if I saw it at all. Maybe it's only my imagination."

"Better we make sure."

He was not wasting any time. He slipped the blade of his machete down into the floor boards and prized one of them up, disclosing the radio in a wood-lined hole dug into the earth, together with a six-volt car battery. He lugged the battery up and said quickly: "You take the radio, O.K.?"

I picked up my jacket and in less than thirty seconds we were clambering through the small window on the other side of the cabin, where the trees came close down to the walls, and pushing our way into the heavy undergrowth. Straining through the thicket, we went deeper into the forest until the ground broke open into a small valley where the shallow stream was running gently at the bottom, then up the steep bank on the other side where coffee bushes were growing wild. He pushed the battery deep into the shrubbery there, took the radio from me and put that in too, and then straightened up and said: "Now. Now you show me where you see this. This way."

We moved round in a circle through the tall slender saplings that quivered and sprang back at us as we pushed past them, and very soon we were moving softly by the edge of the clearing again, close enough to our shack to smell the coffee that was brewing there. I shook my head.

"Not here," I whispered. "There's a break in the forest . . . there. . . ."

Trenko nodded.

"So this way."

We moved further up the incline, keeping close to the trees, until we could see the hill more clearly. Crouching under the bushes, I pointed carefully with my finger.

"There . . . about there somewhere . . ."

"Where the grass is?"

"No . . . to the left. There's a darker patch there. Somewhere there, I think."

He shook his head gravely.

"Up there, there is nothing. If you see something there, then we have trouble. You wait here, I go and see. Maybe take one hour, then I come back. You stay here, in this place."

"Wait," I said. "Don't you think I'd better come with you?"

He scratched his head for a moment.

"Yes, maybe it is better if you come with me. You know how to move without noise?"

"Well . . ."

"No noise at all. Very slowly. Maybe you better wait here."

"I want to see what goes on."

"Then stay close behind me."

He took the pistol from under his jacket and checked it. I hoped he wouldn't have to use it, but there was an alert, angry look in his eye that told me he would if he had half a chance. It was the frightening look of a fanatic.

We pulled back into the bushes and began the slow climb to the top of the hill. He stopped when we had gone a little way, and whistled once, and in a moment Betsa came creeping through after us, her tongue hanging out, her eyes bright. He put a restraining hand on her head, and said something to her, and she almost nodded in reply, crouching down and moving warily after us.

We moved quickly at first, and I knew he was sure that within this circle we were safe as long as the dog was with us. I noticed that he looked round at her from time to time to make certain that she was giving no indication of trouble. Then he raised a warning hand and whispered: "Now . . . now we move very, very quietly. Like Betsa."

Daniel Boone could have learned something from Trenko, the way he moved through those woods.

He sent Betsa in front, now, and we went from tree to tree, standing upright, moving quickly and quietly and then standing stock-still and looking carefully all about us, watching the trees and the shadows—and Betsa—for the slightest sign of anything that hadn't the honest smell of the forest about it. Betsa, too, moved in much the same way, but creeping forward on her belly and then looking back for a silent signal to the left or the right, then moving forward again and waiting for us to catch up. Every time Trenko snapped his fingers, ever so gently, she looked back, took the direction and moved forward again a few yards, then crouched still and alert once more, close to the cover of the greenery. The almost imperceptible sound of his fingers in the silence was more than I could bear. I thought, *If I ever get out of this I'm going to send him a silent dog whistle.*

It was half an hour before we reached the spot I had indicated. Trenko gave a low command to Betsa and she cast about in a circle while we stood and looked around us. I could feel the beating of my heart almost strong enough to knock me off balance, and I was sure that Trenko must be able to hear it too. The impulse to cough was overpowering, but I was glad to be with him rather than down there at the cabin, alone in a strange and dangerous country.

Trenko was looking at the ground, scratching his head and muttering to himself, saying over and over again, "Nothing . . . nothing . . . nothing here . . ."

He looked up at me and said quietly: "Nothing here. Maybe further up? Maybe?"

I whispered anxiously: "Is this where the dark patch is?"

"This is the place. A dead thorn tree, you see?"

"Could be to the left a bit. I hardly saw more than a glimpse. May have imagined the whole thing."

"Better we make sure."

"I hope I did. . . .."

"I hope so too. . . . Soon we find out."

We moved over to the south a little, creeping forward as before, tree by tree, shadow by shadow, with Betsa in the lead and then Trenko, and then me following behind.

If it truly was the flash of binoculars that I had seen, then there was a chink in the curtain and, unknown to us, someone was watching the drama. The prospect terrified me, because if they were watching *here*, then they must know exactly what was going on.

And I knew that this could only mean one thing: we'd never get out of the country alive.

It was the silence of it all that scared me. The feeling that they were all around us and knew exactly what was happening . . . and yet were not moving until they were good and ready. It implied an awful omniscience that made us like rather foolish little ants crawling out of the ground and not knowing that someone was waiting patiently until the line had been established and the whole lot could be wiped out with a blowtorch quickly, neatly and efficiently. It made me feel that it just wasn't worth while being smart, or cunning, or careful; that the results were predestined and fearful. The silence was oppressive, and the insistent sound of the crickets only seemed to heighten it. Somewhere, a bird squawked.

Then I felt a cold tingling creeping over the back of my neck.

Betsa was crouched low on the ground, her belly tight to the hard red sand, her ears pricked up and the hair on her back standing stiff. I looked round in alarm and Trenko was suddenly not there.

Then I saw that he had moved away silently and was close under the cover of a bush, urgently signaling me to keep down. I dropped to my knees, and I knew that I was trembling, terrified of whatever it was that the dog had seen or heard or sensed. There was a constriction in my throat that was choking me.

I could see nothing. I strained every nerve to listen for the slightest sound, but there was only the forest noise of rustling leaves, of the crickets, and an occasional bark of a parrot up in the branches somewhere. I looked over to Trenko again and saw that he was peering into the shrubbery, motionless, his keen eyes fixed on something that he could see and that I could not, and then his eyes moved slowly away, examining every shadow, and I knew that he had seen nothing either, but was following the direction of Betsa's point.

I thought I heard a slight sound behind me and looked over my shoulder in alarm, but it was no more than the stirring of a bush. I saw that Trenko had heard it too, but he shook his head and concentrated his gaze ahead of us again, and after a moment he signaled me to stay put while he crept soundlessly forward to where the dog was. I have never seen a man move so silently. Not a twig cracked under his feet; not a leaf moved with him. He was immobile under the bushes one minute, and streaking forward the next, moving silently and with astonishing speed.

I saw him tap Betsa twice on the shoulder, and she crept forward again, flat on the ground, snaking under the foliage, growling very quietly. For a long time we waited, and then Trenko turned with his finger to his lips and signaled me forward.

Every slight sound I made seemed like a thunderclap. I lost my balance, once, through trying to move too quietly, and then I was in a small clearing, no more than a few feet across, where a gap in the trees showed a long view of the west. Betsa was sniffing at the ground, and looking up and around her, and then sniffing at the ground again. Trenko straightened up and went over to her.

He was staring at the dusty earth and frowning. I came and joined him and saw four or five firm marks of heavy boots deeply imprinted in the dry soil. That was all. Just half a dozen footprints of broad-toed boots with studs in them. I could not determine whether they had all been made by the same man or not.

Trenko dropped to his knees and examined them carefully, looking, I knew, for the answer to the same question: how many men had made them? He stood up and signaled Betsa to cast again, and she went off in a circle once more and when she came back she was sniffing eagerly at the prints and bounding hopefully toward the east. Trenko shook his head. His voice low, he said: "Whoever was here, he has gone now. Betsa is not like this if he is near us."

"Can she follow a scent?" I whispered. I knew it was a foolish question, because that dog could do everything but lay eggs. But I felt the need to say something, to assure myself that there were two of us to help each other out of this trouble that could perhaps have been merely an elongation of my own frightened imagination.

Trenko nodded, standing with his arms akimbo and staring at the ground.

"Yes. She has a good nose, but . . . I think we had better go back. I do not like this. I do not like this at all."

"You think we're being watched?"

"It looks like it. Perhaps not, but . . ."

"It would help if we could find out just who was watching us."

He shook his head again.

"No. Better we go back." I knew he was worried about the radio.

We stood for a moment looking through the gap in the trees at the distant outline of the cabin far below us. It was almost invisible, but if you knew where to look you could see it plainly enough. He took the binoculars from the case which was slung at his back and handed them to me. Looking through them, I could see every plank, every eucalyptus branch of which the shelter was made. I handed them back to him without a word and he looked through them briefly and then put them back in the case.

His voice was forced when he spoke again, displaying a confidence I am sure he did not feel.

"Now we go back," he said. "We will worry after, when we see what we worry about. No good worrying when we don't see anything, eh?"

I said: "To my way of thinking that's exactly when we ought to worry."

"Come, better we go back now. I must get on the air to headquarters."

We went down the hill again a great deal faster than we had gone up it, and when we got to the gully where the radio was, Trenko sent me climbing up a tall mimosa tree to keep watch while he used the set. It was one of those tropical mimosas they call *sensitivo,* and, as I clambered through its foliage, the leaves closed down and folded over each other as though my intrusion were a warning of dreadful things to come. I took the antenna up with me, conscious that the real reason behind my climb was Trenko's need to keep me out of sight if he should be discovered. It made me angry, a little, because it meant that he had seen my fright up there on the hill and was not sure that I could be relied upon in an emergency. He knew that I led an easy, comfortable life, by his standards, and that my nerves were flabby, as well as my muscles. He wasn't taking any chances. I felt resentful; but I knew that he was doing what was best for both of us.

So I climbed to the top of his goddamn mimosa, not without a certain amount of panting and laboring, with the thin wire of the aerial looped over my belt, and soon I was high enough to see all there was to see on every side of us. There wasn't much except trees.

The sky was a light yellow-gray now, with puffs of cumulus cloud dotted about everywhere. The thousand greens of the forest were beginning to take on the friendly somberness of the early evening. As far as I could see there was nothing but forest and hillside and mountain, with a silent, sharp-cut skyline where the ridge stood out clear and distant and somehow fragile, like a stage setting with a faint blue light behind it to make it look real.

Then I heard the subdued chatter of Trenko's key on the set, and in a very few minutes he gave the quick whistle that meant I could come down again.

It seemed a great deal darker when I reached the bottom of the tree. Trenko had put the radio back in its case and was winding in the antenna. I said: "Now what?"

"Now? Now we have a little work to do. Tonight, we sleep in the woods. In the forest, nobody will find us."

"Did you tell them we were being watched?"

"Yes."

"Well, what did they say, for God's sake?"

"They told me to wait and see."

"To wait and see! For God's sake . . ."

He interrupted me angrily. I could see that he was sufficiently disturbed by what we had seen to lose his habitual calm. He said: "My friend . . . we will do exactly as they tell us to do. I told them that perhaps we are being watched, and they told me to wait and see what happens. This I will do."

Conscious of his anger, conscious that he was betraying his own anxiety, he smiled quickly and said: "Believe me, my friend. You are in good hands."

I suddenly realized what a burden I must be to him. The whole complicated operation depended on his keeping me safe and out of sight. I said, and I meant it: "I'm sorry. Of course. Whatever you say."

Still smiling, watching me closely, he said: "If anything has gone wrong, then our friend Lazlo will not be able to come back. It is really quite simple."

"Yes? And what about me? How the hell do I get out of the country without my passport?"

"We will get you out. Never fear."

Never fear... He was gauging my thoughts to a nicety. If Lazlo did not come back, then what Vallance had called the operational epicenter would be alive with troops, with security police and with the special squads... all looking for Lazlo. And we would be right in the middle of them. There'd be a bayonet behind every tree, a hand grenade in every bush and a machine gun at the end of every valley. At *each* end of every valley.

I wished the hell that I knew where DeBries was.

When we got back to the cabin, we moved out all the supplies of food and cached them away in the undergrowth, and we took the cooking pot and a canteen of water. Trenko grinned when I picked up the cognac bottles and stuffed them into my pockets, and we opened a bottle of the imported beer and drank it right there, sharing it out of the bottle. We took the blankets and a length of rope and a supply of matches, and it was quite dark when we got the new hide-out organized.

It wasn't much of a place, just a hollow under a fallen tree where the moss had grown deep and soft and there was plenty of loose foliage to pull around us. I began to get my courage back when Trenko showed me the "back door," as he called it—a way through the trees that led under a tangle of roots, through a maze of liana vines, and into a little valley that led back into the mountain again. There was water there, too, and, as the darkness became deeper and finally impenetrable, I began to feel a lot better. I knew that we could hold out for a long time, provided Trenko was still alive. The border was only—what was it?—a day's hard walk away?

Trenko was watching me in the darkness; I could feel it. I did not believe that he could really see my face, but I sensed that he was aware of the way my mind was working. I felt his hand on my arm. He said quietly:

"Do not worry, my friend. Maybe we think we are in trouble for nothing. Perhaps it is just a false alarm. But we cannot afford not to be careful." He hesitated and went on: "We take all these precautions because we must. But you know? I feel pretty good. I think everything is O.K."

It's funny. You have that feeling when you're doing this sort of thing. If you're at it constantly, that is. It's a sixth sense, or something, like knowing when a person is looking at you without your actually seeing him. I felt it too. I was too cautious to put much faith in my own instincts in that respect, because I'd lost the touch. But I knew that Trenko hadn't. If he felt that all was well, then, by God, all *was* well. I was suddenly absolutely convinced of it.

I took a swig out of the cognac bottle, passed it across to him and lay down on the ground, watching the darkening sky through the trees above me.

The night was quiet and cool, with a dampness coming down from the foliage. I wondered if I could reach the rebel camps in the mountains if anything went wrong, and then I wondered if perhaps everything was as it should be after all. A few footprints in the dusty earth—could it mean so much? Or rather, could what it meant have such awful consequences? It could have been a *cholo* passing by, wearing a pair of stolen army boots.

In that case, the flash of light I had seen? I tried to persuade myself that I had imagined it, but I knew that it had been there all right, and no amount of wishful thinking could make it anything but the sun on a pair of binoculars. In that case . . . it was a logical progression to the fact that they were onto us.

I wished to hell that DeBries were with us.

I wondered what they'd be doing in Trenko's mysterious headquarters, how they could check on just how much the waiting enemy knew. . . . I never did find out how good their intelligence outfit was.

Betsa's breath was close to my face. I stretched out a hand and felt the hairy warmth of her body. She grunted when I touched her and I felt her roll over. I knew she'd be a better guard than a regiment of soldiers. And with the friendly night all about us . . .

In no time at all, I was fretfully asleep.

I dreamed about Madeleine again, and woke up once in the night to wish that she were close beside me, with her long warm body tight against mine. Then I thought of all the money that was going into the bank for me, more than enough to get back home with, but now that I had it coming I knew I'd been fooling myself about going back to Pennsylvania. Not yet, anyhow. Maybe Madeleine and I would go to Europe for the rest of the summer. I'd like her to see the Parthenon, and the way the dark olive trees stand out against the stark uninhabited patches of red sandstone and gray rock, all along the hillsides of Boeotia. Like most people who live in the big towns, Madeleine had always wanted to see a great deal more of the empty, deserted areas where the only person you're liable to meet in the course of the day is a stray goat.

I listened in the night silence for a while, and then went back to sleep, wondering what the day would bring.

As usual, when the bed is different, or the surroundings are strange, I woke early, even before Trenko. There was a dull ache in my side where a small stone had worked its way to the surface under my hip, but I felt refreshed and ready for anything.

For anything, that is, that I thought might be happening.

I stretched and rolled myself out of the blankets. Betsa was watching me. She growled very quietly, just once, her sharp eyes alert, and Trenko was instantly wide awake and sitting up. He saw that it was I who was worrying the dog—she wasn't taking any chances—and he smiled and put out a hand to pat her, then slapped an insect out of his hair.

We rolled up our blankets and stuffed them under the damp bushes, pulling the foliage deep down around them, and then had some hunks of hard salami for breakfast. We debated awhile whether it would be safe to light a fire and make something hot to drink, but decided against it. We drank water instead, and I gloomily inspected the mosquito bites on my arms.

There was something fearfully disturbing in the thought that if the danger was there at all it was all the worse because we might be wrong about it. I believe that had we seen signs, up on the hill there, of any soldiery, or police, or something more solid than just a footprint, we would have felt that we knew just what that danger was; and, knowing this, would be able to combat it. But a mere footprint? We spent a long time arguing about it.

First of all, we decided that it was too much to expect mere coincidence—about the flash of light, I mean. I had seen the reflection of the sun on something shiny, and, when we went up to investigate, there were signs that someone had been there. This much was incontrovertible. And it meant that whoever had been there was carrying something bright enough to reflect the sunlight. Binoculars were the obvious guess. But could it have been, perhaps, just a goatherd? What would a goatherd be carrying that was shiny enough to . . . A water bottle? They all carried them, unless they stuck to the old-fashioned leather bag.

A water bottle could be made of aluminum, and it could possibly be bright enough. I didn't think so. Neither, I could see, did Trenko. He said it could have been a piece of mirror; some of the mestizos carried unexpected things, and it was at least feasible . . . a piece of broken mirror and a razor for the weekly shave? Some of them stayed out on the mountainside for weeks at a time, gathering in their straying herds. . . . Well, it was possible. A drink of water for his mangy dog, tipped out of the eating bowl . . . would it catch the light like that? An old tin can?

Trenko nodded gravely. It was possible. I could see that between us we had entirely different reasons for examining every possibility like this. Trenko wanted to know because if there was danger he would have to report on it and accept the new instructions from his H.Q. And to allow them half a chance to give him the right instructions, he had to assess the degree of that danger. He had to *know*.

There was one thing I didn't tell him. Suppose there was a leak, as I had mentioned to Vallance, somewhere at the other end of the line . . . at the top, wherever that was. Then surely they would never have allowed Lazlo to get over the border, because they must know that if the leak were discovered Lazlo would never come back. But Lazlo was safe now, for the moment. He was out of the country. He'd succeeded in the first half of his plan. Could they be playing it smart and waiting for him to come back, knowing that we could not discover they knew all about it? I didn't think so. Somehow, I couldn't see them running the risk.

Then what was the alternative?

The alternative was far more frightening. It could only mean that they were onto Trenko but knew nothing about Lazlo.

This was the old, old fear. During the war it was the same. You parachuted into somebody else's territory, and, with the best training in the world, the best cover story, the best possible chances of success, you were still at the mercy of your reception committee.

Reception committee. It was a good name for them. They were the people on the ground who lit the signal fires and stood by with a stolen truck or a couple of bicycles to get you away to safety in a hurry, and you were irrevocably in their hands once you jumped out of the aircraft. Usually they were O.K. But sometimes, one of them . . . it happened often enough to be a frightening hazard. Just one man playing a double game and reporting to *them* that you were expected. It happened. . . .

And now, here I was firmly in Trenko's strong hands. He was reliable enough, I knew that. There wasn't a shadow of doubt that he was loyal. But if they were onto him . . . It was a mighty big *if*, and the latent threat of it was terrifying.

Suppose that they'd been onto Trenko long ago . . . had been watching him ever since. They'd know about the sisal cutter's cabin and would want to know what he was using it for. They'd know about Betsa and keep their watchers far enough away to cause us no alarm. Until they were good and ready, that is.

They'd know enough not to act precipitately. They'd keep their distance until they *knew* what was going on. They'd give us enough rope to tie our hands behind our backs, with enough left over to hang us all. They'd be peeking through the curtain that hung over the stage and just biding their time before tearing it down.

I knew they'd never make Trenko talk. But if they got him, they'd get me too, and about myself I wasn't so sure.

Not so sure? Hell, I was damned sure. I knew just how much I'd be able to stand before the breaking point, and it wasn't very much. What's the good of pretending to be a hero? I'm not, and I know it. Some men can stand anything, and Trenko was one of these. He was a fanatic. It's something to do with the ancient heritage of hatred for whoever or whatever represents the tyrant.

It was the thought that they were onto Trenko that worried me. And although I said nothing about it, I knew that he was thinking of this too.

Toward midday he went off to scout around, taking Betsa with him, and he came back an hour later as silently as he had gone, and said with a rueful grin that everything seemed to be all right. He took a stub of pencil and some paper from his radio box and coded a message. It was a simple enough code, deriving from the sequence of letters in a key phrase. I knew all about this kind of code, but of course I didn't know his keys. There'd be several of them, changed daily and never used again. You took a piece of prose you could remember, like the Gettysburg Address or something, and you used a series of three or four words from it, different ones each time. It was rough and ready and not overcomplicated, and it was safe enough unless they caught you and could drag out of you the whole of the essay or jingle or speech which you used for the keys. They could decode these messages, given enough time, but it was a pretty difficult job.

I watched him at work for a while, filling the letters into little squares, reading from right to left and writing from bottom to top. I do not know what he was telling them, but when he got on the air an "A.S. 10" came back, which meant that he was to wait ten minutes for an answer.

When it came, the reply said simply:

Go to the bridge over the stream at two o'clock exactly. Call us again at four o'clock. Ends.

That was all. I could see that he was unhappy about something. When I asked him, he hesitated, and said at last: "I will tell you. If it is true that we are being watched, then I myself can no longer afford to be seen. Before, I have been free to move about because *they* do not know what I am doing. But now . . . I do not know."

"So?"

"The bridge is very easily seen from many places."

I made a wild guess.

"Perhaps they want you to be seen. If someone is watching the bridge . . ."

"Why should they?"

"I was thinking of DeBries."

He said sharply: "DeBries?"

"Yes. Don't you know him?"

"No. Who is this man?"

"Vallance's number-one boy. A smooth operator. He's supposed to be here somewhere."

"I do not know this man. I do not think I want to know him. There are already too many people."

I knew that he was disturbed by the thought of his carefully hatched plan being made common knowledge in a widening circle of plotters. That's the trouble with conspiracy; it tends to be catching.

His voice was sharp and impatient. Again, I was conscious of the breach that lay between my original conception of the wounded man I had dragged to safety, and the moody, inexplicable rebel in whose care I found myself. And, once more, he seemed to sense my disquiet. He looked up at me quickly and smiled and said: "Well . . . if we are lucky. . ."

That was the difference between them, between Trenko and Vallance. To Vallance, luck did not exist. He had to be sure of every single influence that could affect his work; Trenko, on the other hand, would take his support where he found it and he relied quite a bit on chance. Vallance went forward with a competence founded on caution; Trenko with a cool audacity that bordered on recklessness.

I knew that I'd feel a lot safer with Vallance. I knew, too, that I was hopelessly out of place in this angry, desperate quarrel. And I knew that my fear sprang from the obvious corollary of that fact; if they caught me, it was no good pretending to myself or to them that I was merely there for the joy ride. They'd be just as ruthless with me as they would with their own people. Only their own people had built up a sheet-steel plating of protective shell; they were toughened by years of hardship and oppression. I wasn't. I knew that my flesh was as soft and weak and vulnerable as my spirit.

I'm not ashamed of it. There's a limit of pain beyond which

no human being should be expected to go. The apes can suffer more than a civilized man; but that doesn't make their culture better than ours.

chapter 6

It was precisely two o'clock when we came out of the forest and moved onto the bridge.

Trenko had described it as all broken down, but I wouldn't have called it a bridge at all. Maybe a cart could have been dragged over it in the days before the tree trunks, which were not even lashed together, had collapsed into the water. The gravel track that led to it was covered with fine sand and dotted with young cactus plants, and obviously no one had used it for quite a long time. The complete abandon of it gave the place an incredibly lonely air, as though the rest of the world were a long way away. It seemed as if this spot were too remote to be in the least possible danger from anything. The water in the stream was clear and sparkling, meandering quietly over yellow boulders and jagged gray rocks, with smooth round pebbles tumbling over each other occasionally. The sun was quite hot now after the early cold, and steam was rising gently off one end of the decaying logs.

The forest was broken here, with big open spaces clearly visible on three sides of us, and in one green patch there was a long tree trunk that had been felled and left to rot in the sun there, as though whoever had cut it down just couldn't bother to drag it away in the heat. It was all very beautiful and tropical and peaceful; but I couldn't help realizing that we could be seen from a great many places. And my uniform felt very conspicuous.

Worried, I asked Trenko about it. He muttered something under his breath and said: "Why do they send us here? This is not a good place for you, my friend. Those clothes . . . Better you get under cover, no?"

I couldn't have agreed with him more. I went into the nearby forest again and sat down on a bank covered with creepers, no more than twenty yards away from Trenko, where he stood with his hands on his hips, watching the water go by under his feet.

I called softly: "Likely to be anybody about here?"

He looked up and squinted around at the hills, his eyes wrinkled against the bright heat of the day. He shook his head.

"No. Nobody comes here much. A very lonely place. The village is the other side of the hill, but you know . . . very steep; nobody comes up here."

I lay down on the bank and closed my eyes, making sure that the foliage of a thorn bush was close around me. I could still hear Trenko, pacing restlessly up and down on the logs, and I thought what a good soldier he was. Most of us would have chosen to wait under cover, but he'd been told to go to the bridge and that's where he was going to stay, right on it.

I almost dozed off, and I awoke guiltily, wondering if I really had slept, and sat up and examined every inch of the surrounding countryside, looking for a sign of anything, anything at all. There was nothing. Nothing but trees and trees and more trees.

Then suddenly I saw that Betsa had stopped her prowling and was standing alert close beside Trenko, staring, like a pointer, into the thicket. Trenko did not change his pacing; he just went on moving, straight ahead, quite slowly, and did not stop till he was off the bridge and under cover, on the other side of the stream, and, as he disappeared from my sight, I just had time to see that he was slipping his hand into his belt for his pistol. I was panic-stricken. I had the sense not to move any more than was necessary to draw the sharp thorns of the bush closer about me, and then I felt the blood run from my face; I thought I had never been so terrified in my life.

A man was coming down the slope beside me, and out of the corner of my eye I had caught a quickly passing glimpse of a uniform. He was out of sight again almost immediately, but it had been enough. . . . My blood froze, and then I could hear him quite clearly as he slithered down the steep hill, the bushes rustling noisily and the twigs snapping under his feet as though he had nothing at all to hide. I drew deeper into the painful thorns, scratching my face as I wormed deeper under cover.

Then he was suddenly there, a tall man in the gray-green uniform of the secret police, with a queer-shaped cap set jauntily over one side of his forehead. He was neat and dapper, and well-groomed, with a small fair mustache.

The constriction in my throat did not ease as I realized it was DeBries. He stopped a dozen feet away and said cheerfully: "Benasque? Oh, there you are."

I stumbled to my feet and said angrily: "You scared the living daylights out of me. That uniform . . ."

"Yes, I know. You must be getting to be quite a patriot. Fear of this uniform is the honest man's passport. . . . Where's Trenko gone?"

"Over there."

"Well, let's get him in on it, shall we? Would you like to call him? He's probably got a revolver trained on my head."

I swallowed hard and went to the edge of the water. I called out: "It's all right. It's our friend."

Trenko came out of cover, walking very erect, his face stern and unsmiling, one hand restraining Betsa, who was growling most ominously. I realized that it was the uniform; I remembered that he had been training her with an assistant dressed as a policeman, and somehow this struck me as very funny, and I couldn't resist a sudden laugh.

DeBries was smiling, and Trenko stared at him for a moment and then his face suddenly lit up and he ran forward and took DeBries' hand and pumped it up and down as though they were long lost brothers. Speaking rapidly in Spanish, he said: "So it is you, Señor. If I had known . . ."

DeBries slapped him on the back and got down to business right away. He said: "All right, what's gone wrong?"

I said, "Have you been in touch with H.Q., wherever that may be?"

He shook his head.

"Then how did you know that anything was wrong?"

He said gently: "Your presence here . . . That's all I need. This spot is under constant watch, all the time. Your appearance on the bridge . . ."

He spoke in the clipped, precise, rather fussy way that I most remembered him by. I said again: "That uniform . . ."

He smiled in a faintly superior way. "It's the best possible cover. I'm afraid that I would not make a very convincing peasant, but this . . . Now, what's wrong?"

Trenko said: "Yesterday our friend here thought he saw something he should not have seen . . . like the sun on some binoculars. When we went to look, there was the mark of a boot, where one man had been standing . . ."

"One man?"

"I think only one man. It was not easy to see, but I think only one man."

"Hobnails?"

"Yes . . . the same like the soldiers. We moved out of the cottage and went into the woods for the night."

"And this morning?"

"Nothing. I told H.Q. and they told me to come here. They told me also to be on the air at sixteen hundred hours."

Where's the radio?"

"In the woods, hidden."

"I see."

"And that's all?"

"That is all, Señor."

DeBries took a deep breath and began pacing up and down, his head sunk on his slight chest. He said at last: "Just a footprint or two . . . nothing else?"

"Nothing else."

He went on walking up and down for a while, thinking, and then said that there was nothing we could do till four o'clock. He told us to hurry back to the place where the radio was, and wait for the message. He said: "It's probably for me. Whereabouts is it? The hide-out?"

Trenko began to explain. He said: "Behind the cottage, there is a path . . . very hard to see. If you go along this for a little way, there is a bank . . . used to be a stream . . . like a river. If you turn to the right along this little valley, the place is maybe five, six hundred meters down, but I do not think you will find it very easily. . . ."

DeBries interrupted him.

"All right . . . I'll be somewhere in that valley, as close as I can get to where I think you are. You'll hear me. About a quarter to four, all right? Meanwhile . . . Have you any spare clothes there? At the cabin?"

Trenko nodded slowly.

DeBries turned to me. "Then get out of that uniform. Keep it handy, but get out of it and hide it. Get into Trenko's clothes, the spare ones."

I tried to ignore the fear that was creeping up the back of my neck. I said lightly: "I'll make a lousy peasant. . . ."

"Just get into those spare clothes. . . . We'll see at four o'clock what they have to say. And keep out of sight. Anything else?"

"I could do with some of those cigarettes."

"Provided you smoke them. Don't carry them about with you."

"Of course. I'm not moving about anyway, not a yard more than I can help."

"That's fine. Just stay under cover."

He put a hand on Trenko's shoulder and said: "Walk with me a little way, my friend."

I swear that Trenko practically touched his forelock. The deference he was showing DeBries astounded me. They moved off slowly, leaving me standing there feeling rather foolish and helpless, and they talked together very quietly for a while, and once Trenko looked back at me with an uncomfortable expression on his face that told me they were discussing me. Then DeBries waved a hand and stepped into the shade of the trees again, looking incredibly competent in his frightening uniform. Trenko came back with his head sunk on his chest, and, hoping he would tell me something about DeBries, I asked: "Well?"

He shook his head.

"We shall see. At four o'clock we shall hear something."

He would not say anything else.

The walk back to our clearing in the dark-green valley was clouded with a deep oppression. We did not speak to each other, all the way. I wanted badly to ask Trenko what it was that DeBries had said to him, but I knew that he would not have told me—or, at least, would not have told me the truth. I knew that both DeBries and Trenko, the professionals, regarded me as the weak link in the chain, the amateur who would make too many mistakes, might jeopardize the whole operation if that state arose in which it was touch-and-go whether the whole thing came off magnificently or failed abysmally. With our necks as the price of failure.

To do them justice, it did not enter my mind that they might be worried about their own skins. I was the only one who was doing that; all they feared was that the carefully planned scheme would come apart at the seams and then burst open on them.

I wondered again about DeBries . . . exactly who he was. . . . His command of the English language was perfect; there was just a trace of an accent, an intonation rather, with a clipped sort of usage that was the slightest bit foreign to the States. He could have been English; he certainly looked it. Or he could have been an American who had been brought up abroad. I wondered if he was worth worrying about anyway. Whatever he was, he was a pretty cool customer. The way he swaggered about in his police uniform gave me the willies.

We sat on the bank when we got home, still saying nothing. At last, feeling the strain, I imagine, Trenko forced a sort of smile and said: "I'd better go to the cabin and get you those clothes. You wait here."

I said: "Any idea what it's all about?"

Standing up, wanting to move out of the scene simply because he was afraid I would ask something like that, he stopped and stared at the ground for a moment. Then he said slowly: "Maybe we worry for nothing, eh? Maybe there's nothing to worry for at all."

"But if there is?"

He looked up at me as though wondering just how much he could safely tell me. Then he said: "You know you are my good friend. If I know anything, I will tell you, you know that."

It was now or never. I said: "What was it DeBries told you? About me?"

For a long time he did not answer. I could sense the conflict that was going on in his mind, the conflict between friendship and that confounded devotion to the cause . . . to whatever damned political ideal he lived by.

I said shortly: "One of these days, Trenko, you'll realize what that term means—'my good friend.' It means a damn sight more than any purely transient political theory."

He did not know what transient meant. I said: "Friendship has lasted a hell of a lot longer than any goddamn political philosophy."

He was suddenly very angry. I could see a tightening of the taut muscles around his pointed chin. He said sharply: "I think maybe you do not understand what we are doing here."

The anger was gone again before I could reply. He said quickly: "He told me to watch for you very carefully. He said that they must not catch you whatever happens. I think this is a good thing, no?"

"I suppose so. He knows that I'm the weak link. So do you."

He shook his head. He was sorry for flaring up at me, and I think he wondered why I wasn't sorry too.

"It is not this, my friend. It is that . . . well, how shall I say it? For us, there is nothing that we can lose. For you it is different. We have . . . what shall I call it?"

"An obligation?"

"Yes, I think so. . . ."

"Like hell."

"But they will not catch you. They will not catch any of us. It is too important for us to fight. I will see that we will fight for a long time. This I will make sure of. Now . . . now I will get those clothes for you, yes?"

I sighed. "O.K."

As he went off into the woods, I called after him: "Trenko?"

He turned round and I saw that he was grinning at me. He said: "I know. You want to say that you are not angry with me."

"I wanted to say I was sorry."

"For nothing."

"Well, I am, anyway."

"You wait here. I come back soon."

Betsa slunk into the forest after him, and when he came back with the clothes under his arm, I stripped down to the bare skin and held up the hard linen underpants and stood there in the sunlight looking at them and beginning to see the humor in it.

They were long and stiff and white, like something the girls wore to swim in fifty years ago, with tapes dangling from the knees. I said: "In heaven's name . . . where on earth did these come from?"

Trenko was grinning hugely.

"Sometimes we wear them," he said. "It can be very cold here at night."

"I think I'd rather be cold. Ah, well . . ."

I sat down on a smooth yellow boulder that was glistening invitingly in the sun, but leaped to my feet again when I felt the sudden searing heat of it. Trenko's face wrinkled up and he suddenly burst out laughing, and he did not stop after I had put the monstrosities on and was standing there looking for all the world like a caricature of a seventeenth-century dandy in his underwear. Trenko, laughing, threw me a pair of khaki trousers, a cotton shirt and a coarse drill jacket with no sleeves to it. There was a battered hat too, made of tightly woven straw.

We folded my uniform very neatly into a bundle, and stowed it under the bushes, and I slipped my feet into the broad sandals he had brought.

It was half past three when we had finished, and we started getting the radio ready for his four o'clock call. He threw the antenna over a branch and switched it on for testing, and we found that they were already calling us, on what was known as the screamer crystal. This was simply a constant signal that he would get as soon as he switched on, and, if my memory served me right, it usually meant that there was something very nasty about to happen.

On Trenko's signal, I climbed quickly up into the tree again—I was becoming an expert at it—and kept watch, and no sooner had he started tapping at his key than I saw De-Bries coming along the little valley toward us, walking jauntily as though he hadn't a care in the world. I came down from my perch and told Trenko, and he threw the switch that meant "Over" and held out a hand to restrain Betsa, who was already growling angrily.

I slid down the bank onto the floor of the valley, and guided DeBries in. The message was already coming through, followed by an A.S. 5 from them, which meant "Wait five minutes."

Trenko was busily decoding, scribbling the letters onto squared paper, and by the time he had finished, with both of us standing silently by, he was at the set again waiting to receive them. The message read simply:

Following message is personal for DeBries only ends.

We sat down and waited for it, and I wondered if I should get up the tree again, but decided against it. I wanted to see what was going on. It was quite a long message.

When it was over, Trenko passed it over silently, and DeBries took a sheet of paper from his pocket, did a little equation with the figures that had preceded the letters of the message, and then set to work. He used the same kind of code, I noticed, with a different key of course, and I was astonished at the fluency with which he wrote. It's easy enough, when you know how, but it's a slow job. But DeBries was writing at a hell of a lick, as though he had done nothing all his life but decode P.N.M. I never had discovered why it was called P.N.M. Code. We used to call it "Please no mistakes" because one single error in the first cage could throw the whole thing out and make it look like an Ethiopian's recipe for chicken chow mein.

When he had finished it, he read it carefully, looked into the woods for a while as though the secret to it all lay there, read it again and then passed it to me. I was flattered and pleased that I had gotten it before Trenko, and there was just time to realize that this was rather a foolish notion. It read:

Personal to DeBries. Thorough checkup this end indicates no possible leakage here. Have you considered possibility that Trenko has been compromised query. Unless we hear to contrary immediately, we will proceed with Plan B stop. Strongly recommend this but final decision must be yours. Reply at once with co-ordinates and method if necessary. Message ends.

I passed it back to DeBries, who handed it to Trenko. I said: "What's Plan B?"

I remembered Vallance's comment—"a very untidy one; let's hope we don't have to use it."

Whatever it was, there was one thing that was certain: the trip over the border was not going to be as we had arranged. That much was sure. DeBries did not answer. He was watching Trenko carefully.

Trenko handed back the paper and rubbed a hand over his unshaven chin. The shock on his face was quite clear. It was confirmation of what he had suspected from the very first moment of the alarm. He had reasoned, as I had, that the secret police could not have known about Lazlo or they would not have let him cross the border; and that left only one alternative—they knew that Trenko was not what he appeared to be and that he was up to some monkey business. It meant they had followed him to Volvoda, and had been watching him from the very first days of the operation. The sudden breaking of the chain at what he must have thought was the strongest link was a terrible blow to him. He did not wait for DeBries to ask him. I noticed that he seemed ten years older. His face was drawn, his eyes angry. He said slowly:

"No . . . I do not think so."

"The question is," DeBries said, "if so . . . when?"

Trenko nodded unhappily.

"But I do not think so," he said. "I would know this. I think I would know this."

"The important thing," DeBries said again, ignoring the denial, "is *when*. If we assume that they know that there is something about you that requires investigation . . . Let us make this assumption. All right, when did they start investigating? Was it *before*, or *after*, this operation was planned? That is what we must know. And we must know now. You approached Lazlo direct? There was not a third party? No go-between?"

"Nobody."

"Not even one of your own men?"

"Nobody."

"Not even your brother?"

Trenko had been staring at the ground, his face darkly frowning. Now, he looked up slowly, his eyes wide. For a moment I feared a sudden outburst of that anger again, but then the fear was gone and I saw that Trenko was thinking carefully about it, determined not to be swayed from logic by any sentiment for or against. He stared at DeBries for a moment, and then shook his head slowly.

"No," he said stubbornly. "Not even my brother."

"But your brother knows that you are against the regime of the junta?"

"Of course. We have fought them together. But about this operation he knows nothing."

"When did you see him last?"

"A long time ago, after my wife died."

"I see."

There was a little silence. I could hear the tiny gurgle of the water in the stream somewhere, and wondered that I had not heard it before. Then DeBries said: "Are they still on the air?"

Trenko nodded.

"Then tell them to wait . . . to wait fifteen minutes."

Trenko hunched over the set again and sent them an A.S.

15, then sat back and looked at nothing, his face set. I waited, while DeBries put his arms over the low branch of a tree and just stood there, saying nothing, his eyes glazed, not moving.

For a very long time he stood there, silent, morose, calculating, while the minutes dragged by and the silence became almost unbearable. I thought of the phrase, "but final decision must be yours." It was like a military operation . . . putting the onus squarely on the shoulders of the poor guy in the field, who only had one view of the picture. I wondered if the message had come from Vallance. I wondered where Vallance was now . . . where the unidentified "headquarters" was. Havana? Miami? Caracas?

Thinking of Caracas made me wonder how Madeleine was making out in my apartment. I remembered, inconsequentially, that a tube in my German radio had blown, and I wondered if she would know where to look for a replacement.

Abruptly, DeBries stood up and took a map out of his inner pocket. It was a large-scale map of the area we were in, and I saw that it was printed on that special paper that bursts into violent flame if you as much as hold a match, or even a cigarette, within smelling distance of it. Impregnated with magnesium or something, I believe.

He spread it on the ground and tapped at it with the back of his white hands. He said to Trenko: "Here . . . at the foot of this hill . . . Any reason why we shouldn't light fires there? Tonight?"

Trenko frowned over it for a moment. He never was much good at maps. DeBries said gently—he was even smiling: "It's just the other side of the hill . . . over there. . . ."

Indicating with light gestures of his fingers, he said: "Covered by the mountain here . . . on this side there's nothing . . . a run-in along here. The wind's coming up light from the southwest. Could a fire be seen? I think not."

Trenko shook his head.

"No . . . nobody will see, I think. You want to bring aircraft in there?"

"Yes. It's the only way. We've got to get Lazlo back in before they discover what we're up to. Equally urgent, we've got to get you and Benasque out before they can catch you and force you to tell them . . ."

Trenko looked up and began to speak, but changed his mind and said nothing. Seeing the gesture, DeBries said:

"Yes, I know, but there's no reason why . . . We'll get him back by parachute. A small plane can fly down in . . . yes, I think that should do. We,ll drop him as close to his own house as we can, and you'll have to get him in quickly and quietly. He's had the most important of the meetings by now. The operation can still be a success. We'll drop him right there."

He was delicately indicating the map with the side of his fingernail.

"Tonight?"

"Tonight. The moon's up at two-ten. If we bring Lazlo in by parachute before midnight, can you get him back into his house? Before two o'clock?"

"Yes. Can do this."

"Are you sure the house is empty? Still empty?"

"Yes, am sure. I have a man there watching."

"Ah!" It was a triumphant explosion. "A man watching the house?"

Trenko nodded slowly, unperturbed. He said, with the air of a man whose morals have been questioned: "But he does not know that Lazlo is not there. He thinks that he is watching to see if Lazlo goes out. I say again, nobody knows about this. Nobody."

"I see. Well, that's all right then."

He looked at his watch.

"Just time to write a message . . ."

Taking his pencil and paper again, he began scribbling the letters quickly. Watching over his shoulder, I saw that his twelve-letter key was "Save only he di" and I was somehow surprised that DeBries would be a Shakespearean, and more so that the key was in English. Then I remembered the rest of the quotation: "All the conspirators save only he did that they did . . ." It wasn't very conforting to remember that all the conspirators in that caper had met a sticky end.

It's funny how the slightest things can upset your equilibrium when you are sitting on the edge of danger. The thought of Brutus and Cassius and Casca and all the others, lying there in a welter of their own blood, cut down by angry swords or dead at their own hands . . . it seemed too apt to be coincidental. It was an omen.

Of course I don't believe in omens, but I don't walk under ladders without crossing my fingers either. All of a sudden, I was depressed and frightened again, and even the sight of DeBries, cool, dapper, unperturbed, or of Trenko, calm, stubborn, capable, could not disperse the awful cloud of anxiety that was settling over me. Something had gone wrong, terribly wrong, and we didn't even know what it was. And all this stemmed from . . . in God's name, nothing more than a footprint in the hot sand! I could feel the fear creeping back into me and making its home there, as though it knew that there it could rest forever, undisturbed by the intrusion of its enemy, equanimity.

DeBries looked up and said sharply, indicating the map:

"The co-ordinates . . . at the foot of the hill there . . . in the open clearing . . ."

I picked up the map and ran my finger over the line. I found I was stammering: "B-forty-s-s-seven. E-thirty-t-t-two."

DeBries must have noticed it. He said nothing. In a moment he handed the message to Trenko and said briefly: "Send this. Tell them to come back on at three in the morning."

Trenko turned to the set again. DeBries put a match to the papers he had used, ground the ashes under his foot, and said to me: "While he's sending that, let's take a little stroll, shall we?"

My heart was heavy. I turned and followed him a little way along the valley.

The discomfort of my unaccustomed clothes was somehow a reflection of the illness of ease I felt when DeBries started talking.

I was worried about two things: First of all, I knew that I was on the carpet for the simple matter of being scared, and secondly I could not see how Plan B, which Vallance had described as a pretty untidy one, could mean anything but a sick headache for me. I tried to console myself with the thought that this was not really my fight—that I was just a hired hand and that if they didn't like me they could all go to hell; but this only aggravated the worry of the second item—how the devil was I to get out of the country?

I sat down on a round and mossy protuberance that DeBries indicated, and he plucked a thin fan of raffia and played with it idly as he spoke; he did not hide the fact that he was watching me closely. He said carefully:

"We shall bring your friend Lazlo in by parachute, tonight. It looks as if the leak, if there really is one, is in the Trenko water bucket. And that means, probably, that they don't know what it is we're up to. I imagine we've all come to this conclusion by our separate processes."

I said more to establish my independence than anything else: "Don't quite follow your reasoning there."

DeBries said patiently: "It's a fair assumption. If they knew about Lazlo, they would never have let him out of the country."

"They might be playing it carefully. Waiting for him to come back in again."

"No. It's out of the question. If they had the slightest suspicion about him, they would have arrested him at once. At most, they might have let him get to the frontier and then arrested Vallance with him. But to let him get clear . . . It's out of the question."

"Why?"

"Because in this business, as you should well know, there are too many unexpected elements always cropping up. No . . . We're safe in assuming that Lazlo is still in the clear. Therefore, it's Trenko they know about. If they know anything. That's why we're bringing Lazlo back in at once. We'll take Trenko out, out of harm's way. It means a long walk to the frontier, and a difficult crossing, over the Cordillera. But that will have to be done. He won't find it too hard."

"And me? I can hardly go out on the train. My passport will have been stamped 'out' and not back in again."

DeBries smiled thinly.

"You'll go with him, of course."

He was watching me closely. I thought, *So that's it. A nice long walk, pal. Just a matter of fifty miles or so, over the mountains, just a twenty-foot tangle of wire to cross, with border guards and police and Doberman pinschers as big as leopards and twice as savage . . . nothing to it, really.*

I said: "And when does this holiday hike begin?"

"As soon as Lazlo is safe in his house."

I said nothing. I was wondering what our chances were. At last DeBries said: "I'm sorry. But this is one of the risks, no?"

"Uh-huh. At least I'll be in good hands. But if Trenko's suspect, isn't he being closely watched?"

"Of course. But at night—in the forest—how much can they see? No, he'll give them the slip easily enough. But by tomorrow morning, when they find he's no longer where they have come to expect him to be, then they will start looking for him. It's fifty miles to the nearest frontier, and that's one of the places they'll be sure to be waiting. Trenko will know this; so don't be surprised if he chooses another direction altogether."

I knew that he had not said all he wanted to say. I asked: "Something else? You didn't bring me out of Trenko's earshot to tell me this. After all, this is something you'll have to tell him too. That he must know already."

DeBries took a cigarette from his case and passed it across to me, then took one himself. Lighting them, he said slowly: "Would you think me discourteous if I suggested that in an organization like this the weakness is always the amateur? Even the amateur who used to be a pro?"

"Go on."

"I think you've done extraordinarily well so far. I really do. Vallance had the highest praise for you. . . ."

So he'd seen Vallance. I wondered what that meant. He

went on: "But you must realize how essential it is not to get caught. Do I make myself clear?"

"If you etched it out with acid, it couldn't be more painfully so."

The anger was rising inside me. I thought, *What right do they have?* I said bitterly: "I quite realize that I am disposable. They won't catch me."

"I propose to tell Trenko that this must not happen, under any circumstances."

"That's the second time you've had to threaten me."

"The second?"

"In Caracas. You suggested that I might have to be silenced. At least, Vallance did."

"Oh, yes. As you see, it wasn't necessary, was it?"

He was smiling now, quite cheerful about the whole thing. He said: "You do understand, don't you?"

It suddenly dawned on me that his smiling demeanor was no more than a cloak for his embarrassment. He really felt quite diffident and uncomfortable about the whole thing. I said: "Trenko?"

"Yes. If anything goes wrong, then I'm afraid . . . I'm afraid Trenko will automatically shoot himself. It's a reflex these people have. I shall have to tell him that they mustn't get you either. Because only your continued silence can ensure their complete ignorance about Lazlo. An ignorance which must continue at all costs. Not a nice thing to have to tell anybody, is it? But I fear it's the only way."

He brightened suddenly.

"But I don't think it's likely to become necessary. After all, it's only a question of keeping under cover for a few days while you move north. And I can't think of any hands I'd rather be in than Trenko's."

"I'm with you there, anyway."

"But you do understand?"

"For what it's worth, yes."

"Good. I probably won't see you after tonight. And in case I don't have a chance to tell you later, remember this one thing—as though your life depended on it. Which it will. When you get back to safety . . . keep your mouth tight shut, you understand? Tight shut. Don't forget that they'll be wondering what we were doing here. And if they ever link any of us to Trenko . . . then your life won't be worth a bag of nuts. In Caracas, in Miami or even in New York. Their people are everywhere, and a thing like this—they'll move heaven and earth to find out what we've been up to. I can't stress that too much. Their people are *everywhere*. The relentless robots of the regime."

It was strange to hear him use that phrase: that's how I've always thought of them. As robots. It's exactly how they are. Their faces are stern and unsmiling, unmoved by any emotions of hatred or love, of envy or greed or pleasure. The deep lines around their mouths seem to have been there always. And their cold, passionless eyes seem always to be dulled with the constant blindness of obedience.

I got to know them well, later, and the phrase seemed more apt than ever. But perhaps it was DeBries who first used it. Perhaps it is only since I saw them that I realized how right he was in his description. The chronology is confused in my mind; I always feel that I was with Madeleine long after this trouble started, hiding my fears in the warm caress of her love, thrusting my terror aside in the explosive spasm of the rising passion in her . . . but I know that the last of these things ended long before my fears began. So perhaps with DeBries' words it is the same; perhaps the phrase is his and only came to me when I saw that they were after me and knew for the first time that one man cannot fight a regime.

Before I walked back, alone, to where the radio was, DeBries made his point once more. He said carefully: "So you understand? If there's the slightest risk of capture, Trenko will have to shoot you. I'm sorry, but . . . well, I don't think it will be necessary. But I wanted you to know."

Nodding, I turned and left him.

Fifty miles to go. Well, if all went well that night . . . at least, there would be the excitement of a drop. To hear the distant rumble of the plane, and see the angry searchlights shooting up again . . . Would there be guns, too, I wondered? Perhaps not. There might be fighters sent up. So they would make one rapid pass, and the parachute would come floating coldly down, a beautiful eerie bloom in the dark night sky, and there would be hurried buryings of silk and cords, and urgent whisperings in the darkness, and then the long, ice-cold wait in the bushes until Trenko should come back and say: "He's safe. Now, my good friend, we can go."

And after that the long walk would begin, with freedom at the end of it.

Freedom, yes. And a handsome balance in the bank, too. What we could do with that, Madeleine and I! It's a fortune, even today. We wouldn't stay in Caracas, we'd go to Europe, to Paris, perhaps, or Sicily, and watch the olive trees blossom against the black earth and the green grass. She'd have no worries any more, and neither would I. . . .

chapter 7

Well, the operation went off with surprising smoothness.
At eleven o'clock that night we all trooped over to the improvised dropping ground at B47 E32 on the map, and Trenko and I very carefully set small fires of dry brush that would make a bright blaze, three of them set out in cuneiform, with the point of the wedge facing into the wind.

I felt more than ever conspiratorial, and also hopelessly detached from the whole thing. But the cold presence of DeBries was a comfort. It seemed that nothing could perturb him at all. He even lit a calm cigarette while we waited, and stood there, very dapper and distingué in the cold darkness, with the dampness of the night rolling down off the hills that rose up, dark and silent, on all sides around us. The blackness that was the forest seemed to make the clearing a little lighter, and I found myself hoping that the aircraft would be able to find us; the open space seemed far too small for a successful drop, but by now I had grown quite used to the idea that DeBries knew exactly what he was doing—although, when he lit his cigarette, I couldn't help catching Trenko's eye. We were stooped down over one of the set fires, piling up sand beside them so that we could extinguish them quickly, and in the sudden spurt of the match I could see the alarm leap into Trenko's eyes. But he said nothing, though I fancied I heard him mutter something under his breath.

The stillness and the silence were unbelievable. We spoke, when we had to, in whispers, knowing that the cold night air would carry our voices a long way on its absolute quiet. Betsa, of course, was with us, prowling all round the field like a predatory wolf, disappearing into the darkness from time to time and then coming unexpectedly back at us with her white teeth gleaming horribly. I was glad that she was on our side. Trenko had deliberately avoided feeding her during the evening so that she would be at her most alert, and I had the queer feeling that she eyed me hungrily whenever she passed. Once he took some cooked meat scraps from his pocket and gave them to her before she went prowling off again.

A light plane was coming in, DeBries had told us, from up there over the border, with a civilian pilot and no lights. I wondered if they'd found him as they found me, but then I reflected that in this business they probably had quite an organization at hand ready to go to work; there was nothing makeshift about DeBries' methods. It was scheduled to arrive, DeBries said, at a quarter to twelve, and after the fires and their dampeners were all ready we had nothing to do except sit in nervous impatience and wait. It was the waiting I hated more than anything else; it gave me time to reflect on the dangers that surrounded us. And out in the open like that . . .

I knew that if all had gone according to the first simple plan I would never have had a worry in the world. But I hate improvisation, and it seemed . . . Well, there we were, the three of us, crouched in the darkness on the slopes of a foreign valley, committing the most heinous offense imaginable—smuggling an enemy of the state into a closely guarded country where every alien was deeply suspect simply by virtue of his foreign birth. The folly of it appalled me.

And yet I knew that this sort of thing was happening all the time, all over the world. The only thing is, it's usually done by dedicated men working for a cause so vital that their lives no longer count and the risks can therefore be discounted altogether.

The first sign we had was a streak of searchlight, far away to the northeast. I assumed that it was at the border, and I whispered something to that effect to DeBries. He nodded, and then another beam shot out, and then another, and I knew that soon the fighters would be going up, and, if our pilot wasn't mighty careful, there'd be another "incident," with everyone hotly denying that the aircraft had violated the border deliberately, and the other side demanding an inquiry and threatening to take it up with the UN—the same dreary old pattern of charge and countercharge. I wondered how many of these "incidents" the press is always reporting had their beginnings in just such a circumstance as this; but it was small comfort to realize that we were part of the pattern of the daily news.

DeBries looked at his watch, his hand raised, and then said: "Now!" and brought his hand down to his side, and I lit the fire I was standing by, and then raced to the second one and had that going too, just as I saw the third one springing to life over where Trenko crouched. Less than a minute later, there was an ear-splitting roar in the silence as the aircraft came swooping in, incredibly low, skimming the top of the mountain and diving almost on top of us. I threw myself to the ground and it seemed that it pulled up only inches away from me. It stood on its tail and then flattened out for the run-in.

I could not believe that Lazlo, an untrained man, could get

his breath back in time to jump—or be thrown—and sure enough, she came over at about eight hundred feet, moving quite slowly now, and nothing happened.

I was back beside DeBries. He was staring up at the plane open-mouthed. Somehow, that open mouth made him seem more human and fallible than he had been. Then he muttered angrily, "What the devil . . . what the bloody devil . . ." and turned to me with a hopeless gesture as the plane passed overhead and began to circle. He said angrily: "I hope they throw him out this time."

Then the plane was over us again, and this time it was much too low for safey. I could dimly make out the darker patch against the dark sky that was the dark parachute, and then, instinctively, I was running fast along the field to where I could see it would land, no more than a hundred yards off pinpoint, my heart beating fast and my breath straining its way into tortured lungs.

He hit just as I got there. It was a gentle drop, one of those lovely night things when the air is dense enough to make it slow and soft and easy, and I could see the astonishment on Lazlo's face as he landed. He did not even fall to the ground, but stood there, dumfounded, with the silk falling about him in great gentle clouds. I think he had been expecting to be dragged a couple of miles while he struggled out of the chute, but there was no wind at all, and he just stood there gaping. I thumped the box at his chest and the harness fell clear, and he said, in English: "Yes, yes, of course . . ."

I couldn't help laughing. It was the intrusion of the dispatcher's last instruction: "Hit the box, hit it hard, as soon as you land. If you don't want to be dragged . . ." Then Lazlo looked up and saw me, and grasped my hand and said over and over again: "Old friend . . . old friend . . . old friend . . ." And then Trenko was suddenly there, wrapping up the chute and saying: "Quickly, quickly, no time for talk," and the next thing I knew Lazlo was gone and that's all I had seen of the principal in the drama I was playing out.

I stood there foolishly for a moment, wondering how he could have been spirited off so quickly, and then DeBries was beside me, saying: "Come on, come on, into the woods, you know the drill."

I dragged the chute with one hand, clutching a shovel with the other, and together we hurried over to the nearest patch of dark that was the forest, and I started burying the parachute, wondering who had put the fires out and taking comfort in the fact that it wasn't my job; it had been allotted to someone else and someone else had done it. I dug a hole about a couple of feet deep, and shoved the tangled mess of silk and cords down into it, and shoveled earth on top and covered it all over with loose sand and leaves, and knew that they could look for a hundred years and never find it. I said to DeBries, who was standing cool as a cucumber beside me: "Trenko?"

"He's on his way to the house with Lazlo. A nice operation."

A jet plane flew high over our heads with a supersonic rush of sound, and I wondered what were their chances, if any, of finding a small strange aircraft in the darkness. The search lights were still on, and there were others, much nearer now, but I knew that with only fifty miles to go, our plane would be over the border before they could get a fix on him, and I wondered again about the pilot: about how much they were paying *him*.

Lazlo, I remembered, was still wearing his hair piece and his teeth. He looked incredibly like me, and it gave me a most uncanny feeling. . . . I was sorry that I had not had more time with him, but I knew the essential thing was to get him to safety at once, just in case the actual drop had been spotted. Of course, on a dark night, the chances of that are practically negligible. But if anyone had seen what had happened, the place would be swarming with ground troops in no time at all.

I said: "And now?"

"Now, we wait again," DeBries said. "But I think we'll get under cover, just in case of accidents."

"What are we waiting for? Trenko?"

"Yes, Trenko. As soon as he gets Lazlo into the house, he'll be back and you can start moving out. Have to get away from this area as quickly as possible. I doubt if they saw the drop; I doubt it very much."

"If they did, how much danger is Lazlo in?"

"None at all. No reason why they should connect him with any clandestine night activity. None at all. He's in bed with smallpox."

He peered at me in the darkness and said mildly: "I'm glad you're thinking of Lazlo at this time. Shows a nice feeling."

"As long as the operation's a success."

"It will be. I can feel it in my bones."

That feeling again . . . I knew that it was better than anything else. I said: "What about the radio?"

"One of Trenko's men will take over . . . For the time being."

"You seem pretty sure that it's Trenko. The leak, I mean. Come to that, you seem pretty sure that there has been a leak. All we have to go on is one goddamn footprint."

"It's enough. It's more than enough."

"The flash of the sun on binoculars. Could have been a discarded beer can."

"I know that."

"But you're still taking no risks."

"Of course. It's the only possible way."

"It's a long time before you'll catch me at a caper like this again."

"Your nerves?"

"Lousy."

"It's plain sailing now."

"What about you?"

I could sense that he was raising a delicate eyebrow. He wanted to say: "That's none of your business, Benasque," but instead he said, affably enough:

"I have work to do. You and Trenko will move to the border as fast as you can. Through the mountains, it will take you three nights of hard work. After that, remember what I said: in Caracas, mum's the word."

"No fear of that."

Caracas . . . It meant Madeleine again. I was beginning to feel good, really good. There was dark forest all the way to the border, and, with Trenko and Betsa to run the show, there'd only be the actual crossing to worry about. And the worry on that score could wait till we were there.

Trenko came back less than an hour later.

The first sign of him was Betsa's low growl that told us he was coming in. DeBries called out softly from the shadows where we were sitting, and I could see at once that Trenko was a very happy man. DeBries said: "All right?"

"Splendid! Really, it is quite excellent. He is back in the house, and it is all splendid."

I could not believe that it could be so easy. I said: "And nobody knows he was away? Nobody?"

DeBries was slightly patronizing. "Just one of the servants. We had to have a man in the house, of course."

I wondered how many more were in on the secret. I said sourly: "Won't we all be surprised when they arrest him tomorrow."

Trenko refused to be goaded. He shook his head firmly.

"No, my friend," he said. "They will not arrest him. It is all splendid. Really."

Well, there was too much that I didn't know about. I was willing to take it for granted. DeBries said soberly: "Now, all that remains is for you two to get out of the country and see that the secret is kept. When you get to the border, you know what to do, Trenko?"

"I know."

"And you, Benasque, you're free to do what you like. Go back to Caracas and keep very quiet about all this. They've a good many ears to the ground. Everywhere."

"I know."

"Good. Then let's move off. I think we can call it a successful operation. Are we ready?"

Surprised, I said: "Are you coming with us?"

"Only part of the way."

Again, it was a polite way of telling me to mind my own damn business. I was feeling more and more like an intruder. But the prospect of our success was good to gloat over; there was a great deal of comfort in the thought that our little plot had come off successfully. I refused to be fazed by DeBries.

The stupendous impudence of it all was what intrigued me. In less than a couple of days we had spirited one of their ministers—in heaven's name, *a minister!*—out from under their very noses, and had put him back in again. And now, whatever happened, that much had been done successfully, clandestinely and with a great deal of efficiency. I only hoped they'd had enough time, while he was away, to do all that they had planned for him. And however small my own part, they couldn't have done it without me.

As I say, I was beginning to feel very good indeed.

We ran into trouble at daybreak.

All through the dark night we had moved steadily up through the trees and the dense scrub, panting and struggling wearily to get away from the area as fast as possible.

It was terribly slow going. Every hill we climbed had another hill behind it, even higher, and knowing that we had to climb high into the mountains it was sickening to count the number of times we had to move down, instead of up, slithering down into deep valleys to climb out again on the other side.

The night was alive around us. There were millions of insects in the air. There were mosquitoes, and flying night-time ants, and little black bugs that squelched abominably when you slapped at them on your flesh, and stinkbugs that gave off the sickening stench of putrefaction as they died. There were angry cries from disturbed predators, and always there was the constant screeching of crickets and the hoarse complaint of the frogs. The damp dripped from the trees and clung to us.

Trenko moved steadily ahead of us, pausing from time to time for DeBries and me to catch up, just standing there grimly, saying nothing, barely understanding that our city legs were no match for his in the mountains. Even DeBries was feeling the strain, though he still seemed cool and confident.

Only once, when the very first rays of light gray were streaking the east, did he mutter: "Already? A long way to go yet..."

Trenko had cut sticks for us, and we were leaning on them heavily, forcing our way upward. We came to a wide open space, dotted with dark clumps of bushes, and Trenko said harshly: "I think we should have passed here a long time ago, no?"

DeBries nodded, his breath coming fast.

"A long time ago. As the crow flies we've done no more than seven or eight miles."

Ahead of us the hill was open with coarse grass, rising steeply above our heads. It was a formidable climb, and to the flank the slope was gentler, showing eerily gray in the moonlight and the morning glow. Trenko waved his arm and said: "Better we go that way, maybe...."

Then there was a terrifying sound brought to us on the breeze. It was no more than the soft rumble of a motor of some sort, but it sounded appallingly close to us, just beyond the hill we had just come over. Trenko had turned and was frowning in the direction of the sound. DeBries said: "A truck? Is there a road near here?"

Trenko shook his head. "No road. Only hills and mountains."

"Then how the devil..."

Trenko interrupted him brusquely: "Better we move away, Señor, over here."

We turned to the left and headed for the gentler slope of the hill that faced us. Behind us, the sound of the truck was still clear in the silence, its motor coughing noisily, struggling, it seemed, against the difficulties of the terrain. I could imagine it lumbering painfully up the grassy incline of the hill, both its axles engaged, its radiator boiling over, a score of soldiers, ordered out to ease the weight, panting along beside it, leaning into its body from time to time to help it over the steeper grades.

Trenko said quickly: "Better we get back into the woods, as soon as we can."

The gray in the east was getting lighter. His voice now strained and labored, DeBries asked: "How far before the forest gets... gets thick again?"

"Two, three miles."

"We'll never make it. But we must. Keep... keep moving."

We were running now, and the stitch in my lungs was a sharp spasm of unbearable pain. I knew that a danger point was coming—the point of exhaustion at which you say to yourself, unable to go any further, "Well, the hell with it..." and sit down and take what's coming to you. And my fear was overshadowed by the menacing thought that Trenko . . .

"You must not be caught," DeBries had said.

It was enough to keep me moving along fast in spite of the agony in my chest. We pulled ourselves upward, skirting the flank of the hill, praying that the trees would soon close in on us, but the countryside was open and gently undulating, good sheep country, with no more cover than a few scattered thickets which would not have hidden a rabbit. Betsa loped along confidently by our side.

Then, suddenly, we were as high as we could go. I dropped to the ground, exhausted, listening to DeBries' heavy panting beside me. Trenko was pointing at the horizon.

"There," he said. "Over there . . . This is where we must go."

I could not believe that we had climbed so high. The fine ranges of the Cordillera stood out one behind the other in the gray light, somber and distant and lonely, stretching for hundreds of miles as far as we could see. At any other time it would have been an inspiring sight; but now, it served only to show us how vast a land we had to hide in.

The forest was a black, dense wall more than a mile away, across the other side of a wide valley. I said, gasping for breath: "It will take us . . . take us two hours to . . . cross that. . . ."

"One hour, maybe. But here there is no place to hide. We have come very slowly, you know?"

I lay there for a moment, trying to get the breath back into my lungs. The ground was wet and cold under my face and hands, and the sweat on my body was icy; the breeze, or what there was of it, searched my bones out and froze them. I got to my feet heavily, conscious that they were waiting for me. Trying to gain time, I said:

"The truck . . . I don't hear it any more. Have we outdistanced it? Or has it stopped?"

"It's stopped," DeBries said shortly. "Down behind us and to the right."

If only I could see them . . ."

"Thank God you can't," said DeBries grimly. "As long as we keep out of their line of sight . . . their line of fire . . ."

"Better we move," Trenko said.

His wiry frame was sturdy as a rock. I was acutely aware of the difference in our physiques. This was his home, more or less, and a ten-mile climb through the dark mountains was no more than a stroll along the boulevard for him. But for my part, the effort had left me terribly exhausted. There were pains shooting through my legs, my back ached abominably and it seemed as though there were not enough oxygen in the universe to supply the craving my bursting lungs felt. I wondered how high up we were.

Trenko was ahead of us now, running very lightly, slowing to a walk from time to time and waiting for us to catch up. The early gray light in the sky was horrifying, and I knew that our friend the darkness was soon leaving us to our fate; it seemed as though our only ally were deserting us. We were moving downhill, into the valley that lay between us and the friendly forest. I didn't like the idea of going *down*; I knew that if trouble started we would have to climb *up* out of it.

Suddenly there was a sharp retort, like a distant pistol shot, and I was reminded of the friendly firing of the charcoal that had been our signal that all was well. I saw Trenko stop and turn, and then his face was brightly lit with green light that played on his taut cheekbones, giving his features a ghostly look. I just had time to turn my head and see a green flare slowly climbing up into the sky, alarmingly close by to our right, and DeBries said quickly:

"Down. Down to the left. They're on our right."

Trenko turned back and started running, with Betsa beside him, fast, down the hill, twisting his head and calling: "Quick ... this way ... quick ... Across the river ..."

Below us was the steep depth of the valley, the deepest point of it. I was thankful for the increased slope down, just letting my legs fall one in front of the other with gathering speed. DeBries was close beside me, running quite easily, his breath labored but not interfering with the rhythmic movement of his legs and arms. He ran well, like an athlete. I fell once, and rolled a dozen yards or so, and he was suddenly behind me, pulling me to my feet, saying:

"Not much further now ... down the bottom ... there's a river...." I was astonished to see that he was smiling.

It was almost daylight now, clear enough to make out the trees that stood ahead of us and to our right. Then the sun hit the top of the mountain in the distance, glowing a bright-red-gold on the snow at the top, and by the time we reached the bottom of the valley it was light enough all round us to know that we could easily be seen if anyone was looking in the right direction. At the edge of the water, Trenko was standing, waiting for us to get to him. He said:

"We cross over here. It's not too deep, I think. Better we hold hands together ... so."

He held out both his arms, and DeBries took one while I took the other. The water, looking horribly cold, was churning over, running fast, bubbling with little white swirls. Together we slithered down the steep bank. The shock of the ice-cold water was appalling; I did not believe that water could be so cold. Alarmingly, it crept up to our chests almost at once, and I couldn't help thinking that if it were as deep as this at the edges, then at the center . . .

The force of it was surprising too. It tugged at our bodies angrily, and I was thankful for Trenko's firm grasp. Once, DeBries was swept off his feet, and we both struggled to get him steadied again, leaning into the overpowering brute energy of the water; it seemed a live thing, tugging angrily at us, seeking to throw us down among the rough pebbles that twisted and turned under our feet. Sometimes it seemed that Trenko was being physically torn from my grasp, and only the strong vise of his musuclar peasant's hand kept us together. Betsa had swum across already, and was panting on the other bank.

It was deeper now, almost up to our necks, and the cold constriction across my chest was frightening. Then suddenly it was shallow again, and the water streamed off us; we were struggling up the other side, slipping in the wet gray mud that lined the steep slope. I fell exhausted on the ground, heedless of the cold and the wet, and Trenko dragged me to my feet and said: "Up, my friend, up . . . up there . . ."

Looking up at the immensity of the hill facing us, I shook my head. I could feel that my voice was hoarse and choked. I said: "I can't. . . . I can't do it. . . . I can't go on. . . . No further."

DeBries said sharply: "Don't be a fool, Benasque. Get to your feet."

I was aware that they were both standing there waiting for me to move. There was a faint look of contempt on DeBries' fine features. Even with his clothes wet and muddy, his smart military cap lost in the water and his thick hair streaked with dirt, he still contrived to maintain that cold dignity, that air of indisputable authority with which I always associated him.

I struggled up and followed them meekly, though I believe I would have felt happier if the earth had simply opened up and swallowed me there and then. That aloof disdain was unbearable. I could see that Trenko was conscious of it, too. He took my arm gently and helped me along until I shook it roughly loose.

There was no question now of hurrying. The slope was almost a cliff, and it was a matter of clambering hand over hand, clutching at roots and tufts of grass, pulling ourselves up a forty-five-degree incline of wet grasss which was dotted here and there with small bushes of gorse, patches of stinging nettle and clusters of a small round shrub that had a poisonous-looking yellow berry. And there was no attempt at concealment, either. If they could see us, then they could see us, and that's all there was to it.

And not once had we actually seen *them*.

I looked back over my shoulder. The slope we had come down, on the other side of the river, was open and brightly lit now; there was not a sign of life there. I could not see where the flare had been sent up; the configuration of the land was deceptive and I could not easily locate the spot. But I knew that they were all round us. I could feel it in my bones.

Up ahead, incredibly high above us, was the forest. I found myself praying that we should reach it in time. There was something horrifying about the absence of any indication that our enemies were there . . . something frightening in the very efficiency of their concealment. I wondered if they would be up ahead of us too, in the dark forest we were headed for.

How long was it since they had started their search? The plane had come over before midnight . . . six or seven hours? How had they known so quickly where to look? Or was every inch of their damned country covered with troops and police?

It was an indication of the way they worked . . . the relentless flooding of opposition by the sheer force of numbers. And they knew that Trenko was the key to the puzzle that was agitating them.

I could see the way their minds were working. There was one of their men, a peasant, named Trenko, under suspicion for something or other. Perhaps his brother . . . So, watch Trenko. Then Trenko is seen unaccountably waiting in a sisal cutter's hut a dozen miles from his own home. So . . . watch him more closely. Then a stranger appears, a man in a chauffeur's uniform, and the stationmaster says, "Yes, there was a man dressed like that . . . but he caught the train to the border." And someone comes to the logical deduction that it wasn't the chauffeur who left, it was someone else . . . another renegade. "Who?" they would ask. "And why? What's the real chauffeur hanging around for?" Someone else would stare at him for a moment, wondering, and then, admiring his carefully manicured nails, say: "I think we had better put some troops out there. Let them stand by."

And the next thing? A plane swooping over Volvoda in the night, with no lights showing, eluding the fighters sent up to force it down. . . . What could it mean? A drop of some sort? A man, parachuted in? Supplies of weapons for the rebels? They were getting perilously close to the truth. . . .

And I knew that they would go to any lengths to find out exactly what the truth was.

We were close to the top now. Trenko said: "You know ... at this hour there should be shepherds."

DeBries close behind him, nodded shortly.

"I know," he said. "It means only one thing. They've cleared the area."

Trenko said somberly: "You will not get back, now, Señor. To the town. It will not be possible, I think. Nor would it be wise."

"Out of the question," DeBries said. "They will have seen me. I'll have to come with you."

I should have derived comfort from the thought. DeBries' cool efficiency was a wonderful tonic. Nothing seemed to faze him. But it was one more flaw, really, something else going wrong, another departure from the plan and another improvisation, and as such it gave me no cause for satisfaction. All I could see was a net being drawn tighter and tighter around us. And with never so much as a sight of the enemy.

This was the fearful thing—that we had never seen hide nor hair of them, and yet they were slowly and inexorably squeezing us into their trap. First, the abandonment of the wheel-chair scheme, then forcing us down to the valley and away from the hills where we could have found shelter, and now DeBries' change of plan. If it was too dangerous even for him to remain behind as he had intended . . .

We reached the forest at last. There was still no sign of them, and the enveloping shadows of the trees were as welcome as water in the desert. There was comfort in their close proximity, and I felt myself leaning against a tree trunk, assuring myself that we were really there. I felt faint and dizzy, and knew that I was cold and hungry and wet and miserable. But, at least, the horrors of the open country were behind us. We found a dense clump of shrub close to the edge of the trees and waited there, panting, ignoring the icy cold that clung to our soaking clothes. The water was still squelching in my shoes. Even Trenko was tired now, but he lay there on the ground, saying nothing, getting his second wind. I felt that I would never be able to rise again. I sat crouched double, with my head in my hands, watching DeBries. He saw me looking at him, and a faint smile crossed his mouth. I believe he was enjoying himself. He said unnecessarily: "Tired?"

"That's a damn fool question."

"Well, we'll get our breath back. If we can hide up in here for the day . . ."

He said to Trenko: "How big is this forest here? How far to the other side of it?"

Trenko sat up and began massaging Betsa's back, rubbing the warmth back into her. It was strange how much his devotion to Betsa endeared him to me. He said: "Four, five maybe six miles. It is very thick here. But I think there will be patrols. . . . But if they hide carefully, we will hide carefully too. They will never find us here."

"And then?"

"At night, when is dark, we can move on. Move through the trees at night; nobody will find us. We have Betsa here."

I said: "Do you think we are in the clear? From the immediate danger, I mean?"

"It might well be." I could see that DeBries was quite confident about it. Seeking encouragement, I said: "Can't see how they let us get into the woods again. We were out in the open for a long time. Seems to indicate that they're not as smart as they think they are."

DeBries said gently: "They could have got us back there, if they had wanted to."

Trenko was nodding his head. Seeing my look of surprise, DeBries said: "They want us alive. It's the only way they can find out what's going on."

In the uneasy silence that followed, DeBries stood up and went to the edge of the trees, leaning against a sturdy beech trunk, peering out into the valley below us. He said: "Let me have the binoculars, Trenko."

Trenko stood up and handed them to him, and I sat there watching them as they stood there, DeBries with the glasses to his eyes, staring out across the valley. I heard him mutter: "Nothing . . . nothing . . . not a sign of them . . ." There was a tinge of admiration in his voice, as though, had he been on the other side, this was exactly how he would have conducted the operation. He took off his glasses and tried to shake the water from them, fumbling in his pockets for something to wipe them with. He pulled out a handkerchief, squeezed it more or less dry, and began wiping the lenses. He walked over to a better vantage point by the edge of the trees and lay down, easing his body comfortably into the grass, and began studying the landscape again. Betsa stood above him, her head erect. There was humor, if I could have found the enjoyment of it, in the way she was still suspicious of DeBries' uniform. As far as she knew, he was a policeman, and she couldn't quite understand why he was with us.

Then, seeming to come from a long way off, there was a single rifle shot, away to our side. I saw Betsa's alert head swing round quickly as she went automatically into a crouch. Trenko dropped to his knees, his eyes wide, signaling to me urgently to stay where I was. I twisted round, but I could see nothing except the denseness of the trees. DeBries had not moved, and in a moment Trenko muttered: "They cannot see us here. I think a signal, maybe...."

His body was taut, poised, crouched like an animal. He said slowly: "But we'd better move deep into the forest. It will be safer, I think."

I said: "How far away was that shot?"

"Two, three hundred meters, maybe."

"In the forest? You think it was in the forest?"

He shook his head slowly.

"It's hard to know ... a single shot. No, I think it was on the hill there somewhere. Maybe is a signal. Better we move further away from this place."

I was staring at DeBries. He had not moved. I went over to him quickly and bent down.

I cannot describe the shock that hit me. It was the more severe because it was so completely unexpected.

He was dead. There was a tiny mark under his left arm, a huge bloody hole at his shoulder where the bullet had come out, and another one under his ear where it had entered his head again. I stood staring at him stupidly, suddenly conscious that Betsa was whining at him, that Trenko was also staring down at him unbelieving. The binoculars had dropped to the ground close to his face, their strap still round his neck, and it seemed that he was still watching out there. I dared not look at the other side of his head where I knew the slug would have come out of his body. I just stood there, feeling the shock of it sweeping down on me, the horror of it all closing in. I could not believe it. He had just been saying: "They want us alive...." and "Not a sign of them anywhere..." and now he was dead with all the scheming come to nothing, lying silent and still and ugly there on a wet patch of brown dead leaves.

I could feel that the blood had left my face. There was a prickling at the back of my scalp, and I heard Trenko say, seeming far off: "Better get away from here quickly."

His voice was harsh and cold, and, when I did not move, he said it again, then dropped quickly to one knee and gently took the binoculars away from the dead body. I saw him turn it over, an ugly, lifeless thing, and start going through the pockets of the uniform, removing every scrap of paper, everything that he could find. Then he stood up and said roughly: "Let's go. This way."

When I did not answer, he took me angrily by the arm and pulled me with him. The darkness of the forest closed in about us.

chapter 8

I do not think I ever recovered from the shock, the sudden, unexpected horror of DeBries' inexplicable killing.

It was not so much that I had grown dependently close to him. It was more that here again was evidence that the cards were all stacked against us. We had still seen scarcely a sign of *them*. We had known, or guessed, that they were all round us, hidden in the woods, spread out across the fields, with a command post somewhere on top of one of the hills where an officer would be camped elegantly on a shaded blanket with his aide-de-camp standing respectfully beside him and a soldier-servant bringing him his alfresco breakfast; with field telephones laid out and trucks hidden in small thickets with their drivers standing by, smoking their cheap black cigarettes and waiting....

It would be just like a military exercise. But far more deadly.

He had been so coldly competent. Not with Trenko's knowledgeable competence, but with a more precise, detached efficiency that had somehow made him seem invulnerable. Strutting about in his secret-police uniform, he had seemed full of contempt for them, as though there were never any doubt that he would bring us all out of it in spite of their troops and their guards and their watchdogs and the whole paraphernalia of the regime's slick efficiency.

And now he was dead. Whatever plans he was carrying in his head had died with him, and it had left us vulnerable and exposed. And there was no reason for his death; in spite of it, I still believed what he had said: "They want us alive...."

Why, then? And how?

Trenko was carrying a small package of bread an salami, which had become thoroughly soaked when we had crossed the river, but we made a hurried meal of it, huddling on the ground with the marrow freezing in our bones, waiting for the strength to come into the sun and warm us.

On all sides of us the trees were tall and almost impenetrable, standing tightly close together and thickened with bushes and vines. It was a tropical jungle with an equatorial

119

stench. We took off all our wet clothes and spread them out over the rocks to dry, and then lay down, naked, on the rough grass. It seemed years since I had slept. I said: "What are our chances, Trenko?"

Lying there stretched out, with his body brown and lithe, he said slowly: "I think pretty good, if we get out from this forest not too early."

"How's that?"

"I think they are driving us this way . . . you know, like sheep? I think this is what they are doing."

"But, in God's name, we haven't even *seen* them! How could they be driving us?"

Trenko said stubbornly: "This is what I think."

"And so?"

"So, we must stay in the forest till it's very dark. Come out at night. If we get to the other side of the big mountain then we can find the frontier. It is not too far."

Trying to shrink the danger by attention to inessentials, I said: "We shall need some food of some sort. Of course, it's not important. . . . Anything grow wild up here?"

"Some breadfruit. Not much else."

"Raw? We'll have to cook it."

"At this time of the year they are not yet ripe. We can eat them raw."

He knew that I was making conversation to chase the ogre away. He said: "And if that is not enough, there are some small villages. I will steal."

There was great dignity in the way he said "I will steal." There was even a classic simplicity in it. It was as though stealing was, to Trenko, one of the major crimes, but that nothing would stand in the way of the completion of our mission. Completion? It was already completed. I knew that Lazlo's successful installation had finished the operation off nicely, and that all that was left was the escape of the participants—a matter of only secondary importance. I thought again of the instructions that DeBries had left: that we should both die rather than be captured. I said uneasily: "If they catch us, Trenko . . ."

He turned his head and stared at me for a moment.

"They will not catch us," he said somberly. "I think he told you, no?"

"He said he'd instructed you to kill me if necessary." I tried to speak lightly, as though I did not believe he would ever do it.

I said: "But I don't believe you will, old friend."

He stood up and went over to see if the clothes were dry.

He did not reply. I knew that my stated belief was no more than a search for comfort and that none was forthcoming.

Trenko called out that our clothes were dry, and I went over and joined him. I could see he was worried that he had not been able to answer my last question, and as I stood there, holding out my trousers, I said, with an attempt at a joke: "All we want now is a patrol to come marching out of the woods and find us like this."

As though it were a logical contingency, Trenko said: "If so, then we must pick up our clothes and run."

We pushed up through the trees again, with Betsa padding along softly behind us, her tongue hanging out and her eyes bright. I think she was really having fun.

We came out to the edge of the woods again, on the other side, about midday. We stayed there for a long time, watching the rolling country that stretched ahead of us.

It was beautiful. The grass was green and shining in the sun, and there was a white-painted farmhouse halfway up the slope of the hill, with a broken picket fence around it, and a haystack close by a long wooden barn. Beyond it, further up the hill, some sheep were grazing, and after a while I saw the shepherd, too, standing motionless and leaning on a long stick. Two dogs were crouched beside him, and I wondered if we were close enough for them to get our scent. But then I realized that the breeze was blowing from him to us. He was some four or five hundred yards away, and, remembering DeBries' comment about clearing the area to make way for action, I began to derive a certain comfort from the peaceful rusticity of the scene. And then, with a sharpening of the wits I seemed to have acquired in the last few days, it occurred to me that it might not be a shepherd after all. I asked Trenko about it, keeping my voice very low. He said:

"Yes. I think it is a policeman . . . a soldier . . . maybe a scout. I do not know. But now, I think we shall sleep, no? We have plenty of walking to do tonight."

He pulled back a little way into the forest, and found a depression under the roots of a tall chestnut tree. I went over to help him and we pulled off long slender branches and laid them carefully over it, then covered it all with weeds and twigs and vines. Standing back, we saw that the shelter we had made was quite invisible, though under the pile of foliage there was a cavity seven or eight feet long and four or five feet wide. Trenko was staring up at the tops of the trees, and, when he had found what he wanted, he went and cut a thick bush and gave it to me, saying:

"You and Betsa sleep inside there. . . . I will go to the top of the tree here. If anyone come, Betsa will growl; you just put one hand on her back, you know? And do not move, whatever happens. You understand? Whatever happens you don't move at all. Just stay quiet."

"And you?"

"I will be in the tree here, the best place for me. Then I'll see what is happening."

He stood there frowning for a moment, and then said slowly: "If there is trouble, you think you could find your way into Volvoda? Alone?"

Trying to keep the fear from my voice, I said: "I think so. What's on your mind?"

"I think it is necessary that . . . if anything should happen to me, if we should be separated . . . You understand?"

"Go on."

"There is a place in Volvoda. . . . You remember the road that leads from the station into the village?"

"Uh-huh."

"It is called Calle Cuatro de Octubre. There is a small alley there which has no name, but some steps . . . There are some steps that lead down to the village, you remember?"

"Yes. On the left going to the station."

"At the bottom of the steps there is a house, a small white house with some iron bars on the window. It is the only one like this. Some iron bars . . . Go there. If we become separated, go to this house and ask for me. They will let you in and they will know what to do. You understand?"

"The white house with the iron bars on the window. At the bottom of the steps."

"I do not think it will be necessary. But just in case . . ."

"Sure. Sure thing."

I had taken the bush from him, and stood there foolishly holding it, wondering what it was for. Seeing my hesitancy, he smiled quickly and said: "When you get inside, pull this in to hide the entrance, eh?"

We were suddenly laughing. I went inside the hide-out, made room for Betsa and then peered out through the shrubbery and watched Trenko expertly climbing up the tall tree. When he had disappeared from sight, I stretched out on my stomach on the powdery sand, and cradled my head on my arm. Betsa turned round once or twice, and then settled herself tight against me. The last thing I saw before I slept was her bright shining eyes watching me.

I slept like a log.

When I awoke, it was still broad daylight, and the sun was filtering through into the dugout.

I do not know what it was that woke me. It may have been

Betsa, though I think it was not. Or it may have been the sound they made crashing through the underbrush, moving noisily, like untrained soldiers, not caring if the branches rustled mightily as they pushed past them, letting the twigs snap underfoot unheeded. They were moving in single column and there must have been about a dozen of them. They had that untidy, ill-disciplined manner that soldiers often have when there is no officer around, but only a corporal who has just got his stripes and cannot yet assert his authority.

I was astonished to notice that I could even smell the pungent odor of their cigarettes, long before they reached the hide-out. I had my hand on Betsa's back, just as Trenko had said. She turned and looked at me as soon as I touched her, and then growled ever so quietly; I patted her once and she was quiet, but I felt that she was wondering where her master was.

I was terrified. It seemed impossible that they were not marching straight up to where I was . . . and that they would not see the hasty shelter we had thrown up. I watched and listened with a harshness rising in my throat demanding to be coughed free, and a painful crick in my neck where I had lain too long in one position.

And then I saw them. The lead man came first, a tall, black-eyed youngster of twenty or so, with two or three days' growth of beard on his young face, and an ease of movement that showed his mountain upbringing. He was a good-looking boy, and he held his rifle in its sling across his chest.

Behind him, several others broke through the thicket. They were in untidy order, straggling along carelessly, and most of them were smoking. It was hard to see very clearly through the dense bushes that concealed my dugout, but I could sense that they were tired and careless; there seemed to be some comfort in the thought that our pursuers were not the finest troops on the continent, but rather—some of them, at least —a bunch of scruffy and fed-up peasants masquerading in soldiers' uniform. That's the trouble with a totalitarian regime: when *everybody* gets called into the army, there are certain to be a great many of them who would rather be out watching their sheep or fixing the barn.

Then they sat down, some of them, quite close to the edge of the forest, not far from where I was hidden. Some of them had gone to the edge itself, and, although I could not see them, I guessed that they were standing, just as we had stood, and watching the long sweep of the farmland beyond it. There was a certain amount of calling back and forth, and I gathered that one of them, the N.C.O. perhaps, was trying to put them into some sort of order; they were laughing at him and joking among themselves . . . it seemed all so innocent and innocuous.

Then I felt Betsa stiffen under my hand. There was a tremor inside her as though she were growling without letting the sound of it escape from her stomach. With my nerves keyed up as they were, the gentle vibration of it was enough to send a sudden spasm of accented fear shooting through me. I wondered if one of them was peering into the hide-out.

For a long time Betsa just vibrated. There was no sound at all, and the men outside were still sitting around and joking. I simply could not understand what it was that Betsa was making the fuss about. I began to console myself with the fact that Trenko was a fine woodsman, and that they just could not possibly see the slightest sign of the shelter he had built; he was too skilled at the craft, and also, I felt, far too desperate to take any chances. But the soldiers were awfully close.

Then one of them shouted something, and all the others stopped laughing suddenly. The one I could see most clearly, a thin, shrunken old fellow with a white stubble on his chin, was staring over his shoulder, back in the direction from which they had come.

He stood up, then, and moved out of my line of sight, and then the others stood up too, brushing the grass and the leaves from their untidy uniforms.

I was learning to read the signs. If I'd had time to think about it, I would have derived a great deal of satisfaction from the sharpening of my wits, but at that moment I was too frightened to think very much. For I knew what that simple gesture meant; it was a sign that their officer was approaching, and that they'd better get on their feet and look as though they were interested in the job they were doing.

And then I heard the terrifying sound that had first alarmed Betsa. It was the barking of a dog.

I felt the blood draining away from my face. There was panic rising inside me, a cold, senseless, hopeless panic. I've been around dogs long enough to have a great admiration for them. In any case, a half-witted child knows what sort of scent a dog can find, and I had been inside that dugout for no more than a few hours. I knew that if their dog came within fifty yards of it he'd lead them straight there. There was no other course possible. And the soldiers stayed there, fifty feet away, standing around and waiting for the others to catch up. I found myself praying that they would move out into the open, just a few hundred yards away, so that there would be at least a chance that they'd bypass me. I felt the tears coming into my eyes as I realized that there was not the slightest hope of that because their dog was firm on our scent. I could even imagine Trenko, up there in his tree, wide-awake and alert, with his revolver ready. . . .

And then, like a savage beast, Betsa suddenly came to life. At precisely the same instant of time, there was a flurried rustling outside, a furious scuffling at the entrance to the hide-out, a shout, movement and confusion, and a branch was pulled away, savagely. I had just a glimpse of a soldier, his rifle across his chest, tugging away at the shelter, throwing his weight into it to get the untangling done, and then Betsa shot out. The phrase "the dogs of war" went quickly through my mind and I was momentarily startled by her absolute fury. She was foaming at the mouth and her eyes were on fire with rage.

The crouching dog outside was a Doberman, a long, tight-cropped animal with huge white teeth, its lips drawn back in a snarl as it crouched, waiting for Betsa. I saw one of the soldiers swing his rifle round. The dog master, who was on the end of the Doberman's leash, shouted something and pushed heavily at the soldier, swinging the rifle out of the way; then he slipped the nickel fastener at the dog's collar. . . . The soldiers were stumbling around untidily, trying to pull away the tangle of branches that had been the shelter, trying to keep out of the way of the screaming dogs, trying to get their weapons out of the way. . . . One of them leaned down and pulled me by the arm, and I hit out at him with all the force I could muster.

There was something contagious in Betsa's violence. I am not what you'd call a fighting man. The last time I used my fists in anger was when I was a child. I'm not even physically very strong. But there was something in the way she threw herself into the fight that was—what is the word— inspiring? It was an instinctive action, and I hit him as hard as I could on the face, aiming at his jaw in the proper manner but actually hitting his cheekbone just under the eye. He fell back, and someone else grabbed me, and I tore myself loose and ran, ran like the very devil, falling headlong into the thickness of the bushes, and stumbling rather than running, forcing my way blindly, without any kind of reasoning.

I knew that it was fear that was moving me, but I had no time for psychoanalysis; all I knew was that I was momentarily free and that a dozen soldiers were coming after me. I heard a scream and knew that one of the dogs had slashed at someone with razor-sharp teeth. There was a lot of shouting behind me, and more confusion than I had ever heard before in my life. I knew I could not get far with so many men so close behind me, but I ran anyway, moving downhill with the slope of the forest. I did not know where to go or what to do.

The effort to get away was all that I could think about, and there was barely time to wonder why they were not firing, and then, as this thought was flashing through my mind, several shots sounded one after the other, and I heard the sharp clipping of bullets that cut through the leaves well above my head; it was enough to indicate the truth of what DeBries had said: "They want us alive." I knew that at that range they could not have missed unintentionally. I dared not look back to see how close they were behind me, but fell forward all the time, putting my feet down heavily and blindly, not worrying about a twisted ankle that was throbbing painfully, stumbling through the bushes, forcing my way into the denseness, wondering what the next step could possibly be.

I knew it was hopeless, that there were too many of them, that they were too close behind me. I knew that my temporary escape had been a flash in the pan, only occasioned by the alarming savagery of the fighting dogs. I could still hear their yelping and their angry snarling, but it seemed a long way away. I wondered how far I had come.

There was still shouting behind me, and the sound of bodies crashing hurriedly through the thicket, and it seemed a little too much to one side of me, to the right. Then I was tumbling down the steep slope of a bank, with roots and hanging vines and a high canopy above where the trees met thirty feet above it. I fell again, and I picked myself up quickly and saw that no one was in sight behind me, so I turned off to the left and dived under a tangle of thorny vines, tearing my face on the tiny sharp spikes, slithering down on my side and finding myself prone once more, with a sharp root sticking painfully into my chest.

I was about to clamber hurriedly to my feet when the bushes opened just ahead of me and a soldier came through, pushing the bushes apart and moving quickly past me. I froze, and he almost stepped on my hand, and then he was gone. I realized that they were spread out now, beating through the forest systematically, knowing that I could not get very far. There was a single shot, a pistol it sounded like, a long way behind me, followed by a sharp yelp and then silence. . . . I knew that they had shot Betsa.

Poor Betsa! She had fought like a demon. I shall never forget the blind fury in her eyes as she shot out of the dugout, straight for the Doberman's throat. Nor the ripping motion of her head as her teeth tore at his shoulder, nor her sudden startled twisting as the lean Doberman slashed at her stomach with his fangs, fighting, as all Dobermans do, with a kind of cold dispassion that contrasted strangely with Betsa's explosive rage. And now they had shot her. . . .

In the confusion I had burst free, momentarily, and now I lay there, unable to move, with soldiers' hobnailed boots just missing my stretched-out fingers. Another man moved after the first one, almost invisible to me because I had ground my face deep into the soft humus of the leafmold, the gentle ripe stench of it thick in my nostrils, sweetly smelling with a kind of earthy redolence against my cheeks. I wondered how it was that they could not see me. I dared not turn my head, but after a little while, when nothing had happened and they had moved away, I twisted round and saw that I was covered almost completely by the thorns. My slithering body had gathered them tight around me, and only my left foot was sticking out. Gently, very cautiously, I pulled it close under me, and then lay there, not moving any more, wondering how long I could stay there unseen. I thought of the big Doberman and knew that it could not be for long.

And then a brightness came on me suddenly, as though everything were suddenly all right again. There was a picture in my mind of Betsa's teeth ripping into the shoulder of the Doberman, of a lithe and twisting motion, of Betsa's teeth firmly grasped over a foreleg. . . . And the dog master, the man who had angrily pushed away the soldier who was about to fire . . . It was a hope, at least.

Would a man so fond of his dog that he would throw himself at a loaded rifle—would the dog master let his sorely hurt animal go on the scent again? And even if he would, was the Doberman injured enough . . .? Had Betsa earned me a breathing space before she died?

I came to the conclusion that there was no more danger from the dog. And I knew that two of the soldiers had passed me by close enough to smell me—and had not stopped. It was a hope, and, until that moment, there had been no hope at all. I lay very still and waited.

The sounds were still there. Ahead of me, there was considerable movement among the bushes, and from time to time a certain amount of shouting, but it seemed to be getting further away.

Another comforting thought came to me. The brightness had gone from the underside of the leaves, and although I was deep enough within the woods not to see very much of the sun, I was conscious that there was a graying of the atmosphere that could only mean one thing: the sun had gone down.

And now . . . an hour to darkness? No more than an hour to wait for the sheltering comfort of my friend the night? I knew that in the black, moonless night, they would never find me. The stars would be bright, and once clear of the forest I could go north. . . . It would mean that I was alone, but still alive. They hadn't got me yet, and, with all their efficiency, in spite of their huge numbers and their dogs and their field telephones and their trucks . . . I was still free. It was not much, but it was something.

I wondered about Trenko. Had they found him? The tree he was hiding in was a dozen yards from where the dogs had fought, but if the dog master was binding his dog's wound, fussing over him as I expected him to be, then perhaps Trenko too would be safe. There had been only a dozen or so shots, and somehow there was nothing to indicate that they had found him. I tried to figure out if there had been more than one pistol shot . . . most of them had been from rifles. I knew that Trenko would have fired and kept on firing, saving only one round for himself. He used a Luger, and, although I wasn't sure that I could tell a Luger shot from any other pistol, I knew that it didn't sound a bit like a rifle.

So perhaps Trenko, too, was safe. Momentarily.

Then how to make contact? At his little white house with the iron bars over the window? The thought of going back into Volvoda itself terrified me.

I gave up thinking about it. The birds had started whistling and singing again, and somehow this seemed to indicate that the soldiers had gone. Certainly, I could no longer hear them. But I kept still. My fortuitous hiding place was obviously good enough and it was not likely that I could find a better one, even if I could risk the move. And the continued silence of the Doberman back there made me more and more convinced that I was right about it: it was out of the fight altogether. And the darkness was closing in. . . .

I just lay there, absolutely still and silent, watching the grayness go deeper and deeper. It reached a kind of mid-crepuscule, and stayed like that for a long time, not changing, while my limbs grew stiffer and stiffer, and then, suddenly, it was dark. The birds had stopped their friendly sounds and the air was damper than it had been. I was aware of the cold. But still I lay there, not moving. I even closed my eyes and tried to sleep for a while.

At last, very gently, I crawled out from my nest, tearing my face again on the unseen thorns, and stood up. I tried hard to remember which direction I had come from, and for a moment I could not decide where Volvoda lay. Then I realized that it must be to my left, and I wondered if I should go back and try to find Trenko. The fear that they were waiting for me there was overpowering.

The thought of visiting that scene of violence again unnerved me, but I knew that it would be wiser to try and find him here. Not knowing whether or not I would have the final courage to stand on the same dreadful spot again, I went very slowly and cautiously back in the general direction from which I had come. I knew that I could not have moved more than three or four hundred yards away.

It was eerily silent. The darkness was almost absolute, and it was not easy to find the way. I stumbled once into the open, and for a dozen yards or so I walked along the edge of the forest, moving very slowly and carefully. It must have taken me more than half an hour, but I came on a big mimosa that stood by itself a little, and I remembered that I had seen this very tree just before we went into hiding.

Then I saw the white end of a newly cut branch sticking jauntily up into the air, and another and then another, and I knew that I had found the hide-out. I waited a long time, then, wondering if they were there, concealed among the trees and waiting for me to show up. There was no earthly reason why they should be, unless they had found Trenko and guessed that I would come loooking for him. And I was quite sure they thought I had gone far away by now.

I moved forward slowly, and found the body of Betsa. She was lying on her side, with a great deal of blood in evidence, which showed that she had fought for a long time after the Doberman's teeth had ripped her open. As I had thought, she had finally been shot: there was a big hole at the back of her head which could only have been caused by a bullet. On impulse, knowing that Trenko, if I ever saw him again, would want it, I took off her bloody collar and slipped it into my pocket. Of the other dog, there was no sign.

I stood under Trenko's tree for a while, wondering if I had made enough noise for him to have heard me if he was still there. Then I whistled, twice, very softly, but there was no reply. I had not really expected one. I knew that Trenko would be looking for me, and how do you find a hiding man in a forest in the middle of the night? I knew, then, that there was nothing else for it; I had to go back into Volvoda.

I went to the edge of the woods where the fields began and stood for a moment looking at the stars. The Dipper was bright and clear, and I followed the line of its two end pinpoints until I located the North Star, and then stood staring below for a while, trying to see what lay there.

Somewhere over there was the frontier. Thirty miles away? It could not be much more.

The first thing was to get away from that damned forest while it was still dark, and find Trenko. By morning it would be ringed with a thousand troops and there would not be one chance in a hundred of getting out of it.

I suddenly realized how hungry I was. Thinking about it made me hungrier still, so I put it away from my mind altogether and concentrated on getting away.

It was not easy to see very much in the darknesss, even with the darker dark of the forest behind me. I could not help shuddering as I turned and started the long walk across the fields toward the village.

I suppose it was inevitable. I suppose that all my careful reasoning was no more than wishful thinking. I should have known that the net was too tightly spread about me. But I did not know this, and so my sudden capture was a horrifying, desperate shock.

I had gone down to the valley, and was climbing the other side of the hill, climbing wearily upward in the pitch darkness and fighting the tiredness that was oppressing me, keeping an eye from time to time on the North Star, wondering if I could reach the village before light, wondering if I would find the white house. . . .

Suddenly there was a flicker of flame just ahead of me. It startled me and I pulled up short, conscious that it was no more than twenty feet off. I was startled, horrified and full of panic. I looked over my shoulder and could see nothing behind me, so I backed away, and then the tiny light flared more brightly and I saw that it was a match held close to a face, so close to me that it was impossible that I had not been seen. Someone was lighting a cigarette, and, as he puffed, the match flared brightly again and I could see him quite clearly . . . a thin, delicate face with black eyes made satanic by the dancing red glare.

I turned and ran.

It was the only thing I could do. He was so impossibly close to me that I had no other choice. I simply turned and ran back the way I had come, but, before I had gone a dozen panting steps in the darkness, I collided with a sturdy body that gave way unexpectedly before me. We rolled over and over for a few yards, and someone shouted, and then a flare shot up into the sky above us and as the sound of its shot came to me I saw that they were all about me, more than a hundred of them within the circle of greenish light that slowly increased its brightness as the flare came down from the sky. Then a rough hand took my shoulder and jerked me to my feet, and someone hit me hard across the face and started pushing me up the hill again, and there was the beam of a flashlight somewhere, and then suddenly the whole area was lit up as a powerful lamp was switched on not more than a hundred yards away.

I was sick with desperation. The soldiers were milling about and one of them was running his hands over my body, looking for arms I suppose, and then an officer stepped forward and they fell back respectfully as he approached. He stood looking at me for a moment, and said in Spanish: "Well, who are you?"

I shook my head blankly, and he stared harder and then said quietly in English: "So . . . the American."

When I did not answer, he said nothing for a moment, and then said quite affably: "I think we have a lot to talk about, no?"

His voice was soft and effeminate, and his accent was very English, like one of those cosmopolites who have studied in London or at one of the English universities. He said something to the soldiers, and they took me by the arms and shoved me toward a truck that was lumbering down the hill from the edge of the forest. I reflected gloomily that, if they hadn't caught me there, I would have walked straight into them; the truck was coming from the precise point at the top of the hill where I was going. When it stopped, they pushed me aboard, and one of them, a thickset man in civilian clothes, called out angrily to the others, and someone stepped forward and tied my hands together by the wrists, then tied them to the heavy wire framework that was under the truck's canvas canopy.

A moment later we were lumbering off again into the night.

Other trucks were starting up all around us, and their headlights were coming on; wherever they shone there were groups of soldiers. I was astonished that there were so many of them.

We drove to the top of the hill, bounced over a wide ditch, and then turned onto a gravel road. The motor began to whine as we gathered speed, and I realized how desperately tired I was. I closed my eyes and half dozed, feeling the sickness and the weariness and above all the abject fear coming into me like a nausea.

chapter 9

Does it sound strange to say that I felt relieved?
I had spent so much time worrying about what might hap-

pen that now it had come about the worst seemed to be over. I was building up a kind of determination, and somehow I felt a lot better after I had decided that whatever they might do to me the name Lazlo would not pass my lips. DeBries' killing, Betsa's death and Trenko's disappearance had all slowly imbued me with a sort of devotion to what was now becoming my own cause.

Before, I had been just a hireling, a mercenary. But now I was as much a part of the battle as any of them—more so, perhaps, because now I knew that the final delicate thread of success could be broken only by my own irresolution. I spent a long time, on that uncomfortable journey to the prison, trying to figure out some way to mislead them.

We arrived at a big open square in the barracks back in Volvoda, a mere dozen miles or so from the hillside on which they had taken me. There was a sharp pain in my shoulders from the awkward position in which I had been forcibly seated, with my wrists slung to one side and tied to the side of the truck, and, as I stumbled out onto the gravel square, the soldiers were all milling about untidily in the lights of some bare bulbs that were strung along a whitewashed wall. There was a sergeant in charge, a short, stubby man with a hard, deeply lined face and a swarthy complexion that betrayed his Indian origin. He had extraordinarily broad fingers, thick with black hair at the backs of the knuckles. He fumbled with a paper which I imagined to be a receipt of some sort, and handed me over to another N.C.O. inside. I was searched again, quite casually, and then escorted down a long narrow corridor to a small detention cell.

The excitement of the night had brought on its logical effect, and my bladder was near bursting. As the N.C.O. opened the door, I asked him, in English, if I could go to the toilet. He stared at me blankly for a moment, and then motioned me inside. I began to insist, and he said something to one of the soldiers standing by, and the soldier lifted his rifle and drove the butt of it into my stomach. The sudden pain of it was appalling, and, as I stumbled back and gasped for breath, someone slammed the heavy wooden door shut and I was left in complete and utter darkness. When I had recovered my breath, I groped about and found a sort of bed, just a wooden bench fastened to the walls at both ends, on which there was a blanket that was thinly shredded and odious; the stench in the place was overwhelming, an ammoniac sort of smell that clogged the nostrils almost to the point of suffocation. Groping about again, I found that it came from a wooden bucket in the corner that was full to the very brim and was overflowing onto the floor. It had obviously not been emptied for a long time, and in the confined, six-foot space, its effect was nauseating. I was soon gasping for air, but I knew that so slight a thing as a bad smell would be the least of my worries.

There was nothing I could do. I knew that I had to avoid all thought until I was thoroughly rested and my mind was clear of the awful depression that had set in on me. I lay down on the wooden planks, pulled the thin blanket over my body and slept.

Slept? I suppose that is the word for it, but all night long I woke again and again in acute discomfort, trying to puzzle out what was the best course to take—if, indeed, I had any choice.

Thinking back on what DeBries had said, I knew there was one thing they *had* to find out—what we had been up to. And whatever else they forced from me, I was determined that I would say nothing about this.

When they came for me I had been awake for at least an hour, though I had no way of knowing whether it was daylight outside or not. It was the sergeant again—the man with the hair on his knuckles. He took me to a cheaply furnished office, and I was immensely and foolishly relieved to see that it was not a cellar lined with medieval instruments. . . . It all seemed impossibly *casual*.

Then the officer came in, the same man whose face I had briefly seen the night before. In daylight, he seemed even more effeminate than I had imagined him, a slight, good-looking man, whose high boots were brightly polished and whose fancy uniform was clean and freshly pressed. He carried a file under his arm and was smoking an American cigarette. He smiled at me very good-naturedly, pulled out a chair and sat down, indicating another chair in the friendliest possible fashion. He was so friendly that I was at once put on my guard. He put the file of papers on the table, shuffled them around and said:

"Now, where shall we begin?"

His voice was soft and well-modulated; there was even a slight lisp to it.

"Mr. . . ." He looked at the papers again. "Ah, yes, Mr. Benasque."

As if he did not know! I do not know what effect he was trying to achieve, but that slight break in his voice made me feel as though I were merely another case that had to be decided as quickly as possible so that more pressing matters could be attended to. He said:

"Michael Benasque, 32 Calle Sofía, Caracas. You're a long

way from home, aren't you?" It was an expression of sympathy more than a question.

He said: "Now, let's see. You arrived here five days ago on the train from Encino, and someone else left in your place. The stationmaster should have noticed . . . peasants, you know, no intelligence at all. So . . . What we want to know, first of all, is—who was the man who took your place? Let's deal with that first, shall we?"

I said shortly: "I've nothing to say to you."

His smile was wide and affable. "Come now," he said, "let's not be melodramatic." He was genuinely amused, trying to make friends, trying to make me one of the group he belonged to.

He said: "You're a journalist, not a politician, and you were hired by some enemies of the state to do a job. Now, you've been caught. Isn't it rather foolish not to make a clean breast of the whole thing? To disassociate yourself from them, so to speak? Otherwise . . . would you have us believe that you are one of *them*? Is that what you want? Of course not. Now, who was the deserter? And who was it hired you?"

An idea came into my mind and I seized on it before I could think much about it. I said: "I don't know who he was. I was just told to come in and give my passport to another man to get out with."

"And who told you to do this?"

"The man you shot. I met him in Caracas."

"Ah, yes. That one. That was a major mistake, wasn't it?"

Now, he was seeking sympathy. It was all supposed to mean: "We've both got out troubles, so why don't we help each other out?"

He said sadly: "You can't trust anyone, can you? Our best shot . . . an expert marksman. He was trying to get the dog, of course, and no one was more surprised than we were to find the body. In one of our own uniforms, if you please."

So that was it . . . they were after Betsa. It should have been obvious. He offered me a cigarette and lit it for me, and said affably: "You know, I knew from the very beginning that we'd have trouble with that dog. Where's Sassini now?"

Surprised, I said, "Sassini? I've never heard of him."

An acute discomfort crossed my mind at once. I knew that I would have to plead ignorance of a good many things; it did not improve matters to be asked questions I genuinely could not answer. An unnecessary "I don't know . . ."

Watching me carefully, he said: "Miguel Sassini. Perhaps you know him by his rebel name. He calls himself Trenko."

I could not help nodding my head. I said: "I don't know where he is."

But you admit that you know him?"

What was the use of denying it? I said briefly: "I know him."

"So do we, Mr. Benasque. We've known him for a long time. But what we'd like to know is just what he has been doing these last few weeks. And frankly, when we catch him, I don't expect he'll have much to say to us . . . another stubborn peasant. So you see, you are really our only source, aren't you? I'm afraid it puts rather a heavy load on your shoulders, but . . . well, you understand, don't you. You got yourself into this thing, so you have only yourself to blame. However . . . let's hope that you'll co-operate with us. It'll be easier for all of us, won't it?"

He had the most extraordinary eyes. They were dark brown, rather bigger than usual, and set quite close to the bridge of his nose. A woman would have been delighted with such eyes, but they were much too close together. And they moved too much, always flickering from side to side without a corresponding movement of the head.

He said: "Of course, you and I both understand that our present regime is not popular with everybody, although we try to do the best for the greatest number. Some malcontents prefer to fight us, and so . . . But for you to go to all this trouble to smuggle someone out . . . I suppose time will tell who is missing, but . . . It's not enough, you know. We'd like to know *now*, so that we can forestall any political advantage our enemies might make out of it."

He leaned back in his chair, tilting it to bring his feet up on the table, and put his hands behind his head. He said dreamily: "Political advantage . . . that's all it is. It's a strange game, isn't it? The juxtaposition of divergent political theories, no more, and yet it can cause all this trouble. So, you don't know the name of the man who took your passport?"

"No, I don't."

"Well, that's as may be. We'll find out, of course. Now, the second point. What was the name of the man who hired you? The unfortunate one we shot?"

"I knew him as Emerson. Probably not his real name."

"A little hesitation, Mr. Benasque. It gives the game away. I should tell you that we are more accustomed than you to deceit. Try again."

"Emerson."

"Ah well . . . And how were *you* supposed to leave the country?"

"I was going to walk to the frontier and cross over where I could."

"You see how much easier it is when you tell the truth?

But I wonder, all the same, why it should be easier for you to cross the border illegally than for this mysterious deserter of ours. That's the crux of the matter, isn't it? However, I suppose that could be easily enough explained. And the name of the man who found you your nursing job?"

"Nursing job?"

"Pushing Mr. Vallance's wheel chair."

"Oh, that. That was Emerson."

Was I right in assuming that Vallance was in the clear? They knew his name, of course, from his passport. We'd stayed at the hotel and they'd had ample time to get both our names.... Conscious that he was watching me through the haze of his cigarette smoke, I brought the mythical Emerson in again.

"Emerson arranged the job for me. He said it was a good way to get here. Then I handed over my passport to him and he gave it to the other man . . . whose name I don't know."

"I see." He stared at the ceiling for a while. Then he said cheerfully: "I think I detect signs of co-operation. So much the better. What was Emerson's real name?"

"I don't know."

"Well, we'll come back to it later. Now, where is Trenko?"

"I don't know."

"Presumably you had arranged a meeting point. In case you got separated. Where was that to be?"

"We did not expect to be separated."

"Your operation, though somewhat simple, bears a professional stamp, you know. I can't believe that this contingency would not have been taken care of."

"None the less, it's the truth."

"I see. Now, what else is there?"

He let his chair down with a bang and looked at his papers again. As though he had forgotten all about it, he said: "Oh, yes, of course, the aircraft. Tell me, what was dropped—a man? Arms? Supplies to the rebels?"

"A man. But I don't know who he was."

Smiling, he said: "That hesitancy again, Mr. Benasque. Were you wondering, perhaps, if you should lie or not?"

He stood up and began to wander about the bare room, his delicate frame mincing slightly. He said airly: "All right, I know you're telling the truth. We found the parachute. Twenty-eight feet across. That means a man weighing about a hundred and seventy-five pounds. Simple, isn't it? I wonder who he was.... You really don't know?"

"No, I don't."

"Ah well, we'll just have to assume that you do. But that can wait. What else was there? Oh, yes."

He went back to the table and shuffled his file again. Then he took out a paper and handed it to me.

"Can you read this?"

It was an official document, and my own name had been typed in on the dotted line. My blood ran cold.

I knew that he wanted to find out if I could read Spanish, but this was a detail of no importance at all. It was impossible to keep up a pretense that I could not read it; it was a death certificate. My own.

He said gently: "I'm afraid we've had to inform your consul that you met with an accident. It's the proper procedure, you know. We said that you were in the country illegally, that you were asked for your papers, that you resisted arrest and that you were shot trying to escape. We added a handsome apology, but insisted that we could not accept responsibility for this result of an illegal act on your part. The letter has already been sent off."

I couldn't help stammering. I said angrily: "And . . . and what do you expect to gain by that?"

I knew damned well what they expected to gain. He was still smiling affably at me. He said smoothly: "Of course, if necessary, we can always say that some fool of a clerk made some stupid mistake, can't we? And apologize again. But I show you this in order to make the point that as far as we are concerned, Mr. Benasque, you are already dead. You're just a body now. Now, doesn't that present the problem in a rather new light? Do you really think you won't tell us what we want to know? It's simple, isn't it?"

I said angrily: "I've nothing more to tell you. I've . . . I've told you all that I know. As you said, I have no interest in all this; I'm just a hired hand. If I knew any more, I'd tell you."

The smile had gone from his face and he looked unbelievably cruel. He said softly: "You will tell us, Mr. Benasque. Sooner or later, believe me, you will tell us. And remember what I said: we want to know *now*. We want to find out all we can with the minimum waste of time. And you are the only source we have. So if we have to be . . . to be a little unfriendly, then I want you to know that the solution to your problems lies entirely in your own hands. Tomorrow morning, we shall take you to another place. And there, please believe me, they will not be so lenient. Do I make myself clear?"

He rang a bell on the table, a little bronze sheep bell, and stood up to signify that the interview was over. He did not look at me again. When I turned at the door with the soldier who came running in, he was looking at his carefully manicured fingernails. The soldier jerked his head at the door, and hustled me out of the room.

In the stinking darkness of the cell I sat down on the edge of the bed and started thinking. It was quite obvious that I had to get out of there one way or another. It was terrifying to think of that fearful death certificate. I was now mere flesh and blood with no living entity to worry about—they could do what they liked with me with no holds barred. There was no one I could turn to; there was no glimmer of hope. No hope at all.

No hope? Impossible! If I could get out of my prison . . . there was no window to the cell. The door was of solid hardwood, an inch thick and heavily reinforced with iron straps. The floor was concrete. It seemed as if not even the air could come in. How, then, could I get out? The answer was obvious: I couldn't.

But there was one thing I remembered from the days of the war, when a good deal of expensive training had been drummed into my negligent ears. One thing I remembered: they had said—Was it Colonel Matley? Yes, I believe it was. He had said: "Remember this: your guards are worrying about their wine ration, or their women, or when they're going to be relieved. But you—you've got nothing to worry about at all except the process of getting out. There's nothing else to exclude that problem from your mind, so you start off with an enormous advantage. Sure, they've got the keys; but use your brains, boy. Use your brains."

Well, it was true enough; there was nothing else to think about. But how do you get out of a six-foot-square box with no window?

I lay back on the bed, feeling lost and dejected, and terribly empty.

It was a long, long time before they came for me again.

I was starving. I had had no food of any sort for nearly two days, and now I was thirsty too. My body was beginning to itch, and I knew that I had picked up some lice off that filthy blanket. I hammered on the door once, yelling myself hoarse, but there was no reply at all. The place could have been deserted for all the sounds I heard. And there was a horror growing within me that they were going to leave me here in the darkness to die, no more than a corpse shut up in a dark square room not much bigger than a coffin. I tried yelling again later on, but still there was no response, and at last I gave it up.

They came, then, two of them, the sergeant and a civilian whom the sergeant treated with a great deal of respect. They threw the door open and motioned me outside, and, as I stood there wondering, staring at them, the civilian said, in Spanish: "My name is Weber. Weber. You will be my guest."

His Spanish was atrocious. It was labored and slow, and he had the most throaty accent I had ever heard. It was almost comical. He seemed to search for the words before he used them, as though he had learned no more than a few phrases. . . . But there was nothing comical about the man himself. He was short and fat and solid on his heels, standing there like a block of gray stone. His face was gray in the dim light, and his belted jacket was gray too. His once-black shoes were gray, and so was his hat. It was almost as though his face had to be looked for in the stodgy gray mass before you could find it, and then only by knowing where it ought to be. But his tiny, porcine eyes were sharp and sullen at the same time, and his gray lips were thin out of all proportion to his flabby gray chins. The corners of them turned down, and there was a most disagreeable odor about him. It occurrred to me that I had just left a very fetid sort of smell behind me, the ancient smell of an overflowing latrine bucket in a confined space, and yet here, in the comparative cleanliness of the corridor, an equally unpleasant odor was emanating from this wretched man. It was the smell of plain body odor, and it came off him in waves every time he moved.

He raised his plump hand and laid it gently on my cheek, and spoke in his comic-opera accent; he pretended to ignore my instinctive wincing as his arm came up. He said: "So that we will understand one another . . ."

Then, hardly moving his body, he chopped twice in rapid succession with the edge of his hand at my throat. The pain shot through my head, tearing at my brain, blinding me for a moment, and I was aware that I was on the cold concrete floor with my head reeling and the agony moving down my sides to my chest as I gasped for air. All I could see was the gray outline of his feet, and I was inexplicably startled by the tiny size of them. Then they turned to red suddenly, and then to yellow, and I felt myself falling from my hands and knees and tumbling sideways so that my head hit the floor painfully, and I heard him say: "Now get up, we go to another place from here."

I staggered to my feet, wanting to vomit, and fell again, and then picked myself up and just stood there feeling sick and scared. There is something terrible about a callous, cold-blooded beating. I sensed that he was wanting me to hit back at him so that he could really go to work on me. He said something to the sergeant, and the sergeant stepped behind me and took hold of my arms above the elbows, and then Weber stepped forward and rapped the side of his hand several times across the bridge of my nose, just between the eyes, not very hard, but with lightning speed. I felt the senses leaving my brain with the agony of it, and I struggled to get my arms free, and I yelled at him, and finally I fell to the floor again and Weber just stood there looking at me, and then turned his back and walked away.

The sergeant bent down and yanked me to my feet, and I was aware that his oafish face showed a certain sympathy; there was an unexpected gentleness to his touch and he would not look me in the face. He propelled me quite carefully after the retreating figure of Weber, and I stumbled along feeling as though all the devils of hell were racing round in my head. I was conscious of a screaming sound that seemed to be coming from beyond a door we were passing, and I wondered if the awful noise were in my own head. And then the door opened, and the screams grew louder and suddenly stopped, and, as we stood there, waiting, a policeman came out and leaned against the wall looking at us. He was grinning foolishly, and I heard him say to the sergeant:

"She's ugly as sin. Why do I always get the ugly ones?"

Then he saw Weber and he stiffened. He went back into the room and closed the door. But I had seen the most frightening object I ever laid eyes on in my life. It was a stick, about two feet long and an inch or so thick; it was tightly bound with ordinary barbed wire, and the policeman was holding it lightly by its leather thong. It sent a shudder of revulsion through my veins. Then the main door was thrown open and the sergeant pushed me forward. We reached the outside of the building and an ancient pickup was there waiting for us. I clambered in the back with the sergeant and a policeman, and Weber stood staring at me with absolutely no expression at all on his evil face; it seemed that his features were not physically capable of leaving the form of the unpleasant mold in which they had been cast.

He climbed in the front with the driver, and we set off. Someone opened the big iron gates that led into the barracks square, and the truck turned out and along a gravel road in the darkness and soon the lights of the buildings were far behind us.

We had gone, I suppose, half a dozen miles or so when the motor stalled, and the driver slammed on the brakes to stop us running back down the hill. We sat there waiting while he ground at the starter, quite uselessly, and then he climbed out and spoke to the sergeant, and then Weber got out and stood by the side of the road with his hands in his pockets and said something to the sergeant too, and finally we all got out and started pushing to get the truck up to the top of the hill so that it could get a decent run down for a start. I began to wonder what the devil I was doing pushing a truck for *them* in the middle of the night, and my heart was pounding with the thought that there were only four of them. . . .

Weber was walking slowly along with us, hands deep in pockets, and the sergeant, the policeman and I were shoving at the back, with the driver forward so that he could push and use the steering wheel at the same time. I knew that it was now or never.

It was the sight of the sergeant's rifle that made up my mind for me, though not to do the thing I should have done. He was holding his rifle quite loosely in his left hand, and leaning his shoulder into the truck. The weapon was close by my side, and I knew that in a matter of seconds I could have snatched it away from him, pumped a round into the breech—if there was not one already there—and killed Weber.

It did not occur to me, at first, merely to use this chance for escape. Though my fear was great, my hatred was greater, and the urge to kill Weber . . . It was something to do with the complete dispassion on his face as he had listened to the awful screams that came out of that room, under the barracks. It was the thought of the dreadful weapon Weber's policeman had been so nonchalantly holding. I swear that it was not the pain that was still racking my head from the coldly scientific blows he had struck at the bridge of my nose—nor the knowledge that he was taking me to "another place," as he had called it, where he could do what he liked with me. There was a feeling of altruism in my hatred for him which I must insist upon because I am a little proud of it. At that moment, I wanted to kill Weber more than I have ever wanted to do anything in my whole life; it was the sudden flash of a neurotic obsession.

Instead, I took the easier course, and I shall never know why I did. Nor shall I ever forgive myself.

Well, what's the use?

We were climbing high in the mountains, only a few miles from Volvoda itself, where Trenko's little white house was. I knew that this would be my only chance. The road was winding steeply round the hill, and on one side there was a black drop into the darkness; it might have been a few feet down or a hundred. . . . I had no way of telling. I tried to visualize the road as it had been in the glare of the headlights, and then, without thinking any more about it, I made a sudden dive for the side of the road and threw myself over the edge.

I know that if I had believed it to be a thousand feet down, I would still have done the same thing; my state of mind was such that anything was preferable to Weber's merciless attentions. But to my astonishment I landed on my feet almost at once, slithered another dozen yards or so on the damp grass and felt the earth straighten out under my feet as I started running. There was a shout behind me, an angry, violent shout, and then two shots were fired in rapid succession, but I did not even hear the whine of the bullets. I heard Weber's thin voice raised in terrible anger, and some more shots were fired, and then a submachine gun opened up and I still did not hear the bullets.

They say it's the one you don't hear that gets you, but don't you believe it. There is no more vicious sound in nature than the sharp clip of lead cutting through the leaves of the trees about you, and as long as I did not hear this I knew that I was safe again. It had seemed incredibly careless of them to let me get away so easily, and I wondered for a moment if it had been intentional. But, intentional or not, I was determined to stay away from them now. I knew that if Weber set eyes on me again . . . I threw out my hands and blundered into the bushes.

Weber . . . Thinking back, I know that he is the man with the brains and with the evil. Of course, over there there are hundreds of Webers; there have to be, to keep the people in check. But, as far as I am concerned, he was the one man among all of them on whom I could concentrate my hatred. The little officer with the big brown eyes and the effeminate voice—well, he was just trying to scare the daylights out of me, and trying to solve his own problem in his own way. The sergeant, he wasn't a bad sort of fellow; there had been genuine sympathy in his eyes when he had picked me up after Weber had struck me across the nose like that. And all the others . . . But Weber's immobile face remains as a nightmare with me. The callous and quite dispassionate terror that he deliberately inspired . . . Weber was the man for whom I reserved all the hate that was left inside me.

I reached Volvoda with surprisingly little difficulty. I took the easy way, keeping close to the road and simply retracing the way we had come. . . . I even ran part of the way, though the pounding in my head was appalling. Once, a truckload of troops passed me in the darkness, and I flung myself flat on my face in the scrub at the side of the track, not breathing until their lights had passed me and the sound of the broken-down motor had faded into the distance, and the crickets had resumed the interrupted insistence of their strident voices. Then the frogs started up close beside me in the water, and somehow there was comfort in the sound. I moved as fast as I could, with a desperation born of terror. I knew that they had dogs. . . .

I stopped and rested as soon as the mountain flattened out

into the valley where Volvoda was, lying on the ground like a discarded bundle, all doubled up and not caring about anything but the luxury of rest and the relief of air that could stay for a while in the body and not be used up by a pounding heart before it could bring any comfort. The lights of the railway station were dim in the distance, but I could clearly make out the long, winding road that led to it. "Calle Cuatro de Octubre," Trenko had called it. It was named after another of their damned revolutions.

The streets of the village were deserted and quiet when I moved in, keeping silently to the shadows wherever I could. I knew that whatever forces they had at their disposal would be crowding into the hills to look for me, and there was some comfort in the thought that therefore the village itself was probably the safest place. I could not believe that I had escaped so easily, and the knowledge of my accomplishment gave me strength and courage and confidence. The emptiness and the silence and the darkness bolstered my hopes. I was suddenly full of assurance.

I found the little alleyway Trenko had mentioned, with the steps leading down from it, and, as I began the descent, I pulled up short and almost turned and ran. Just around the corner, a man was lying asleep in the shadows; I almost fell over him, and I was about to turn and run from sheer unexpected alarm when I heard him say, very quickly and very quietly:

"Do not enter the house, Señor. The police are behind you. Keep walking straight ahead."

As I stood there, momentarily startled into stupidity, he said again urgently: "Keep walking straight ahead, Señor."

The confidence fell from my shoulders like a discarded cloak. A moment ago, there had been an assumption that the danger and the fright had receded into the background, to be remembered only when the urgent light of morning came. The ease with which I had slipped away from them . . . Not since the days of the war had I played this sort of game, and I had begun to believe that some of the old, forgotten skills were coming back to me. And now a dark and somber shadow had fallen across my well-being.

It was not only the thought that they were playing with me like this, letting me escape to lead them to Trenko . . .

Sassini, Miguel Sassini, they had called him, and the awareness that this was the first time I had heard his real name widened the gulf between us. But it was more than this. It meant that they knew I could not get far, that they were securely on my trail and quite competent to pick me up whenever they wanted to. It presupposed an omnipotence on their part that was terrifying. It made me no more than a puppet on the end of a string.

The man was still lying there, unmoving, sleeping. I could not help staring at him, and then I pulled myself together quickly and moved away from him, wondering if I had interrupted my movements long enough to be suspicious . . . if the sleeping man would have gone by the time the police behind me passed the spot. . . . My heart was playing up again, but I kept on walking quickly and quietly as I had done before, down to the bottom of the steps, catching a glimpse out of the corner of my eye of the friendly house I could not enter, and straight on to the end of the alleyway, not daring to look to the left or the right. I did not even know which way to turn, and as I momentarily hesitated, a shadow moved beside me and a child's voice said:

"To the left, Señor, to the left."

I did not see the owner of the voice, but, dazed and miserable, I turned to the left and went round the corner, and nearly collided with Trenko.

He stepped out of the darkness close beside me and seized my arm and whispered urgently: "Run . . . run with me . . . fast . . ." and still holding tight to my arm he half dragged me with him, moving off into the darkness between the rows of dreary whitewashed adobe buildings. Still holding my arm in a vise, he lugged me round a corner, moving fast, and then another, and soon we were doubling back on our tracks again, running through the shadows, and I glimpsed the beam of a flashlight far ahead of us where the steps lay. We ran fast to the left, not talking, moving like an unlikely four-legged creature with two heads and two bodies but only one brain. And not till we were clear of the village and my lungs were bursting out of my chest did Trenko slow down a little.

The moon was up now, and in its blue light I could see the sweat pouring down off his face. He stood a moment with his arms akimbo, his breath coming fast, his mouth open to suck in the air. I was startled to see that he, too, was human enough to feel the strain of the desperate course we had run. For my part, the constriction in my chest was creeping up through my throat to my dried mouth. My limbs were numb with exhaustion. He dragged me close under the shadow of a clump of banana trees where the thin trickle of a shallow stream made the soil soft and squelchy, and we bent down and scooped some water up and splashed it into our faces, and then he said:

"My friend . . . you give me plenty of trouble tonight, no?"

He was actually smiling. He slapped some water over his chest and said: "Come on, we must get to the coast tonight."

I could hardly catch my breath. The words choked in my throat. I said hoarsely: "The coast? That's . . . that's a hell of a long way to go. We'll . . . we'll never get there tonight."

Scooping some of the filthy water into his mouth, he nodded his head, and the sight of the water trickling down his chin as he tried to drink and talk at the same time . . .

He said: "I know. It is too far. But let us get as far as we can. We must."

"What's . . . what's at the coast . . . for God's sake?"

He said grimly: "It is the only way. I do not know how many troops or police they have here. There are thousands of them. At the coast . . . maybe we can find a boat. We will steal one."

There was a painful stitch in my side. I said: "You're the boss. Whatever you say."

There were a hundred questions I wanted to ask. But the breath inside me was painfully short. He moved off and I followed him blindly.

We kept to the road, because Trenko said it was the shortest route and it was the one place where they would probably not be looking for us—at least, only in trucks. And once or twice we hid in the ditch while cars rumbled past, and then we stumbled on again, not caring about the intense fatigue that made every footstep an agony.

There was a river to cross, and, once again, fearing the bridge would be guarded, we made a detour and stumbled through the water. It was not very deep and it was warmer here on the plain. We fell exhausted on the other side and rested for a while. Then we filled our bellies with water and staggered wearily on.

Trenko was like a man possessed. He spoke hardly a word, but urged me on with short, silent gestures, over the hills and down into the valleys, pushing our way blindly through the scrub every time we came to a village, detouring over plowed fields to avoid the scattered farmhouses. We moved with quite unbelievable speed, and Trenko dragged his bad leg after him like a wolf that has left one paw in a trap. He was absolutely tireless.

We had our first piece of luck when we had covered perhaps ten miles. A truck was coming along the road behind us and we had flattened ourselves in the bottom of the ditch that ran by the side of the gravel road. By the grace of God, we were halfway up a short, steep hill, and as the truck overtook us and ground its gears down for the sharp rise, I saw

Trenko lift his head and heard him whisper: "Quickly . . . on the truck . . ."

I saw him bent double in the moonlight as he leaped out of the ditch and raced after the lorry, and, as I jumped up and followed him, the truck moved ahead with a loud coughing of its broken-down motor, then faltered, slipped back a few feet, and with a roar began the climb again. But Trenko was already aboard, clinging onto the back and holding out one arm to help me. I grabbed his strong hand and swung myself aboard just as we reached the top of the rise and gathered momentum for the run down on the other side. We pulled ourselves over the tail gate, and flopped exhausted on top of the bulky load.

It was melons. There must have been a couple of hundred of them, big and hard and round and green. I was still trying to get my breath, gasping for air and near to collapse, when Trenko pulled out his knife and sliced one open. I heard the squelch of his blade as it ripped at the soft meat, and when he held out a long crescent for me to take, I shook my head; I was too exhausted to move.

He pushed it toward me and said: "Go on, eat. Eat now, while we can."

I knew that it could easily be our last chance for a long time. I knew too that I was desperately hungry. I twisted into a less awkward position, finding that a pile of melons is not the best bed in the world, and we lay on our backs there, letting the sweet red juice trickle down the sides of our necks as we ate, cooling ourselves off and filling our empty stomachs. The sky was moon-bright, and the air was cool and fresh. We just lay still and rested when we had eaten all we could manage, staring up at the sky and saying nothing.

At last, when I felt refreshed, I rolled over uncomfortably onto my stomach and said quietly: "So . . . they let me escape, is that it?"

Trenko looked at me somberly and nodded.

"Otherwise . . . if they had not wanted it, you would not have escaped."

"To lead them to you?"

"Of course. I was quite sure they would do this. There were only two things they could do. One, to force you to talk. Two, to let you go free and follow you. I think perhaps they believed the second way would be quicker."

If only he had known! I did not tell him how sure I was that I would have broken down long before they had stripped my clothes off me. Instead, I said: "You know a guy called Weber? A foreigner?"

His eyes were suddenly gleaming.

"I know him," he said. "We must not let him catch you again, my friend."

"How did you know they were following me?"

"I waited near the police barracks. After you had gone in the truck, I was certain that they were letting you get away. So I went to the place where we were to meet, and my friend from the white house . . . his wife, his son, his three daughters . . . they were all waiting for you. Whichever way you came from . . . waiting to stop you from going into the house and giving it away to the police. The rest you know. They were very close behind you. I am surprised that you did not know this."

"I know. I guess I was feeling too smug. That bastard Weber . . ."

"Weber . . . He is a sadist. He is obscene. Many times we have tried to kill him. One day we shall succeed."

"I took Betsa's collar for you, but they took it away from me at the barracks."

He said nothing. I said awkwardly: "I'm sorry about Betsa. She was a good dog."

"The best I had."

"She saved our lives."

"Yes."

"Poor Betsa."

"She was a good dog. Better you try and get some sleep."

"I wonder where this truck's going?"

"To Braca, perhaps."

"Braca?"

"Braca del Mar. A fishing village on the coast. It is not too far, now."

"How long to daybreak?"

He looked at his watch.

"Twenty minutes to three. Another three hours."

"If this truck's going all the way . . ."

"Yes, I know. In one hour we shall be there."

"About time we had some luck."

Trenko said solemnly: "This night we have had more than our share of luck. Without it, my friend, you would not be here now. You would be in one of their cellars, with Colonel Weber."

I noticed his use of the army rank. It was as though the army epitomized his hatred of the regime. My own loathing for Weber was more personal. I told Trenko about the barbed-wire stick I had seen. I told him too of another little thing I had noticed. Lying there with the cold night air under the dark friendliness of the sky, the revolting picture was coming into its proper perspective, no longer distorted by

147

immediate fear. I told Trenko that I had seen him, Weber, standing by the door to the other room when it opened, listening impassively to the screams that came from inside. And when the policeman, grinning obscenely, had said: "Why do I always get the ugly ones? She's as ugly as sin...."

I swear that, at that moment, Weber had been about to go into the room and see what was being done to her. And, when he heard the words of the grinning policeman, he had changed his mind and decided it wasn't worth while. It was a small thing, but it was part of the picture. I told Trenko about that too. He said nothing, but stared gloomily into the night. Then he put out his hand and touched my shoulder, and he said:

"Colonel Carlo San-Verde Weber . . . One day, my friend, he will pay the price for these things."

He fell morosely silent again, and I dozed for a little while, listening to the rumble of the motor, lying sprawled out exhausted on a bed of watermelons, then fell fretfully asleep. When I awoke, a long narrow building was flashing past us, and I felt Trenko's urgent hand on my arm. He was sitting up and looking along the road.

He whispered: "Braca del Mar. We are lucky."

"What time is it?"

"Half past three."

"And it's the coast?"

"Yes. If we are still lucky . . . before it is light we shall be far out to sea. But first, we must jump. It is a little fast, I think."

Fast? That damned truck was doing forty miles an hour, trying to get in for the early-morning market. We leaped over the side together, and I rolled over on my back and let the momentum carry me along like a sack of flour. The gravel surface ripped at my face and my hands, and the road struck me a cruel blow on the side of the head, but in a moment I had rolled into the grassy ditch and hit the muddy bottom with an awful whack.

It knocked the breath out of me, and, as I lay there coughing, Trenko came over and stood above me, grinning down at me and telling me to keep quiet. He crouched down and held out a hand, squatting on his haunches, and, as I clambered to my feet, he said softly: "We must hurry. We do not have very much time."

"Can we find a boat? Have you got friends here?"

He shook his head.

"We have very few sympathizers down here. They are too far from our territory. We must steal."

Again, there was that impressive, tight-lipped dignity when he said "We must steal."

"What about the police? Will they be looking for us down here?"

His face was grim.

"They will be looking for us here. And everywhere. But if we can get a boat . . . the frontier is only twelve miles along the coast, and beyond that we can land. There we shall be safe. For a little while."

"Know where we can find a boat?"

"At the wharf there will be the police. But there are some places . . . a little to the north of town. . . ."

"North? Well, that's a good direction, anyway."

We walked quickly through the village. There were one or two early risers about, fishermen for the most part, going down to the beach with their nets, but they paid us no attention.

It was not surprising. In my grubby clothes, and with a long stubble of beard on my chin, I looked exactly like one of them. Trenko made no effort at concealment. But one thing he did say: "Get ready to run. Always be ready for running."

We saw a police patrol, once, three men together, in dark gray uniforms carrying rifles, but we swung quickly round a corner and they did not see us. We came to the beach and Trenko took a couple of small round nets from the sticks on which they were strung out to dry, and we walked brazenly along the sand, carrying them over our shoulders. Some of the fishermen were already at work, standing thigh-deep in the surf and casting in slow and rhythmic movements. And already the first red streaks of dawn were showing in the sky.

We came at last to a small jetty that stuck out for a hundred feet or so into the ocean. We clambered over it quickly, and walked past it, keeping a sharp lookout for any patrols, and then came back and clambered over it again, looking some more without seeing anything to cause us alarm.

Not stopping, Trenko said quietly: "I think there is no one here. The last boat . . . the one with the single mast."

We turned, now, and walked along to the end of the jetty. The silence was unbearable. It was the last moment of acute danger, and once this was behind us . . .

The boat was a small one, with a Bermuda rig, one of those raked-masted vessels that handle so easily. It had a sprit instead of a boom, but there was a big outboard motor behind it that augured well for a speedy getaway. There were several other boats tied up alongside it, but this was the one that had caught Trenko's expert eye.

He said softly: "See anybody?"

I shook my head.

"Not a sign of life anywhere."

"The fishermen down the beach?"

"Too far off to worry us."

"Keep a good lookout. As soon as I start the motor, jump in."

"O.K."

He had already slithered aboard and was checking that the tiller was in position and the centerboard down, and loosening the ropes that tied her to the wharf.

There was an adobe shack on the beach by the jetty, and I was watching it with an apprehensive eye. I just could not believe that it would be so easy. . . . Trenko had the rope coiled round the starter, and he was looking up at me excitedly, his eyes gleaming in the half-light. He said: "Ready?"

I nodded and the motor roared out, coughed, spluttered and fell silent. I heard Trenko curse softly, and saw him winding the rope again. For the second time the engine failed to start. He was swearing volubly now, but the third time it caught and held. He shouted: "Jump in! Quickly . . ." and I slipped off the wharf and into the boat. He swung the tiller over and the craft shot forward and then stopped with a sickening thud that threw us off our feet and sent us floundering in the bottom helplessly. I saw him staring in wonderment behind us, and then I saw what it was; there was a padlocked chain that fastened the boat to the side of the jetty.

We should have known it, of course, so small a thing . . . a rusty padlock . . . It caused us so much trouble and heartbreak when we were almost free. It was no good trying to hide our movements now. Trenko pulled out an oar and thrust it down between the gunwale and the jetty, and we both threw our weight against it, trying to pull the staple out of the rotting timbers. Behind us, on shore, there was a commotion in the shack, and Trenko yelled, "Now . . . pull . . ." I tugged at that damned oar as though my life depended on it. Which it did, of course.

The chain pulled free suddenly, and the boat swung round with its propeller, and Trenko nearly went overboard, and I looked up beyond him and there was a policeman running down the wharf toward us, struggling into his jacket and lugging a submachine gun at the same time; if it had not been so desperate it would have been comical, the way he was worrying about his uniform, as if it were essential that he be properly dressed for what he was about to do. He was a matter of thirty or forty feet away from us and I stood rooted with a sort of sudden shock, and, as I watched, two more men, fishermen, came running out of the shack, screaming at us, and the policeman was shouting *"Alto! Alto!"* and Trenko was yelling at me at the same time, something about "In my way . . ."

The policeman slung his gun round and started firing, wildly, flustered by a situation he was not sure how to handle. I dropped to the bottom of the boat, getting mixed up with some rope and Trenko's thrashing legs, and I heard the bullets smacking into the timber with an ugly, frightening sound, and then Trenko had his revolver free and was taking aim, with the long barrel close alongside my face. When the shot went off, the sudden explosion of it nearly blew my eardrums out, and then he fired again, and once again. I saw the policeman double up like a collapsed dummy and fall to the ground, with his gun still firing and the bullets thudding into the wharf, smacking into the side of the boat, splashing into the water. . . . The gun was running away with his finger still clenched tightly round the trigger, and I saw the trail the bullets were making in the water as they cut across toward us.

There was another sound in my ear, close beside me, a horrible sound that was like a madwoman's screaming, and I knew in that dreadful moment of clarity that it came from Trenko.

The boat was slewing round out of control, and I pushed the tiller over and tried to reach him at the same time. It was an awful moment. I knew how badly he had been hurt, and as the boat shot away from the jetty I dropped the tiller again and bent down over him. He stopped his screaming suddenly, and his eyes rolled up and I thought he was dead, but his arms moved convulsively and clutched at his stomach, and then some dark blood started pumping out of his mouth, and he tried to say something, the words spluttering horribly.

He said: "Out . . . out to sea . . . to sea . . . to sea . . ."

He kept saying "To sea . . ." over and over again, and I pulled him straight in the bottom of the boat and wound a rope quickly round the tiller as best I could, and then pulled open his jacket. . . . His bare stomach was a bloody mess where the bullets had cut across him, and I found it hard to speak, not knowing what to say and not knowing what to do. . . . What could I do?

In the cold early morning, in a speeding boat that was cutting through the swelling water like a wild thing, with the white tops of the waves splashing over us and a dying man lying in six inches of dirty salt water . . . The sound of his screams had stopped, but they were carved deeply into my mind.

I headed the boat into the waves and tightened up the rope around the tiller. When she was steady, I crouched down beside him and took his hand and I said: "What can I do, Trenko? What can I do? Tell me what to do?"

My voice sounded as though it came from someone else, and I knew that I was shaking.

For a long time he did not answer. Whether it was the pain, or that he was in a coma, I shall never know. Then his eyes opened again, and he looked at me and he almost smiled. His face was white and drawn, and he looked once at his bloody hands and then put them back to his stomach. He said hoarsely, his voice hardly more than a whisper:

"You can do nothing, my friend. You can do nothing."

I said desperately: "Can I . . . can I land you somewhere? Can we do that? A doctor . . . some help of some sort . . . I don't know what to do. Tell me, Trenko. Tell me what to do. . . ."

His head rolled sideways as if he were trying to shake it and could not control the movement. I could hardly hear the whisper. He said: "Go north. . . . In three, four hours . . . go north until midday; you will be safe. . . ." His face was screwed up tightly with the pain. I saw then that he was dying, and in the moment of helpless anguish that came with this knowledge I knew also that there was only one thing I could say.

I put my hand on his cheek and said: "Maria-Anna, old friend. Maria-Anna."

He nodded then, a twisted, jerky nod, and his eyes clouded for a moment and then closed, and he was quiet and still for a moment.

Then he looked at me and said slowly: "Yes . . . Maria-Anna. You are a good man, Michael. Maria-Anna. Maria-Anna."

It was an almost inaudible whisper. The boat started rocking violently and he grimaced horribly. I turned to the tiller quickly and thrust it over so that we cut deeply into the waves, and she steadied up, and when I turned back to him he said once more: "Maria-Anna. Maria-Anna."

And then he was dead.

I sat there, then, leaning into the tiller, staring at his crumpled body with the water gently lapping about it, feeling a great emptiness inside me, watching the way the blood had, mixed with the water that swirled about there, looking at his tightly clenched hands, hoping that the policeman who had killed him was dead too, and knowing that there was no comfort in this angry, bitter hope.

I felt too that there was a—how shall I put it?—a rounding off of the Trenko episode. When I had first met him, he had been lying in the gutter, cut down by bullets, and I had pulled him away into the shadows. The shadows had never left him, and now, once more, he was lying there in the half-light with bilge water sucking the useless blood out of him and his dead hands clutching at the ugly wounds in his stomach. The life was gone from him, and I knew that part of my own life had gone too.

I could not bear to look at his face.

chapter 10

The sun beat mercilessly down on the small craft and my throat was parched and dry.

I ran a hand over the stubble on my chin, wondering how long it would be before I'd be able to shave again; I would have given my soul for a canteen of water.

Long ago, I had cut the motor and was using only the sail, which billowed out splendidly from the sprit; under other circumstances I would have felt a certain relish at the way the small craft was handling in a stiff breeze that whipped the tops of the waves and sent her hurtling north at a hell of a lick. The sea was not too rough, but she was not built for open waters, and it was all I could do to keep her headed into the swell. I had encountered one or two fishing vessels during the morning, and once I thought I saw a patrol boat, but it passed me by harmlessly a long way off. I already knew what to do if I should find myself being chased; I was going to open up the motor and run with the wind, heading straight for the broken, craggy shore in the hope that with the centerboard up I could find shelter in the treacherous waters of the shallow rocky shelf that ran along under the cliffs and where no bigger boat would dare trespass.

But no one bothered me. For all they knew, I could have been an innocent helmsman out for a day's spin under the sun.

There's something inspiring about a sailing boat in a good wind and deep water. The wind had a freshness to it that was somehow clean after the frightful events that had preceded the flight from Volvoda, and the harsh tragedy of Trenko's death.

Poor Trenko . . . He was a truly fine fellow. The cause he fought for was an obsession, and there was some slight comfort in the thought that he could never have expected to die in any other fashion than from a police bullet. And his slaying of the policeman had gained me some time; I knew the fishermen would soon report what had happened, but it would not be so fast nor so efficient a report as that which would have come from the policeman himself. They would know, of course, that I had gone north, because no one in his right mind would try the long haul south along their coast, and in any case it would have meant driving slowly into the wind.

No, I was quite sure they knew which way I was going, and I kept a weather eye open for anything that didn't look like an innocent fishing vessel. Fortunately, there were a good number of yachts about, just like this one, and if they had to investigate every single one of them . . .

I do not know how long I had sat at the tiller there, afraid to look at Trenko's face or to touch his dead body. It was a long, long time. But at last I had secured the rudder and buried him.

Buried? Is that the right word? I had waited for more than an hour because the idea of bundling him over the gunwale somehow smacked of indecency. There could be no elaborate ritual, no consigning to the waters, no flag-draped body. . . . I could do no more than lift him bodily up and drop him overboard, and the thought of this unseemliness was almost more than I could bear. But I knew it had to be done.

Finally, I compromised. I said a sort of prayer first, mumbling a little and feeling awkward about it, but halfway through I realized that I was not impressing anyone, not even myself, so I gave it up and spoke to him instead, just as though he could hear every word I said. I told him that he had been a good friend to me, that he had not died for nothing, that he was going to join Maria-Anna in whatever corner of heaven may be reserved for rebels, that I would never forget him; and then all this seemed foolish too, and I lifted him up, cold and stiff and soggy and somehow ugly, and slid him as gently as I could into the water.

I had not fastened the tiller too well, and the boat was slewing round into the wind, so that for a little while his body stayed with us and bumped against the bottom of the boat as though he were still trying to nudge me in the right direction; as though, even after death, his one concern were to fulfill the task he had been given—to look after me and see that I did not fall into their hands. I watched him for a while, letting the sadness seep into me, and then I swung the craft north again and left him far behind me, a brown bundle swaying up and down with every movement of the waves. I found that my cheeks were wet and knew that I had been crying, and I let the tears come for no other reason than that I could no longer stifle them. But, at last, the bobbing speck had disappeared and it was at this moment that I saw the launch way off to the east that made me come to my senses again and begin running for the shore.

But the alarm passed, and the sleek launch kept her direction, and by the time I was back on course myself the immediate anguish over Trenko had condensed itself into the dull ache of sorrow.

By midday, which Trenko had told me would be the limit of danger, I was close inshore again, sailing under the high cliffs and looking for a place to land. I knew that I had long passed the frontier, and that I was well within the territorial waters of a friendly state, and, in spite of the tragic events of the past, the future was imposing itself upon me with a great deal of satisfaction. I knew that I had come through a terrible ordeal by the grace of God and the skin of my teeth; that I had emerged from those frightful events unharmed and with the knowledge that what we had set out to do had been achieved; that the operation had succeeded in spite of the most fearful dangers. I tried hard not to think of the money that was waiting for me, my share of the profits and my recompense for the fears I had suffered. But I could not entirely dismiss it from my mind, try as I might. There was too much of it, and too much that could be done with it.

I started making plans. Daydreaming, watching the waves slip by, I was in Paris again, with Madeleine beside me, and then on the steep sandy mountainsides of Sicily, admiring the vast panorama of the empty hills and listening to the pleasant sound of the sheep bells in the distance. And in Athens, feeling with my fingertips the subtle smooth texture of those huge white stones on the Acropolis that seem to breathe with an uncanny life, deriving almost as much sensual pleasure from the touch of them as there was in Madeleine's own white skin that was so eerily like them. What was it she had said to me as I left?

"I will be here when you return, *mon amour.*"

The thought that I was on my way to her drove away all thoughts of tragedy or sorrow and left me with a feeling of overpowering excitement.

I headed into the little bay just as the sun was hitting the water.

It was a coaling station, and I did not even know its name. There were four or five big ships tied up there, freighters all of them, and as I sailed among them, waiting for some petty customs or immigration official to come out in his motorboat and ask me what the devil I was doing, I wondered how I could explain my absence of papers. No passport . . . no money . . . no harbor clearance . . .

But the problem solved itself. I hit the small wharf between two dirty freighters, and jumped up onto the oily wooden planks. No one bothered me. There were no police, no guards. I began to realize that I had already become accustomed to that fear of the police that is the hallmark of the rebel.

There was a harbor rat sitting on an upturned box in the long gray shadow of a warehouse, a *cholo* with a broad-brimmed hat thrust to the back of his head and his wizened face deeply lined and pock-marked. I walked over to him and said: "Where are we, *amigo?*"

He opened his drowsy eyes and looked at me as though wondering how much money he could get from me. He took off his hat and scratched his head, and put it back on again and said: "Marena."

"Good."

"Where do you come from, Señor?"

"Down south. What's going north?"

He jerked his head at a grubby tug that was tied up close by. It was a Panamanian vessel. I said: "What about the others?"

He jerked his head again as if it was too much effort to take his hands from his pockets and point.

"That one there. The French one."

"Oh? When does she sail?"

He grinned at me owlishly.

"Yesterday. She is one day late already."

"Good. God take care of you."

As I started to walk away he called out, whining: "A long time I do not eat, Señor."

"You and me both, brother."

I walked along the wharf to where the French ship was tied up. She was the *Solange*, out of Marseille. It felt like going home again. I went over the narrow gangplank and asked the hand there where the skipper was. I spoke in French, and he clapped me on the back and asked me what *le diable* a Frenchman was doing in this Godforsaken hole. I told him I was trying to get out of it, and he grinned and pointed to the companionway and told me to see the first mate.

It is a funny thing about Frenchmen. They're the same the world over. It's enough to talk French and they're on your side at once. The mate was a shriveled-up little man with scars all over his wiry arms, and he wore one of those comic striped T-shirts that fit tight to the torso, with a scarf round his scraggy neck and a cap pushed to the back of his skull. He was sitting in his cabin with his feet up on the bunk, drinking wine out of a bottle. I told him I wanted to go north, to Venezuela if possible, and what about it?

He stared at me for a moment, took another swig out of his bottle and passed it across to me. I drank greedily and he said: "Where are you from, *mon ami?*"

"Paris."

"Ah . . . Paris. Nothing but mackerels on board."

When someone calls a Marseillaise a "mackerel" it means only one thing—he's from Parris. I was halfway home already. He said: "Passenger? Or are you looking for a job?"

"Whichever's easier."

"Seaman's Union?"

"No papers."

He raised his eyebrows, then, and said sharply: "And the police? Are they looking for you?"

"No."

"Passport?"

"No papers."

"Money?"

"Nothing."

"*Ça alors . . .*"

"It's a wonderful phrase. It means "So that's it" and you can take it from there.

He switched the subject and started talking about Paris, and I knew he was trying to find out if I was a nice guy or not. We talked for more than an hour, and he broke out two more bottles of wine, and I knew that my passage was secured.

He grumbled when I told him I knew nothing about seaman's work, and muttered something about the uselessness of landlubbers, and then the captain came aboard and I was introduced and we had a good many more drinks, and before long I was incapably drunk. I had not eaten for a long, long time, and the heavy wine went straight to my legs. I remember hearing the captain say: "And how's he going to get ashore at La Guaira?"

The mate had shrugged his shoulders in that beautiful French fashion that means "who cares?" and then I felt someone roll me bodily onto a bunk, and I just let the sleepiness overcome me and thought no more about it.

And when I awoke, we were under way and far out to sea.

I staggered on deck, feeling the rolling of the ship in the heavy swell, and found my way to the wheelhouse.

My friend the mate was there, grinning at me and not asking questions, and I left well enough alone and merely thanked him for the party the night before. He asked if I was hungry and when I told him how long it was since I had eaten he nodded wisely as if he had known this all along, and sent me down to the galley for a meal. I filled my stomach, then, with good hard bread and a hunk of rich cheese, with an onion thrown in for good measure and a mug of coarse red wine to wash it all down. And, when I went back to the wheelhouse to ask what I could do to earn my keep, the friendly mate shook his head and told me he was always glad to help a fellow Parisian. When I insisted, he shrugged his shoulders eloquently and said if I could find anything to do . . . provided I didn't get in anybody's way . . .

I went below and helped one of the crew swab the decks, and then someone gave me a paintbrush and a can of rust remover, and I went to work on some of the jobs that had needed doing for a hundred years. It was merely a matter of relief, I think, at being able to behave like a reasonable man again. I felt that I had to employ my hands, and I scrubbed at that damned rust with a wire brush until the metalwork shone like new. I knew that it wouldn't last long, that it wasn't important; but I needed the relief that came with senseless work.

The journey took two days. I lived with the crew, and slept on the spare bunk in the mate's quarters. I ate like a horse, and someone handed me out a pair of drill pants and a clean shirt, and by the time we steamed into the welcome harbor of La Guaira I was a new man. The hunger had gone, and the fear had gone too, and, as I had scrubbed the filth and the lice from my body, the pain of all that I had left behind me was no more than a memory.

As we tied up, the mate asked the same question again: "How will you get ashore, *mon ami?*"

I said: "You've done a great deal for me. Can I get a seaman's card?"

He laughed then, a great guffaw that burst out of his shriveled body like a thunderclap. I knew what it was that amused him: I wasn't exactly his idea of a good seaman. But he rummaged through a drawer, and came up with a dog-eared card that would do to show the policeman at the dock gates. Once ashore, I knew, I'd soon straighten things out at the American Consulate. I was already dreaming up likely stories to account for the loss of my papers. I went ashore.

The first man I saw on the dock was 'Arry.

He was standing on the wharf at the foot of the gangway, neat and dapper and looking like a gigolo in a clean white suit. A tremendous excitement welled up inside me, not because of 'Arry, because, to tell the truth, I never liked him very much, but simply because it meant I was home again.

I pumped his hand up and down and said: "It's good to see you.... How's everybody?"

His sly face was cold and unwelcoming. He said: "Good to see you, Mike.... Brother, the trouble you've given us."

"How's that?"

"All the boys out looking for you."

I stared at him and began to stammer something, and he said quickly: "Well, this ain't the healthiest spot to stand around in. Let's get going."

I said: "But . . . but . . . what's all the trouble about?"

"All the boys out looking for you," he said again. "Pedro's out at the airport, meeting every plane; Rafael's at the railway station.... Brother, Digger's really laying on an operation."

"But . . . but in God's name, what for? What's happening?"

He took hold of my arm and pulled me away. He said: "Let's get on the phone to Digger."

He would say no more until we had found a telephone. My heart was beating fast again, but I could not for the life of me relate his concern with the events I had left behind me. It just didn't make sense. But he would not answer my questions. He just dragged me along with him, quickly, secretly, urgently, and when we squeezed into the phone box and called Digger's number, he said: "I've found him, Digger. Came in by ship."

He passed me the receiver, and I said irritably: "Digger! What the hell's all this about?"

His voice was full of concern. He said: "Mike . . . All kinds of things are happening. 'Arry will bring you right around. Keep out of sight."

"But . . . but what's it all about, for God's sake?"

"Lots of jokers looking for you, Mike. Keep out of sight until you've seen me. Come round right away. I'll tell you all about it."

He rang off and I dialed my own apartment. 'Arry was trying to urge me away from the lighted phone box, but I pushed his restraining hand away angrily and listened to the ringing of the phone at the other end. I said: "What time is it?

'Arry twisted his wrist round and looked at his watch. He always wore it strapped on the wrong way round.

"Just after midnight."

"Madeleine's not answering the phone."

He said nothing and I shook him by the arm and said angrily: "What the devil's it all about, 'Arry?"

He shook his head, then, and said slowly: "I don't know, Mike. Honest, I don't. Let's go and see Digger."

I put back the phone and we drove over in 'Arry's beat-up jalopy. We were silent, and morose, and worried. We drove down the alleyway past the bar and went round the back where there was an outside stairway leading up to Digger's quarters upstairs. I saw that 'Arry looked anxiously around before we climbed up. I was getting angrier every minute.

Digger and Rosa were waiting for us in the bedroom. I knew that it must be serious if Rosa had left the cash register at a time when the bar was beginning to get crowded. She flung her enormous arms round my neck and kissed me like a long-lost son, and Digger shook hands solemnly and said: "All right, Mike, let's get down to business."

"Business? For crissake, what the hell's going on?"

Rosa plumped her huge weight on the bed and said: "Where you been, Mike? What you been doing, eh?"

"Why? What's this all about?"

Digger was pouring out some brandy. He said slowly: "All kinds of people have been asking for you, chum. It looks like you're in trouble."

I could feel my heart pounding hard. I said stupidly: "Trouble?"

"You know about your friend Vallance?"

My throat was suddenly dry. I said: "Go on."

"He's dead, chum. Did you know that?"

"No, I didn't know that."

There was a horrible tingling sensation at the back of my scalp. I said: "Here? Here in Caracas?"

"Yeah. Three days ago. They picked him off the rocks down on the beach."

"Drowned?"

"That's what they thought. But there was an autopsy. His stomach was full of poison."

I knew then that it could mean only one thing. Almost in a daze, I heard myself asking: "Cyanide? Cyanide of potassium?"

Digger's heavy eyebrows shot up.

"How did you know that?"

"Oh . . . it's one of those things. People in Vallance's business carry it, in little phials. Under the tongue sometimes. It's an easy way out."

"And a lot of strangers in town have been looking for you."

I could do no more than stare at him and wait. He went on: "I don't know what it's all about, Mike. Maybe I'm putting two and two together and making a dozen. But a copper came in the bar looking for you, and I told him you'd gone away, and I didn't know where to. Then, the next day, this little fat joker comes in, early in the morning, and starts asking the same questions."

I swear I almost fainted with sudden fright. I heard myself saying: "What . . . what did he look like?"

"Little fat joker. Spoke Spanish with a hell of an accent, sounded like a Czech or a Russian or something."

"German?"

"Could be. You know who it is?"

"Yes. I know who it is. Go on."

"Well, he sat there at the bar drinking Coca-Cola, and, you know how it is, I never trust a bastard who drinks soft in a bar, and he started asking where he could find you, said he was a friend of yours from San Antonio. Well, I know as well as the next man about all the trouble there is down there, and with this guy nursing a soft drink . . . Well, I told him to go to hell. Then he came out into the open. He laid a big fat wad of currency on the counter, Mike, and said: 'Take it. Tell me where he is and take it.'

"I told him to go to hell again, and he looked at me and tried to smile, you know how it is . . . some men, it just ain't natural to smile; he emptied all the cash out of his pockets onto the bar, and he said his time cost too much money to fool around. I tell you, Mike, there was a lot of the folding stuff there. That's when I sent the boys out looking for you. They don't spend that sort of money just to find friends."

I said: "Digger . . . Where's Madeleine?"

He exchanged glances with Rosa, then, and poured himself another brandy, waiting for her to tell me. Rosa laid a huge hand on my knee and said: "We don't know, Mike. We don't know where she's at. First thing after this man go, I say to Digger, you get round to Mike's apartment and get that girl outa there. Maybe they make some trouble for her."

"So I went round," Digger said quickly, "but she wasn't there. I spoke to the landlady, and she said she'd gone out on a job somewhere. I don't know, some modeling job."

He looked away awkwardly as though this were a euphemism for something else. I said steadily: "It was a modeling job, Digger. Nothing else."

"Sure, Mike, sure. I didn't mean anything."

"Go on."

"Well, we've called the apartment a dozen times since then. But nobody answers."

"Have you been round there?"

"Sure. I went round three or four times. This little fat joker's there, Mike. Got a couple of other men there with him, strangers by the looks of it. At least, I never seen either of them around before."

"Did you call the modeling agency?"

He shook his head.

"Didn't think of it, Mike. Come to that I don't think I know who she works for."

"If she's gone away somewhere . . . I don't know where the hell it could be. We've got to find her, Digger. We've got to find her before Weber does."

"Weber?"

"The little fat bastard."

I took the telephone book and looked up the man who ran the modeling agency. When I called him, at his house, he was sleepy and angry at being disturbed at one o'clock in the morning. I cut short his protests and asked him where Madeleine had gone. He told me she'd gone over to Maracaibo on a publicity job for one of the oil companies there.

The fear drained out of me and I felt a sudden elation. I said cheerfully: "Good . . . So that's all right. When's she due back in Caracas?"

He said: "She came back this evening. Now, do you mind if I get back to sleep?"

He hung up on me and left me holding the receiver, staring at it as though it were responsible for the news that had come from its coldly inanimate body. The terror was creeping up on me again. I said to Digger: "I'm going round there. She came back this evening"

Digger looked at Rosa and then back at me. He said slowly: "All right, Mike. I don't want to ask too many questions, but . . . You remember once you asked me about a guy called DeBries?"

"Well?"

"Is this . . . is this one of his capers?"

"It was. DeBries is dead."

Digger looked embarrassed. He said: "You're on your own, Mike. I suppose you know that?"

"So I'm on my own."

"It's not that I'm scared or anything. . . . But that monkey's tied up with . . . Well, it just isn't healthy to mess around in the things he gets involved in. It's common knowledge, Mike, all over town. You won't find anybody's going to help you if you're in one of DeBries' kettles of fish."

Then Rosa did an astonishing thing. She pushed her great weight up off the bed and waddled over to where Digger was standing, and gave him a great clout across the ear. I was too astonished to do anything but stare. She said sharply: "You go with Mike, Digger. You go along with him."

I have never seen a man look so awkward. He stood there like a chastised schoolboy for a moment, and then he drank his brandy down with a gulp and said, rubbing his ear: "Sure, Rosa, sure, anything you say. You're the boss."

"Is right," she said. "And you not forgetting it, either."

She waddled over to the ancient mahogany wardrobe that

stood in the corner of the room and took a revolver from the bottom drawer. I was surprised to see her check it expertly, and then she slipped in a full clip of shells and handed it to me.

"Better you take this," she said. "If Digger take it, he gonna get hurt. You got more sense."

I nodded at her and we went outside into the cold darkness. As we went down the stairway, Digger said unhappily: "I'd have come along if you'd asked me, you know that."

"Sure, Digger. Sure."

"Well, so I would. But we better take it canny. Too many of your friends getting killed. DeBries too, you said?"

"Yes. They shot him. Thought he was a dog called Betsa."

Digger looked at me and said nothing. I told him about Trenko too. I thought he'd better know that we were playing for keeps.

We drove over to the apartment in Digger's Chevy, and drove past it twice to see if there was any sign of Weber. I knew precisely what I would do if he was there. I was going to shoot at once, and the hell with the consequences. He was certain to be armed, and I could plead self-defense. I told Digger about it and he nodded miserably and said: "That Rosa. She'll be the death of me yet."

I knew that I could count on Digger.

We went up to the apartment and stood outside the door listening. I rang the bell and pounded on the door, but there was no reply. I called out "Madeleine . . . Madeleine," several times, feeling the urgency mounting with each unanswered call, feeling the fear for her like a spasm of pain in the pit of my stomach.

We went downstairs again, and I hammered on the door of the janitor's room, and, when it opened, his wife was there, a little old woman who looked like a witch. Behind her, I could see the janitor playing cards with three other old men. I pushed inside, followed by Digger, and the janitor got to his feet and touched his forehead. I said: "Where's the girl I left in my apartment?"

He grinned at me stupidly.

"She went out, Señor Mike."

"When?"

"Little while ago."

"Oh? Then she got back? From Maracaibo?"

"I don't know, Señor Mike. She come back from someplace, this evening, seven o'clock, but she go out again."

"Alone?"

"No, Señor. Friend of yours go with her."

I felt my blood running cold. I knew that my face was white. I said: "A friend of mine?"

"Yes, Señor. A very fat gentleman who has been here looking for you. She go with him."

He was actually chuckling, tickled pink by my distress. He said: "One of those things, Señor Mike. . . . But there are many other pretty women, no? When you are my age, you know that you must not leave a pretty woman. . . ."

I do not know what came over me. I stepped up to him and hit him hard on the mouth with all the strength I had. He fell down and lay there on the floor, spitting out a broken tooth, clutching at his spectacles, a white-haired old man cruelly beaten. The other old men at the table stood up quickly, pushing back their chairs, standing there frightened by the sudden violence, and the wife too stood there unmoving, not helping her husband, staring at me in shock. I felt Digger's hand on my arm, and I looked down at the janitor, eighty years old if he was a day, watching him fumble for his broken glasses, not sure what had happened to him.

I cannot describe the shame I felt. I bent down and helped him to his feet. I could feel him trembling; he did not weigh more than a hundred pounds, and his bones were thin and almost bare of flesh. I mumbled: "I'm . . . I'm sorry. . . . Forgive me. . . . Don't know what . . . I'm sorry. . . ."

What can you say? A man old enough to be your grandfather . . . a delicate structure of skeleton almost at the end of its life? My blow could have killed him. I said again: "I'm sorry . . . truly sorry. It's just that . . . Tell me what happened. Tell me about this man who came for her. . . . "

He wasn't a bad old stick He used to come up sometimes and run errands for me, fetch cigarettes or newspapers when I was too lazy to go out. I always paid him well, and sometimes I slipped him a bottle of gin when times were good.

He stood there trembling, looking at the others from time to time as they stood in a silently reproachful circle round me. He said hesitantly:

"This man came, Señor . . . to look for you. He told me he was a friend of yours and he asked me where you were. I told him I did not know and he wanted the key to the apartment, and I gave it to him because he was your friend."

He would not look at me, and I knew that Weber had paid him for the key and for his silence. I wondered how much he had been given. He went on: "And then, when the lady came back . . . He went out with her."

His voice trailed off and he started coughing again. Digger silently passed him a handkerchief, and the janitor dabbed at the blood on his mouth with it. I said hoarsely: "Where . . . where did they go?"

"I do not know, Señor. She got into his car and they drove away. I do not know where they went."

I sat down, then, and buried my face in my hands. I knew just what had happened. Madeleine had arrived at the apartment and found Weber there and he had said:

"I am a friend of Michael Benasque's, Mademoiselle. He will arrive on the plane from San Antonio, and I thought you would like to meet him? My car is at your disposal. . . ."

I said: "Where? Where in Caracas? A town this size . . ."

I felt Digger's hand on my shoulder again, and I got up to leave. The old men were still standing there silent and reproving. Hardly conscious of what I was saying, I told the old janitor I would make all this up to him. I told him I was sorry again, knowing that I was only talking to prevent a complete breakdown.

He nodded his old head, still unsmiling, still dabbing at his mouth with Digger's handkerchief.

We stood outside for a moment, feeling the cold of the night, leaning against the scarred brickwork of the building, wondering what to do next. Wondering if it was worth while even thinking about it.

Digger said gently: "You'd better come back to my place, Mike. Maybe Rosa can think of something."

"No . . . No. I'll stay here. Maybe . . . maybe if I stay in the apartment . . . if I put all the lights on . . . they'll know I'm there."

"They won't be watching any more."

"Maybe. But if they are . . . they'll find me and let her go."

"I don't think so, Mike."

"Get the key from the old man, Digger, will you? Please?"

He hesitated a bit, awkwardly fidgeting, and then went inside again. He was gone a long time, and when he came back he silently handed me the key. Not looking at him, I said: "See you in the morning?"

"Sure. Maybe Rosa will think of something."

"I'll be in the apartment."

"O.K."

I turned and left him and ran up the stairs, feeling the need to get into my rooms before I broke down. I went straight to the bedroom and threw myself on the bed, which was still sweet with the scent of her, and I cried like a baby. I felt the spasms of hysteria rising inside me and I let them come, and when they had passed I switched on all the lights and turned on the radio loud, and I took a shower and lay down on the empty bed dry-eyed in the last depths of despair.

Why had they taken her? Why?

Did they think I was back in Caracas and hiding out? Would I have left her there if that were so? Did they think that a threat to her would bring me out from under? Or was it . . .? I thought I could see the way his mind was working. She was a girl, and helpless, and she was close enough to me to permit at least a possibility that she might know where to find me. And such a possibility was all he would require. Life was cheap to the Webers. If she could tell him nothing and died in the process, then what was the loss of a life?

I knew the suppressed excitement she would feel, sliding softly across the seat of his car, ready to meet the man who loved her, ready to start a new sort of life that perhaps she had always wanted. Knowing nothing, unsuspecting . . . It was foolish enough to drive off like that, with a stranger, but how should she know? What could she suspect of the terrors that boiled inside the brain of a man like Weber?

And now? In a city of nearly a million people, where should I start looking? I knew she would be waiting for me to come and save her from whatever agony she was in, that her trust in me . . .

I felt the tears coming again.

chapter 11

I do not know how long I lay there. The radio was blazing a modern composition of brasses and strings from the all-night station on top of the hill, a nerve-shattering cacophony that somehow fitted the dark mood of desperation that was on me.

I got up after a while and went downstairs, leaving the bright lights of the apartment still burning so that *they*, wherever they were, should know that I was there waiting for them. I walked up and down outside in the darkness, hoping that someone, *anyone,* was still watching the house. But after a couple of hours I knew that I was wasting my time. They were gone.

I walked round to Digger's place, climbed up the back stairway and banged on the door there. It was opened by Lala, the dark-skinned girl, who was sleeping in the room next to Digger and Rosa's. I pushed past her and started for the bedroom door, but she stopped me and said: "He is not there, Michael. He went out."

She was wearing one of Digger's old dressing gowns, and it hung long on her slight figure, and trailed on the floor. Fiddling with the arms, trying to turn them up, she said: "Only Rosa is here. You want to see her?"

I nodded and knocked on the door. I heard the creaking of the bedsprings as she turned her huge weight over and then she sleepily called out: "Well? Who is it?"

I said: "It's me. Mike."

"Come on in, Mike. Come in."

She was sitting up in the middle huge bed, dressed in an old-fashioned woolen nightgown, and spreading monstrously in all directions. Her hair, which was pretty ragged at the best of times, was in tight curlers, and there was grease all over her huge cheeks. The reading lamp beside the bed was just a bare bulb on a chipped ceramic stand. She said, grimacing: "I thought you come here soon. You got plenty bad news, Michael."

"What are we going to do, Rosa?"

"I dunno. Digger go out to round up some of the boys; maybe they find her. You want to tell me what you been doing down there? In San Antonio? Maybe will help."

I sat on the edge of the bed then, and told her almost all of it. I told her that DeBries had wanted me to help smuggle a man out of the country. I told her about Vallance, and about Trenko, and about Weber and the barracks where the ugly woman was screaming herself to death, and about the policeman who was grinning stupidly as he swung his barbed-wire stick while he complained because she wasn't pretty. . . . I did not tell her about Lazlo. I did not say that we had smuggled the man back in again. I merely said that he was what they called down there an enemy of the people. She listened without interruption, and when I had finished she leaned over and thumped the wall with her gigantic fist, and, when the door opened and Lala came in, pulling Digger's robe on, she sent her down to the kitchen to make some coffee.

She scratched at her tremendous stomach, and rubbed a hand over her greasy face, and said: "Four o'clock. Only for you I get up at four o'clock."

"I don't know what to do, Rosa. I left the lights on in the apartment. I figured if they were still watching the place . . ."

"I know. But no good they find you, Michael. We gotta find them. Is different, no?"

"I guess so. But how, Rosa? How? And we have no time. By morning . . ."

I could feel the shuddering inside me. Rosa said again:

"Digger round up some of the boys. Maybe they know where to look. Down on the waterfront, I bet. This man DeBries. I know him good. He get mixed up in plenty trouble, Michael. Smart man, make plenty dough. But dangerous."

"The people on the other side of his fence. Where do they hang out?"

She shrugged enormously. It was like a minor earthquake.

"Your guess better like mine. On the waterfront I bet. We send the boys down there to look, but, you know, some of them ain't going there, not with this kind trouble. Some of them too scared silly. Like my Digger. He pretty damn scared too, you know that?"

"Digger's O.K."

"Sure . . . sure. He not helping you, I take Lala away from him, he know this. But is a good guy. He's O.K. When I first come this country, Digger always been pretty good to me."

"Where did you come from, Rosa?"

She raised her eyebrows as if this were common knowledge.

"All this time I know you, Michael, this the first time you ask me. You just wanna talk, eh? Make conversation?"

"I guess so. It's this waiting . . . not knowing what to do . . . knowing that . . ." I threw up my hands.

Lala came in with the coffee, and Rosa told her to stay. She sat on the edge of the bed too, pouring the coffee into mugs on the end table. Watching her, Rosa said: "I come here from Sofia, long time ago. Digger pretty good to me then, help me plenty. That's why he got these girls. What good I am for a man like Digger, eh, you tell me that."

There was just a trace of pathos in her voice. Lala sat there with her eyes cast down, saying nothing, drinking her coffee with us. Rosa sniffled once, and then forgot her miseries.

Digger came back and joined us, and told me what he'd been doing. He said: "I got five or six of the boys out, Mike. Don't know if it'll do any good, but . . ."

"Where do we start looking? In a place this size, for God's sake, where do we start looking?"

"Well, 'Arry's down in La Guaira with Pedro and Sam da Costa, Rafael's over on the east side and Cristobal's over at police headquarters . . . got a few friends there who might know something. It's not much, Mike, but it's the best we can do. Waterfront's the best bet, but you know what it's like down there.

"Yes. I know. Think I'll go down there myself. . . ."

Rosa said roughly: "You wait here. We get news from one of the boys, you and Digger gotta be ready. You stay here."

I knew it was the best thing. It was hard to wait there doing nothing. I said again: "It's the waiting. . . ."

"Nothing else to do, chum. Just wait. Maybe Cristobal will find out something. He's got some pretty good friends down there."

"The police won't help. Didn't you say there was one of them looking for me?"

Digger nodded.

"Don't mean a thing though. This guy . . . What's his name? The Czech or whatever he is?"

"Weber."

"Yes . . . He'll have some friends among the coppers, but not too many. Most of them will be ready to help."

"Any good if I go over and talk to them?"

"You stay here, Mike, like Rosa says."

"O.K. It's the first time in my life I've felt like praying. A girl like Madeleine . . ."

"I know. Don't talk about it. Try not to think about it. There's nothing we can do but wait."

Try not to think about it. . . . It was easy to say.

It was almost dawn when Cristobal appeared, and it had started to rain heavily.

He was a big, heavy-set man with very long arms, who'd come from over the border, from Colombia. They'd thrown him out some years since, and he'd found refuge in Caracas and learned how to make a living by stealing. He spoke in a slow sort of drawl that was more American than Spanish. His face was heavy and lugubrious and looking at Cristobal you always had the feeling that tragedy was happening all about you.

He knocked on the door and when Digger jumped up and opened it Cristobal looked inside, saw me and went to the top of the steps again, calling out to someone down below: "He's here."

Then he came back into the room, and looked at me and then at Digger, and lastly at Rosa, waiting for encouragement to speak. I said: "Well, for God's sake . . . have you found anything?"

He knocked on the door and when Digger jumped up and she saw just what he was thinking and turned to me saying gently: "You want to wait outside, Michael? Maybe I think is better."

"No. I want to hear what he has to say."

My heart was pounding again, and there was a dreadful dryness in my throat. Cristobal said bluntly: "They find her. The police find her."

He looked down at his toes and Digger shook him roughly and said: "Go on. What else? Where is she?"

Cristobal's spaniel eyes were worried and frightened. He said: "She's dead. I got a police car downstairs you want to go there."

There was a terrible silence in the room. I was conscious that only Lala was looking at me, her big child's eyes wide and solemn and unmoving. I could hear the ticking of the alarm clock on the table, loud and clear and relentless, and in the silence there was the heavy sound of someone climbing the stairs outside, and, when the knock came on the door and Digger went silently across to open it, a policeman was there, a man from the transport section whom I'd run into once or twice. He was about to speak, but somehow the silence seemed to take hold of him, too, and he just stood there waiting, looking at Cristobal and trying to catch his eye. At last I heard him mumble, speaking in a whisper as though he were in church:

"Does he want to come? I better get back there."

Not saying anything, I nodded and turned away from them, and went with him down the wooden stairway, feeling the shaking of the fragile, rotten supports that Digger was always just going to get fixed, wondering if the shaking inside me was as violent.

I climbed into the car beside him, and we drove off through the gray, deserted, early-morning streets, with the first yellow glow trying to force its way through the wet clouds that hung over the city, but only succeeding in casting a grayness over the shiny pavement. He said nothing, the policeman, and we went down to La Guaira and turned along the waterfront till we came to the old Paseta wharf which has been closed down for I don't know how long, and we got out of the car and went down some steps that were rotted clean through with age so that nothing but the barnacles and the stench of decaying fish was holding them together, and there under the oily black planks there was a room....

It was a cellar, of sorts. As we stepped down into it, the word flashed into my mind with all the horrors of it lighted by the brilliance of my memories. The sound of the sea was gentle against the timber, and the rain was dripping through the ceiling and lying in wet patches on the concrete floor that had broken up into muddy holes. It would have been dark there, very dark, but the police had rigged up some lights from an old socket that was hanging from the wall on a broken wire that stuck out of the rotting plaster, just a couple of bare bulbs that threw their eerie shadows on the group of people huddled here.

There were eight or ten of them, mostly in police uniforms, with a guy I knew slightly from one of the newspapers taking pictures with a flash bulb and getting in the way of the police photographer. The sergeant said something as I came in, and they all fell back, making way for me.

He was an elderly man, the sergeant, with a stolid, patient look about him. He wore old-fashioned spectacles that were fastened to his ears with a cord, a thickset, slow-moving man of sixty with thirty or forty years of plodding police work behind him. In his quiet sort of way he was very much in charge of what was happening there. He took me by the arm and said gently: "Señor Benasque?"

I could only nod my head. I was staring at the disclosure the widening gap in the little crowd had made. He said very quietly: "I think you would want to see this before we take her away. . . ."

He let go of my arm, then, and I moved over to the bench and stood there looking down on her. There was a white handkerchief over her face and she wore the green Grecian dress that I'd always been so fond of. She was lying straight and slim on a narrow wooden bench that was fastened to four concrete posts set in the floor, and at the feet of the two posts below her ankles there were tightly knotted strings that had been cut with a knife, one on each side of the two-foot-wide bench. A longer piece was lying on the floor below her head, and I knew with a shudder of revulsion just how they had been used. When I took the handkerchief off her face and looked at the marks across her lovely features, I could feel the sergeant's hand on my arm again, and then I saw where her underwear lay, carelessly tossed into a corner. The sergeant said very gently:

"I put her dress back on again. . . . You would not like to see her body."

His voice was very slow and soft, but there was a restrained anger there. I leaned over and pulled the green dress down from her shoulders, and lifted the smooth drapes of it high above her waist, and then I felt myself falling and the sergeant took the strain of my weight before I hit the ground, and the next thing I knew was that someone was holding a flask of brandy to my lips and I was feeling the sharp sting of it in my mouth and the fire of it in my throat.

Somebody helped me to my feet, and I saw that they had covered her up again. The sergeant was fussing over me like a mother hen, his arm over my shoulder, and I took hold of his jacket and pulled him toward the door, and when we were outside I said hoarsely: "Did you find them . . . the men who did this?"

He shook his head. He said: "If you know anything . . . if there is something you can tell us . . ."

I blinked at him and heard him say bitterly: "The kind of men who can do this to a woman . . ."

When I did not answer, he said:

"I myself, Señor, have a daughter who is not very much older. A man like that . . . If there is anything you can tell us . . ."

"His name is Weber."

"Weber? He is not from here."

"No. From San Antonio."

He took off his spectacles and wiped them on the sleeve of his coat. He said slowly: "I think, Señor, that we will not find him."

"He has friends here. In the police."

"I know. I am very sorry. If there is anything I can do . . .'

"There is nothing you can do. You were very kind to bring me here."

"I thought it was better that you should know."

"Of course."

"If there are any relatives . . ."

"No one. We were going to be married."

"I know. The man Cristobal told me. I am very sorry. My own daughter . . ."

"And now?"

"The police doctor . . . They will take her away. Tomorrow, if you wish . . ."

"Of course."

"Shall I send the car to take you to your house? It is a long way."

"No. No, I'd rather walk."

"It is a long way."

"I'll walk."

"And if there is anything I can do . . ."

"Nothing. There is nothing you can do."

"A little brandy, perhaps?"

"Not now."

He did not know how to break off the conversation. I turned and left him there, a kindly, elderly man full of sorrow and sympathy and a bitter, subdued anger. I fel tthat his watery eyes were fixed on my back, and I wondered what it was like to be a policeman in a country such as this, where men like Weber could have friends in high places that would cause an elderly career sergeant to say, regretfully, feeling the shame of it: "I think, Señor, that we will not find him . . ."

I cannot describe the condition I was in as I walked back into town. One minute it was still gray with the rain and the early morning light, and I was in La Guaira . . . and the next moment the sun was hot and strong and I found myself in the Plaza Bolívar up in Caracas.

I have no recollection of walking there at all, nor do I know what it was that made my feet turn in that direction. I was in a sort of blind coma, and I was conscious once or twice that I was walking into people instead of round them. I pulled myself together and went back to Digger's Place.

The bar was closed at this hour of the morning, but the *cholo* was there, swabbing the floor with a rag on a long pole, and the smell of the kerosene he was using was strong in the air. I walked past him and up the stairs to the bedrooms.

Digger was standing at the top of the stairs, watching me, a brush and comb in his hands, with his huge chest naked and wet from his early-morning shower. He said nothing, but moved back as I approached, making way for me. His face was lined and troubled. He put a hand on my shoulder and said: "Cristobal told me. I'm sorry, Mike. Anything I can do?"

It was what the sergeant had said. It's a funny thing how people always want to help when there is nothing that can be done to ease the savage strings that constrict your chest and tie up your loins in agonizing knots. I said: "Just one thing, Digger. Can you go to the bank for me?"

"Sure, Mike, sure. If you want some money . . ."

"I've got it. Plenty. Give me a pen and ink, will you? And a blank check form?"

He went into the bedroom and I followed him and sat down on the bed where Rosa was fast asleep. I wrote a check and a letter to the assistant manager down at the bank, asking him to give Digger all the money that was in the account. There was a good deal there. I said to Digger:

"I got ten thousand dollars paid in for that job I did. I want it all out. I'm going to France, Digger. I've had it here."

"Sure, Mike. Best thing you can do. Get away from it."

"But there are some things to be done first. I want Weber."

Digger said slowly: "What's happened, Mike . . . it's got the boys more scared than before. I'll help, of course, you know that. So will Rosa. The others . . . well, they're scared, Mike."

"Just tell them there's ten thousand dollars in it."

"That's a lot of money for one of the boys."

"That's what I figured. It's the only thing I want to do with it. I want him myself, but if one of the boys gets there first . . . I'm not proud. I'm not fussy. I just want him dead, that's all. One way or another. Get the money, Digger. Keep it for me."

We were whispering so as not to wake Rosa. I looked up

173

and saw Lala standing in the doorway looking at me and saying nothing. She was still wearing Digger's dressing gown, and she was just looking at me and crying.

Digger folded the note up and put it in his pocket, looked at the ten-thousand-dollar check for a while and then put that away too, and I pushed past Lala and went out into the hot bright sun.

It was strange to feel the everyday bustle of the city going on all around me. It was as though the only world that had come to an end were my own little world; somehow, it made it seem small and insignificant. The sights and the sounds of people moving all about me as though nothing at all had happened, as though this were normal life in Caracas, as though the brutal death of the girl I had loved were no concern of theirs . . . as though they were unaware that such things could happen. I could not control the emotions that crowded into my mind, and the gray face of the crowd was hateful and repulsive.

I went round to the apartment. It was broad daylight and the lights were still on. The radio was still blaring, martial music now, as though it were urging me to fight.

I opened the drawers of the closet where Madeleine had kept her clothes, and I ran my hands through them, trying to persuade myself that she was still with me, that she had merely stepped out for a while, down to the market to get some fruit. . . . I felt the soft stuff of her dresses and tried to convince myself that she would come back to me soon. There was a cigarette butt in the ash tray that was stained with the red of her lips, and on the stove there was a saucepan with some hard-boiled eggs in it, and some lettuce was on the cutting board with a sliced tomato and a bright green pepper.

It was a dead and empty and dreadful house.

Digger came over at midday. He looked solemn and angry. He held out a check for me to see. It was one of my own checks, from the spare book that I kept in the bureau drawer.

It was made out to Carlo San-Verde Weber and was for the sum of ten thousand dollars.

I stared at it and stammered: "But . . . what the hell . . . what the devil's all this?"

He spread his hands expressively. He said: "I tried to cash the check you gave me. . . . There were no funds. So I saw the manager. I told him you'd said there was a big deposit made a week or two ago. . . . He showed me this check, and said you'd withdrawn it all."

I stood staring at it unbelieving. It looked like my signature, very much like it. And it was on one of my own checks with my name and address printed across the top. I went over to the bureau and pulled open the drawer; the checkbook was still there, but the first check had been taken out. Digger was droning on, telling me about the trouble he'd had getting the evidence from the manager . . . He'd had to promise to return it as soon as he'd seen me. . . . Would I go round and talk to him about it . . . ? If it was a forgery, the police would have to be notified. They were very sorry about it but could not accept responsibility.

I said: "It doesn't matter. It's not important any more."

"You mean he just signed your name on a check like that? That's a pretty good forgery, Mike. Looks like your signature."

"I can see that."

"If you want any money . . . I haven't got this much, but I guess Rosa and I could dredge up a couple of thousand."

"It doesn't matter."

He said awkwardly: "Well . . . I guess I better get back . . ."

"Sure . . . Thanks a lot, Digger."

"Why don't you come and stay with us? We got plenty of room."

"I've got to find Weber."

"Cristobal's making a few inquiries. 'Arry and Pedro have backed out, but . . . well, there's still me and Cristobal."

"I'll find him."

"How, Mike? How?"

"He'll come looking for me. He's got to."

"He might not. He might give up and go back."

"Are you mad? Now that it's all cut and dried? He's got to find out what was going on down there, and I'm the only one who can tell him. I'm the only one left to tell him. That's what he came up here for. When he couldn't immediately find me, he assumed I was hiding out somewhere, so he tried to find out where. He took Madeleine away and tried to find . . . But now he won't have to look so hard. He'll soon find out where I am. I'm making it easy for him."

"He won't just walk in and wait for you to shoot him."

"I know that."

"Come round to my place. At least there'll be some help there."

"I don't need help."

"You do, Mike. You do."

"I'll manage."

"Hell, Mike, he can just loose off a couple of rounds at you through the window. You won't even see him."

"He's got to get me alive. He's got to find out what we were doing down there."

"Your friend Vallance may have told him."

"No. That cyanide means only one thing. Vallance killed himself so that he wouldn't talk. And that means Weber still doesn't know."

"You're a sitting duck for them, you know that."

"I know. That's how I want it."

He scratched his heavy chin for a while, looking at me, wondering what to do. He said at last, using his hands to press home the point: "Come back with me, Mike. There'll be two of us. And in a pinch . . . if the need arises . . . maybe 'Arry will forget he's scared. You know how he likes a fight. Between us we can manage something."

"Such as?"

"Well . . . I don't know. Something. At least we can keep you alive, maybe."

"No, Digger. I'll get Weber, but someone else will come up. It's a slug. You cut off its head and it grows again. Let's face it, they'll get me sooner or later. But I don't mind any more. I'm not frightened of them any more. All I want is Weber. After that, I don't give a damn what happens."

There was a long pause, then. He said at last: "I'm sorry about the money. That's a lot of currency."

"I know."

"And of all people to get it . . ."

"He won't live long enough to enjoy it."

"Sure you won't come round with me?"

"Quite sure. Thanks anyway."

"O.K. If that's the way you want it."

"Thanks for the offer."

"Rosa will be mad at me if I don't bring you back."

"I'll see you both soon."

"O.K. See you, then."

He turned round and went out. His great bulk stopped in the doorway as though he were going to say something, but he gave up the idea and went out.

I could not understand why they did not come for me. Then I realized that they were waiting for the dark, so, when I had thought about this for a while and was quite sure that it was true, I lay down on the bed in my clothes and slept a little. I did not even dream.

I woke soon after five, and then went down into the street, looking for them, looking to see if they'd come back to take up their positions, and as I walked up and down, quite openly, with my hand clenched round Rosa's pistol in my jacket pocket, I was aware that someone was in the courtyard of the building on the other side of the road, standing in the shadows of the clump of bamboo that sprayed out just inside the gateway. I walked over there, quite unafraid, but it was only Cristobal.

I said: "Well, what goes on?"

His heavy face was solemn and lugubrious. He said slowly: "Digger tells me maybe I better stay here awhile. I'm not afraid of them, Mike."

"Go back. I don't need any help."

"You be surprised how much help you going to need. There are four of them, Mike. Four of them."

I said sharply: "Have you seen them?"

He shook his head.

"Not this time. Before."

"How long have you been here?"

"I came over with Digger. He left this for you."

He held out his hand and offered the keys to the old car. I said, surprised: "I don't need a car."

"Maybe you need it. Digger tell me to give you the keys. It's over there. Maybe you want to go down to the waterfront."

You could never tell with Cristobal. He's one of those people who never come right out and say what they mean. I asked him: "You know something, Cristobal? You know where they are?"

"No. Only I think they hang out down there."

"Maybe, but they'll come here looking for me. They must know I'm here."

"Maybe. Anyway, you take the car if you want it. And if you want me, you just shout, Mike. Shout good and loud."

"O.K., Cristobal. Thanks."

He moved back into the shadows as I walked away. I went over to where Digger's car was parked and looked in it. I had the crazy idea that Weber would be sitting in the back, waiting for me. Maybe it wasn't such a crazy idea at that; it was just the kind of thing he'd do. But there was no one there.

I wondered again what they were waiting for. It was almost dark now, and the red lights of the cabaret down the street came blinking on—the place where I'd taken Vallance on the night of the first meeting with DeBries.

On an impulse, I went down the alleyway there and stood looking inside for a minute. The barman saw me and called out a greeting, asking me if I wanted a drink, on the house. He did not know what had been happening. I shook my head and walked away, and then I saw them.

There were two of them, thickset men with clothes that were not made in Caracas, gray silk suits and white panama hats. One of them had a thin black mustache, and the other was smoking a long cheroot. They were walking toward me on

177

opposite sides of the street. For a moment, panic took hold of me, but it did not last for long. I almost ran into the cabaret, but, before I could make up my mind that this was the best thing to do, it was too late, for one of the men was passing the entrance himself.

I looked quickly behind me, expecting to see Weber or the fourth man there, but there was no one in sight. The man with the cheroot took it out of his mouth and threw it away, and made a brief signal to the other one. I looked behind me again, and there at the far end of the alleyway was a policeman, standing and watching us. There was something about him . . .

How shall I explain it? Is it an awareness of the enemy that comes over you? I do not know. I only know that I was quite sure that this one was one of Weber's friends. The police in these parts always patrolled in pairs, and, in any case, at this time of the evening, a solitary policeman standing close to the wall of the building and watching . . . It could not have been anything else.

The two men were coming closer, now, on opposite sides of the street, moving off the broken sidewalk and walking along in the gutter. I pulled out the pistol and cocked it, pointing at the one nearest to me, and, as he stopped and held his hands away from his sides, I heard a thin, sharp retort quite close by, and at the same time I felt a sudden heat in my left arm. It was not much, not very painful, but as I stared at my forearm and saw the blood on the back of my wrist, I knew that I had been hit. I knew, too, that it was a small-caliber rifle, probably a .22 that could not really do much damage, and knowing that this was the one way they could disarm me I started shooting.

I fired rapidly at the nearest man, and he ducked into the roadway and threw himself flat on his belly, bringing out a revolver expertly at the same time and firing. The other man was running up, charging into my gun, and I slewed round on him, still shooting, and I felt a surge of unbelievable pleasure as he suddenly stopped short and then toppled over backward.

I yelled "Cristobal!" as loudly as I could, and turned round to see where the rifle shot had come from, and a bullet smacked into the wall close beside my legs and I knew the man on the ground was trying to cripple me. I was pulling the trigger as fast as the gun would fire, and when it stopped I could not believe that I had fired the full complement of the clip. I tried to pull back the barrel to check, but I could not use my left hand, so I dropped it then and turned to run.

The policeman at the end of the alleyway had gone, and a

couple of passers-by, who looked like American tourists, were standing there staring at me, their horrified expressions telling me that they probably thought a revolution was beginning.

I saw Weber then, running out of the shadows with a light rifle in his hand, and then I was more sure than ever that the policeman I had seen was there to provide him with cover. A man with a rifle, on the streets of the city? It could not have been anything else. I nearly fell over the man I had shot as I swerved round and ran toward the car, and then Cristobal was suddenly in front of me, flinging open the door of the jalopy and running round to the other side, and when I fell into the front seat he was already revving her up and slipping in the clutch. The car shot forward and screeched round the corner, and somewhere a thin voice shouted and a police whistle blew, and then we were speeding along the Calle Pullata toward the hills.

We did not stop until we were clear of the city.

I tore a piece off my shirt and bound it round my arm, and tried to flex the fingers of my left hand, but I could not easily move them. There was no great pain, and the bones seemed all right, but the little slug had torn its way in just below the elbow, on the fleshy part of the forearm, and come out above the wrist. It was no more painful than a really bad scratch.

I told Cristobal to stop the car then, and I took over the driver's seat and turned him loose. He would not go at first, insisting that he stay with me. But I knew that I was better off on my own. I asked him if he had a gun, and he shook his head. He held up his big hands and said: "Only these, Mike. Only these. But better if I stay with you."

But at last he gave way to my urgent insistence, and, as I drove off up to the Silla, I just caught a glimpse of his bulky figure diving headlong into the bushes.

It was dark now, but I drove without lights, knowing that they would follow me anyway, and once I saw them far below me on the hairpin bend by the baobab tree, driving a jeep, also without lights. The moon was full and the sky was still pale and silver over to the west above the mountain. I stepped on the gas and hoped the tank was full. The gauge on the dashboard had been out of commission for ten years or more.

The moon was lower when I turned onto the sandy track that led to the barn, and the yellow dust whirled up behind me as we bounced off the road and drove fast along the small valley. I left the car outside the barn, in full sight, and went in through the small door at the side, using the big iron key that Digger kept hidden under a flat stone over by the well.

The heavy door swung to behind me, but I stuck my foot in the opening and prevented it from slamming shut; because once you were inside, that door automatically locked itself.

Actually, it was no particular scheming of Digger's that caused it to slam shut like that. But in the course of the years the supporting posts in one corner of the building had sunk a little into the soft earth. Not much—an inch or two perhaps. But it was enough to twist the door frame so that it hung at a slight angle, and, if you weren't ready for it, as soon as you let go it swung back shut and jammed tight. And when I say jammed, I mean just that. From inside, there wasn't a hope in hell of getting it open; you had to go outside again and sort of twist the wooden catch round a bit to free it.

Across on the other side of the barn there was a huge double door big enough to let a truck in when the stolen gasoline had to be delivered, but here there was a big iron padlock and a chain. I knew then that if I let the door stick shut, I was there until someone came to let me out . . . except for the high window.

The window was up on the raised floor where all the corn shucks and the bales of hay and the coils of rope were, where Digger kept just one drum of gasoline for his own use. It was a proper window, of dusty glass, big enough to climb through, and it led onto the long steep slope of roof, from which you could slither down, if you so wanted, and take the ten- or fifteen-foot drop to the soft sand below, over by the shallow well. There was another window over on the other side, but this one was heavily covered with rusty iron bars, and you couldn't get up to it anyway.

I knew exactly what I had to do.

I stuck a piece of wood under the small door to stop it from shutting, just in case of accidents, and then I opened up the heavy planks of the trap-door arrangement that led to the lower floor where all the barrels were. It was a long, dark, narrow corridor, really, with the forty-gallon drums all lined up along one side in five rows. Some hundred and twenty of them, all told.

It was very dark down there, and I lit the kerosene-lamp carefully and placed it up on the high shelf where it was out of harm's way, and then I took the big spanner and opened up seven or eight of the drums. I wanted to open them all, but I was worried about time. I left the lamp burning there, and hurried back up the steep ramp to the main floor. There was a horrible moment when I thought I heard their jeep outside, but it was only a sudden and unexpected noise that came up on the wind from the road below. I went to the door and looked out, but I could see no sign of anything.

Standing in the doorway, looking back into the barn, I could just see the dim light cast by the lamp down there, a feeble ray coming up from the basement through the open trap door.

Then I heard them clearly, as they rounded the steep bend about half a mile down the gravel road. I could hear the whine of the engine and the change of its note as the driver slipped into first gear for the steep hairpin; I could even hear the tires slipping as it swung round at speed. I saw them then, for one brief moment before they passed out of sight under the bluff, and I knew that in a moment or two they would be there, outside, looking at my car, peering in through the doorway of the barn, gripping their firearms and watching.

There was not much time to be lost.

The pain in my arm was coming on now, an uncomfortable stiffness that rendered it almost useless, but I pulled myself slowly up the ladder to the upper floor, to the loft, and braced myself hard against the stout wooden walls, with my feet wedged against the side of that one half-empty drum. It moved more easily than I had expected, and though the pain was severe now, shooting through my arm when I moved, I shoved it close against the edge of the platform so that it was almost ready to fall. I felt the balance of it carefully, and pushed it a little closer. I nearly lost it then, when the movement of the gasoline inside it almost sent it spinning over the edge, and I threw my arms round it and held it there until the slopping motion inside had stopped.

It was right over the edge of the entrance to the cellar below. Laboriously I pulled up the ladder after me. It was a slow and painful task.

There was only one more thing to be done.

I found another lamp, groping for it in the darkness where I knew it would be, and took the glass shade off it and turned up the wick. I put it on the floor close to my side, put a box of matches from my pocket close beside it, and waited. I was suddenly aware that I was trembling.

The silence was insufferable now. The crickets had stopped their shrilling, and I knew that my enemies could not move silently enough for me not to hear them. I wondered if they would even want to. They must know that I was alone there. Or if they thought that Cristobal was still with me . . . But what would it matter?

The smell of gasoline was overpowering, and in a moment of alarm I wondered if it would frighten them away. And then I knew that *nothing* would frighten them away until they had done what they had come here to achieve.

Now, the silence was slowly broken by the growing sound of the jeep as it pulled up outside. It seemed to come into the yard in a leisurely sort of way, and even after it stopped the motor was still turning over for a moment or two. Then someone switched it off and there was silence.

I craned my neck, stretching to look out of the window; and down across the shingle roof on the ground below I could just see them, the jeep cutting across the corner of my vision, so to speak, with Digger's old jalopy close behind it and the picturesque tile edging of the well behind that. The dark outline of the forested mountainslope was a backdrop under the cold pale blue of a night sky that was faintly luminescent.

There were three of them. I could see Weber clearly. He stood there silently, his hands thrust in his pockets now, staring at the barn. One of the other men had his rifle and the other one was carrying what looked like a Luger pistol with the butt attached. I waited for them to spread out and cover the back of the barn, but, surprisingly, they did not. I puzzled about this for a while, and then I came to the conclusion that it was the inevitability of my capture that was making them careless. They knew that I was wounded, though they did not know whether it was a bad wound or not. They knew that I had emptied my gun, and I think they believed that if I had been able to get another from Cristobal I would have fired at them at once when they arrived; certainly the frantic wildness of my shooting down in the town justified this assumption. So they did not even bother to cover the back of the barn properly. They knew that now it was only a matter of time, a matter of following an unarmed, wounded man into his last refuge and going to work on him.

And so, Weber was standing there nonchalantly, with his hands in his pockets and a cigarette in his mouth.

The faint glow of the cigarette fascinated me.

Then one of the men ran round to the back while the others waited, and I heard him rattle the chain on the main entrance. But in a moment he reappeared and I saw one of them point to the door. I could not hear what they said, but Weber jerked his head and the two men moved slowly toward it.

I was fascinated, too, by the way they walked, without any of the animal grace that you would expect to see in stalking men. "The relentless robots of the regime," DeBries had called them, and watching them now, watching their steady advance on the door of the barn, with no crouching or hiding or hesitating, with nothing more than a straight-line movement forward, it struck me forcibly how apt a phrase it was. It was not only an uncanny movement; it was almost unholy, as though it implied the very abnegation of their human origins.

They disappeared from sight then, and in a moment the moonlight streamed into the barn through the door that they had opened, and I heard one of them call out to Weber: "There's a light down there."

Weber moved out of my range of vision too, and I wriggled quickly over to the edge of the loft, tight against my half-full gasoline barrel, and peered carefully down below me. The two men stood by the trap door staring down into the lamplit, inviting mystery of it. They were not hesitating; they were only waiting for their master. Then Weber came through the door and it slammed shut behind him and he ignored it completely and I knew that now he was mine.

It was as inevitable as a vendetta could be. The sullen sound of that ominous thud that meant, to me, that the heavy door was firmly wedged shut and would not open for them again was like the near sound of a church bell to a dying sinner. I could feel the excitement and the triumph and the expectation almost crowding the hate out of my heart as they moved in beside it and waited there, with it, for complete fulfillment. I was trembling again, and I pulled closer back into the darkness of my shelter.

There was a temptation to ease myself under the friendly cover of some straw that was close by, but I knew that the slightest sound I made . . . I dared not even breathe, but watched them, almost hypnotized by the sight of dead men who were still alive and glowing with ignorance of the fate that was inevitably theirs. It made me shudder.

Then Weber said something quietly, and punched out his cigarette, and I knew that he had smelled the heavy stench of the gasoline. It did not worry me. I was well aware that Weber would know exactly what this place was, that it was a storehouse for stolen gas, an underworld hide-out where a man like myself would feel safe, foolishly safe, from pursuit. I could even sense his contempt. And then he said, quite clearly, quite coldly, and without a trace of excitement in his voice:

"Get down there and bring him up. This is as good a place as any."

I do not know what obscene mutilations he was planning for me. I know only that at this moment he was quite sure that the one question he *had* to have answered was about to be put. And, as I thought of this, the aptness of the phrase almost made me laugh: "putting the question"—the old terror of the Inquisition that had started the long history of tragedy and violence and ruthless oppression that produced, over the centuries, the men like Weber. There was even a warmth in the imagery of the Inquisition's fire.

He was standing there coldly, dispassionately, saying: "Get down there and bring him up," and as the light from below lit up their features faintly in the surrounding darkness, I could almost imagine that they wore the black hoods that would mask their mortality.

Weber was still standing there. I wished for a moment that he would go down the ramp too, and thus have further to run and longer to wait in terror before he found that his way was blocked . . . But I could not run the risk of waiting. The trap was set and all that was left was the springing.

I leaned against the solid timber wall at my back and strained my feet against the half-empty drum that was hiding me. It moved easily, now that I did not have to be careful about it. It rocked for the briefest instant of time as though it were animate enough to gloat over the fearful uproar that would follow its fall, and then it toppled over and hit the floor below with a resounding crash that must have scared the living daylights out of them. I heard Weber yell, and I believe that he thought I was trying to drop it on his head, for he was quite close to the spot where it landed. I was watching as he looked up to see where it had come from, and I could dimly see the surprise on his face. But it was surprise, not fear, and even the surprise was only momentary. Then he looked down at the gasoline that was pouring out of the drum and sloshing about his feet; it was spreading fluidly all over the floor, indicating its encroachment by sound and smell rather than by sight, for it was black against the blackness of the floor, and I could not really see it except in imagery.

Then, I think, it suddenly struck him.

In that moment he could not really have known what I was doing; he may even have briefly thought it was an accident that had emptied gasoline all over the place. But he became acutely aware of the sudden danger. After all, the light that he was looking for me by was an exposed flame in a kerosene lamp, well secured high on the wall of the cellar, but an exposed flame none the less. He shouted out to the others and began to run for the door, for the heavy timber door that was so solidly jammed tight behind him, and I heard the commotion as the other two men began falling over themselves to get up and out of there.

I did not wait any longer.

The matches were under my hand, and so was the lamp with the wick turned high and the glass abandoned. I put two or three matches together in a bundle and struck them, and held them to the soaking wick, and as the fire flared smokily I stood up and looked down on Weber, and for one short instant of perpetuity we were facing each other. He was at the door, his hand outstretched to open it, and the sudden flaring of light behind him made him half turn and stare up at me where I stood in the loft, holding my flare up high for him to see. He stood rigid for that instant, not frozen by surprise but merely not understanding, and, when the understanding came to him, he turned away from me and pushed at the door and I waited only long enough to see that it would not open and to watch for one split second of triumph as he threw himself against it in sudden panic, and then I brought back my arm and hurled my flaming light as far as I could to the other side of the barn where the hay was.

It was an elongation of the same movement, really, that sent me crashing through the wide, dusty glass window and onto the steep shingle roof, and as I rolled over and down, quite uncontrolled and with sharp spasms of sudden agony shooting through my damaged arm each time I hit it, I could still hear his shouts and the heavy, useless thudding of his body against the door.

The broken gutter that dangled along the edge of the roof caught at my coat as I went past it, and I was conscious of a ripping sound that seemed to be an overture to the fearful shock as the sandy ground came at me and knocked the breath out of my limp body with a blow that I thought I could not possibly survive. I dared not wait, and with a strength that could only have come to me through utter desperation I threw myself at the wall of the shallow well, conscious that a broken leg was dragging behind me and shooting vicious stabs of pain along my spine and into my head, conscious too that there was blood in my mouth and a sharp sting at the side of my tongue where my teeth had bitten deeply into it as I hit the ground.

I went over the little adobe wall head first, and I hit the water just as the barn went up.

It made the most fearful noise I had ever heard.

First, there was a rushing sound, like the noise of water suddenly streaming out of a hose, that grew in intensity and was suddenly overwhelmed by a great roar that seemed to split the sky itself. And above and behind the roar was the long thin scream of a man's voice, a high-pitched, weirdly mechanical sound, as though even in death he could not get back to his human heritage. Then the fierce crackling and the sound of falling timber took over, and even down there in the minor depth of the well, with water lapping at my face and limbs, the sudden blast of heat was overpowering. I could see planks that were on fire and trailing sparks behind them soaring through the sky and I could hear their angry, heavy thudding as they struck the sandy ground again. The drums were going off one by one, exploding with magnificent anger and raining a Pompeian fury all around.

Then, through it all, surprising, horrifying and unbelievably close, came a repetition of that frightful scream.

Perhaps it was my imagination. I do not know. But it seemed to me that the wild and horrifying sound came closer and closer as though, on fire and charred like a barbecued steak that has fallen into the coals, someone, somehow, had managed to get clear and was struggling hopelessly toward the friendly cold of the night that would be drawing back from him in equal horror. . . .

I found that I had covered my ears and was pressing myself into the muddy brickwork to hide the dreadful sound, and at last, when I uncovered again, all was silent except for the steady noise of the flames and the slight hissing that came from a piece of burning timber that had dropped unheeded into the water close beside me. The crackling was muted and soft and I wondered if I had fainted.

And then I wondered, too, if I would ever get out of that well alive, for when I tried to move I found that there was an insufferable pain in my leg, and I did not have the strength in my one good arm to pull myself up to the wall and clamber over. Nor did I really want to. My head was resting on a wet and muddy edge of broken brick, my limbs were cold and drenched, and above me I could see the red brightness in the sky as the fire raged on, casting its vivid, mobile lights high up to the clouds, and I knew that sooner or later someone would come up from the town to see what the blaze was. The fire brigade would be there, and the police, and Digger . . . Digger, wondering what had happened to his barn and his precious gasoline, and wondering, above all, what had happened to me.

He would find me, then, lying in six inches of wet mud, broken and bruised and bloody, but somehow finally at peace.

At peace? For how long? They'll send others after me, of that I'm sure. But I don't care any more. One man cannot fight a regime, but it's the effort that counts, and the drop in the ocean that will somehow swell to the force of a tidal wave and wipe them out forever. They'll frantically shake their robot arms and scream their mechanical screams as they go down, but one day . . .

Who can tell? Trenko, DeBries, Vallance . . . there are men like these all over. They fight for different reasons, and some of us fight only for money. Or used to. And some of us are lovely women who die bewildered and not understanding, in terror and in agony and in helplessness.

And for what?

Vendetta is a balsam and a sedative. It counters horror with horror, and does this reduce us to the savage level too?

I suppose it does. But the only panacea is the abnegation of thought, an induced emptiness of mind. . . . I lay there in the slimy darkness and heard a lonely frog close beside me start a hesitant croaking as though he, too, were looking for sympathy and were not sure that he could find it. I watched the lights in the sky and thought about Madeleine, and the image that came to me was no longer the broken idol of her body, but it was instead the clean warm presence of the happiness that could have been ours.

It seemed that she was close beside me once more, and as the sky grew suddenly darker I knew that the merciful oblivion of coma was slowly covering me with its gentle cloak.

It was like an eyelid softly closing.

The face that was peering into mine seemed to be Weber's and I screamed out and struck at it, feeling the pain shoot through my arm as I tried to move it.

And then he was holding my wrist and saying, "Gently, now . . . Easy," and I was conscious enough to feel the small sharp sting of a needle in my flesh. Then the face was gone and the bed I was lying on was not mud and water any more but clean white linen, and I twisted my head round and saw a blur above me that could have been a woman's face. I heard myself say, my voice coming deep down from the bottom of a chasm, not like my own voice at all:

"That was a needle. I know . . . A hypodermic."

I tried to twist myself free of the pressure that was holding my legs down, but I could not move them, and suddenly the fog cleared and there was Lala, Digger's girl, bending over me with her smooth brown face streaked with tears. She put a hand to her eye with an eternally feminine gesture and said: "A needle? What do you mean, Mike?"

I could not answer, and the bed I was on was swaying madly as though I had been drinking too much bad liquor. I shook my head, feeling the pains go through it, and then it was no longer Lala, but Rosa, and she was saying crazily: "That was two days ago, Michael . . . two days ago . . . two days ago . . . two days ago . . ."

Her voice droned on and on, until the oblivion hit me again, and then I suddenly woke up and it was dark, and I was frightened in the darkness, like a child who wakes in a nightmare. The heavy, gasping breath that I heard was my own. A chair scraped somewhere and there was a gentle weight pushing down the springs beside me so that the bed tipped down ever so slightly. I imagined that it was Madeleine climbing quietly in with me, and then the light of the chipped ceramic lamp went on and I saw that it was Lala again, and she was looking at me sadly and saying nothing.

She put her hand on my head, and began to move away quickly, and I put out my hand with a painful movement and held her thin wrist and said: "Lala?"

She nodded, then, and smiled, and broke away from me and ran to the door, moving out of the circle of light, looking back over her shoulder with the tears beginning to come again. I heard her voice as I closed my eyes: "Digger! He is awake...."

It all tumbled back into focus then, and I still felt the fear that Weber had inspired, so that when Digger came in I knew I was trembling. He said cheerfully, awkwardly: "Three o'clock in the morning. Mighta known you'd pick a time like that to come round. Just getting to bed.... How d'you feel, Mike?"

The room swimming about me, I said: "That's a damn fool question."

It was an effort to speak. He was standing there grinning at me, doing up the cord of his pajamas, not knowing what to say. I heard the slap as he struck Lala lightly across the buttocks, and he said: "Go on . . . Get the brandy. And get Rosa, too."

She stood there for a moment, smiling at me and repeating the gesture I had seen before, the back of her slim hand to her eyes, and then turned away quickly and went out.

Digger sat down heavily on the edge of the bed. It sank down mightily under his weight, and he said again: "Well, how d'you feel, Mike?"

I could feel the hard bulk of the cast on my leg, and my left arm was strapped tightly to my chest. I said: "Was it a doctor I saw here just now? He looked like Weber."

"Just now? That was three days ago. Brother, the sleep of the just . . ."

"What happened, Digger? What happened up there?"

"At the barn?" He shrugged. "Someone blew up about five thousand gallons of my bread and butter, that's what happened."

"Yes, I know."

"I figured you did."

"Did they find . . . did they find any . . . any bodies?"

It seemed like a foolish question. I could sense Digger's repressed excitement. He said: "Are you kidding? You never saw such a bonfire."

"Sorry about that. About the gasoline, I mean."

He threw back his head and laughed boisterously. He said

happily: "I'm only sorry I wasn't there. Were they all inside?"
"Three of them."
"They picked up one off the streets. Outside the apartment. A hole in his head."
"I know about that too."
"Sure you do."
"What about the police?"
"They should worry."

The fear of *them* was coming back into me again. My mouth was dry. I said: "I've got to get out of here, Digger. There'll be more of them. It's still unfinished business. They'll still be after me."

He was grinning like a Cheshire cat. He swung round as the door opened and Rosa came running in. Running's the right word, too; the floor was fairly shaking with it. She plunked herself down beside me and threw her gigantic arms round my neck, smothering me in her warm embrace, and by the time I got my breath back Digger was pulling her away and Lala was standing there with a tray of glasses and a bottle of cognac.

As he poured out the drinks he said: "May as well tell you right away, Mike. . . . There's no need to run any more."

"How's that?"

Rosa said: "San Antonio. In the newspapers there is nothing except San Antonio."

"About me?" I felt I was staring at her.

"Why should they write about you?"

"So?"

"A revolution. Another one."

So . . . They'd started again.

I sank back on the pillows while they told me about it. There were names in the press that I knew of . . . Maduso, who had been captured when Trenko's girl Maria-Anna had been shot; they'd found him in one of their cellars, twenty years older but still alive and virile. They'd found José Uraca too, with both legs broken and his fingers useless. Hernando Riego, emaciated, blind and castrated. . . . I could not place him at first, and then I remembered. Riego was the fiery young boy who had helped me pull Trenko to safety that far-off time on the steps of the railway station. I listened to the tale of sudden and successful revolt, and when I'd emptied my glass I said:

"And the new Premier?"

My voice was shaking.

Digger got up and went to the rickety dressing table, opened a paper and folded it neatly to show me.

"Joker called Lazlo," he said. "Looks like you, a bit, doesn't he?"

I stared at the picture for a long time, savoring the thought of the name I was about to speak. I remembered I had promised myself . . . his name would not pass my lips. . . . Even when I had told Rosa the story behind all my troubles. . . . I said slowly: "José Lazlo. . . . I wrote some articles about him once."

I felt that Digger was looking at me questioningly, probing, wondering, hesitating to ask for a downright honest answer, even from me. I said again: "I'm sorry about all that gasoline."

He nodded then, closing the incident forever. And closing, too, the question of my business in San Antonio.

I said: "How long before I get out of this harness?"

"A few days. A week, perhaps. What's on your mind?"

"I can't stay here indefinitely."

"Why not?"

The warmth of the cognac was seeping into me. There was warmth, too, in their friendship. Digger, and Rosa, and Lala . . . Rosa said: "You stay here as long as you want, Michael. When you ready to go . . . you go."

"As soon as I'm fit to travel . . ."

"Sure. But you come back sometime, no?"

"You bet."

"You are not forgetting you got friends in Caracas too, good friends."

"Of course not. I'll be back again."

Digger said wrathfully: "Will some joker tell me what you're talking about?"

I said: "San Antonio, Digger."

"Oh."

"I told them I'd be back one day."

"Oh."

"I'm well in with the new government. Too good a chance to miss."

"I see. Be going down there alone?"

The pause was heavy.

"Yes."

The thought of Madeleine was painfully throbbing. An induced emptiness of mind . . . I wondered if I'd ever forget the warm vision of her delicate loveliness . . . her hair piled high and her solemn, restful eyes. I said aloud: "An induced emptiness of mind . . . Sometimes, it's the only answer."

"Another cognac?"

I shook my head and lay back on the pillows.

"Some food? You must be hungry. Three days . . ."

"No. Not now."

My voice was very far away.

I felt the springs rising gently as Rosa got up off the bed. I heard her say: "Lala will be here if anything you want, Michael."

I did not answer. I was thinking of Madeleine, knowing that the sensuous touch of her was still imprinted deeply on my flesh. They went out quietly, both of them, good friends leaving a man with his thoughts, and in the silence I saw Lala's hand move to the lamp, and then it was dark again.

She crossed softly and sat by the window where the moonlight was streaming in, and let its gentle brilliance fall about her shoulders. She did not move, then, but sat there, silent and still and expectant . . . and, somehow, eternally sad.

About the Author

Alan Caillou is an author with a thirst for adventure. During World War II he served with the British Intelligence Corps behind enemy lines in North Africa, was captured by the Italians, and escaped just before his scheduled execution. He then joined the guerillas to fight in Yugoslavia and Italy. After the War, he returned to Africa to become a safari guide. Mr. Caillou now makes his home in Arizona.